JUST ONE MOMENT

Praise for Dena Blake

Friends Without Benefits

"This is the book when the Friends to Lovers trope doesn't work out. When you tell your best friend you are in love with her and she doesn't return your feelings. This book is real life and I think I loved it more for that."—*Les Rêveur*

A Country Girl's Heart

"Dena Blake just goes from strength to strength."—*Les Reveur*

Unchained Memories

"There is a lot of angst and the book covers some difficult topics but it does that well. The writing is gripping and the plot flows."—*Melina Bickard, Librarian, Waterloo Library (UK)*

"This story had me cycling between lovely romantic scenes to white-knuckle gripping, on the edge of the seat (or in my case, the bed) scenarios. This story had me rooting for a sequel and I can certainly place my stamp of approval on this novel as a must read book." —*The Lesbian Review*

"The pace and character development was perfect for such an involved story line, I couldn't help but turn each page. This book has so many wonderful plot twists that you will be in suspense with every chapter that follows."—*Les Reveur*

Where the Light Glows

"From first time author Dena Blake, *Where the Light Glows* is a sure winner."—*A Bookworm's Loft*

"[T]he vivid descriptions of the Pacific Northwest will make readers hungry for food and travel. The chemistry between Mel and Izzy is palpable."—*RT Book Reviews*

"I'm still shocked this was Dena Blake's first novel…It was fantastic… It was written extremely well and more than once I wondered if this was a true account of someone close to the author because it was really raw and realistic. It seemed to flow very naturally and I am truly surprised that this is the author's first novel as it reads like a seasoned writer." —*Les Reveur*

By the Author

Where the Light Glows

Unchained Memories

A Country Girl's Heart

Racing Hearts

Friends Without Benefits

Just One Moment

Visit us at www.boldstrokesbooks.com

JUST ONE MOMENT

by
Dena Blake

2019

JUST ONE MOMENT
© 2019 By Dena Blake. All Rights Reserved.

ISBN 13: 978-1-63555-387-1

This Trade Paperback Original Is Published By
Bold Strokes Books, Inc.
P.O. Box 249
Valley Falls, NY 12185

First Edition: July 2019

Credits
Editor: Shelley Thrasher
Production Design: Stacia Seaman
Cover Design by Tammy Seidick

Acknowledgments

Thanks to Len Barot, Sandy Lowe, and the rest of the Bold Strokes Books team. You all have a hand in making my stories come to life. I will always be grateful for how seamless you make it happen.

To Shelley Thrasher, my grammar guru aka my editor extraordinaire—you make me a better writer.

Thanks to my BSB family. You are truly supportive in every way. I'm glad to be part of such a wonderful family.

To my family, Kate, Wes, and Haley, for always encouraging me to write the stories that constantly fill my head and for putting up with my quirky habits. You're the ones who get it when I break into song or recite random movie dialogue at inappropriate times.

To my readers, all I can say is that you're simply awesome. Thanks for being there and reading.

This book is dedicated to those
who have the strength to follow their heart,
even if it leads back to the person who broke it.
Forgiveness never comes easily,
but sometimes it's worth the effort.

CHAPTER ONE

Chloe flopped into the lounger on the deck and breathed in the salty air. She wiped the moisture from the back of her neck. It wasn't hot, just above seventy degrees, the usual for March. She'd just moved the second carload of her belongings from their apartment in Tampa to the beach house in Clearwater. She thought about Shay and her stomach knotted. When they'd gotten together so many years ago, never in a million years had she seen this future for them. The split seemed to be the only way to move forward. She shook her head. How had they reached this point?

"Is that all of it?" Erica's voice startled her from behind.

She shook her head. "It's enough for now." She wasn't up to destroying the life she'd planned to live more than she already had today.

Erica handed her a glass of wine and kissed her lips lightly. "I moved a few of my things into the other half of the closet." She sat in the chair adjacent. "I hope you don't mind."

Chloe stiffened. "You shouldn't have done that. What did you do with the clothes that were in there?" Shay hadn't cleared hers out yet because she hadn't been ready to make things quite so final. But after their last discussion, the same circular one they'd been having for the past few weeks, Chloe had decided to separate. She'd needed some distance. She hadn't given Erica the go-ahead to change anything, but wasn't surprised that she'd taken the liberty of moving some of her things in.

"I bought a plastic tub to put them in." Erica stared out at the ocean as she took a sip of wine. "I'll pack them up and have it delivered to her."

"No," she said, her voice louder than she'd expected. "I'll take care of it." She hadn't told Shay how involved she'd become with Erica and wasn't sure she wanted her to know. If she did, all the questions and suspicions Shay had confronted her with over the past year would be vindicated in her mind. She'd denied them because they weren't true until a few months ago when she'd discovered Shay's indiscretion. At that moment, she'd been absolutely crushed, and she'd gone to see Erica for comfort. At first it had been just that, comfort, but eventually she'd given in to Erica's charms, emotionally and sexually.

She wished she'd been stronger. She'd never had the guts to confront Shay until she'd walked in on them. The text messages, lies, and lack of intimacy should've made it perfectly clear that Shay had found someone else—someone smarter and more suited for Shay than herself. She glanced over at Erica. Would she ever have the same passion for her as she'd had for Shay? Not that it really mattered. This was her life now, whether she liked it or not.

"Don't forget Jackson is having a little get-together tonight. I replied to the email he sent you and told him we'd be there," Erica said.

Fuck. She closed her eyes, cursing herself for forgetting to log out of her email again. "Tonight? Where?"

"At his place. Just a few people, including us," Erica said.

"I'm not really up to socializing tonight. Can we just stay in?" After the day she'd had, she just wanted to stay home, relax, watch a movie, and forget about reality for a while.

"You told him you'd bring wine," Erica said.

"In your response to email he sent *me*?"

Erica nodded.

She hated it when Erica didn't check with her first, which she did all the time. "Why don't you go ahead without me? I don't think I'd be very good company tonight."

"It's exactly what you need to get you out of this funk."

She closed her eyes and took a deep breath. Erica had no idea how hard the day had been for her, and she didn't seem to care.

Erica squatted down in front of her. "Come on. You know Jackson's humor always lightens your mood, and his wife will be there. Isn't she your best friend?"

She was right. Jackson always had a way of making her feel better, no matter what she was dealing with at the time. His wife Whitney had been a friend since they were roommates in college, and they had been inseparable ever since. The night out with them would probably do her good. "Okay. Maybe just for a little while."

Erica took her face in her hands and pulled her into a deep kiss, which prompted all kinds of reactions from her body that she wasn't quite comfortable with. Guilt washed through her, and she broke the kiss. Today wasn't the day to enjoy sex with Erica. "I need to shower and change." She smiled softly as she stood up. "You want to pick out the wine?"

"Yeah. I'll get it." Erica kissed her lightly on the cheek, then turned and went into the house.

❖

After Chloe knocked on the door to Jackson and Whitney's apartment, they stood for a few minutes waiting for someone to answer. Any other time she would just let herself in, but since she wasn't alone tonight, waiting seemed more appropriate. From the number of cars parked along the street, the party seemed to be in full swing already. It was past eight o'clock, and Chloe had intended to be there much earlier, but they were late again—the way Erica liked it.

She'd taken over an hour choosing her outfit—a multicolored, oversized silk blouse, white leggings, and a pair of slip-on sandals. It honestly didn't seem much different than what she'd had on earlier in the day, but she'd said it was much more fashionable for an evening event. Erica liked to make an entrance wherever she went, and there was no making her move any faster. Chloe, on the other hand, had chosen comfortable black jeans and a short-sleeved, powder-blue, V-neck top, and her favorite pair of black Vans loafers. She didn't need to impress anyone at her brother's party.

She hadn't seen Jackson or Whitney since she'd started seeing Erica because she wasn't sure where this thing with Erica was leading. She'd come out tonight instead of watching a movie at home only because Erica had responded to the invitation.

The door swung open, and Whitney greeted Chloe with a huge hug. "Oh my God. It seems like forever since I've seen you. I've missed you," she whispered in her ear as she held her tight. "You can't stay away this long ever again."

"I won't. I promise," she whispered back. "It's just been a tough month."

Whitney released her and gave her a sad smile, then turned her attention to Erica. "And who's this?"

"This is Erica," she said, not daring to look at her. Erica was certain to be shooting daggers at her because she hadn't mentioned anything about her to Whitney before.

"It's so nice to meet you." Whitney held out her hand and Erica shook it.

"Nice to meet you as well." Erica handed her the bottle of cabernet they'd brought. "Chloe's told me so much about you. It's nice to finally put a face to the stories."

Chloe rolled her eyes when Whitney glanced at her.

Whitney accepted the bottle of wine. "Well, this was totally unnecessary. Come on in. There's food in the dining room and drinks in the kitchen," Whitney said as she pointed Erica that way and then whispered in Chloe's ear again. "I'm sorry. I didn't know you were bringing someone. Shay's here." Apparently, Jackson hadn't filled her in on the finality of everything between her and Shay or about her moving on with Erica. Probably wishful thinking on his part that she wouldn't bring her tonight. He was still rooting for the other camp.

She headed straight for the wine, poured herself a glass from an open bottle of merlot, and took a big gulp. She was thankful Shay hadn't been home today when she'd picked up her things, but she'd known she was going to run into her sooner or later, though sooner hadn't been her preference. It was going to be a long night.

Jackson raced across the room to see her as she entered the living room. "Did you see Shay when you came in?" Jackson asked, hitting her with the question before she'd even had a chance to say hello. "She came alone. She's devastated." He shook his head.

Erica interjected herself into the conversation. "She could've brought someone."

"But she chose *not to*," Jackson said, narrowing his eyes before he turned his attention to Chloe and whispered, "She's not over you."

I know. She closed her eyes and held back the tears as she tried to suppress the pain ripping through her heart. This was the first semi-public event she'd been to without Shay, and seeing her tonight was going to be absolute misery, even if she *had* come alone.

"She needs to go home to…what's her name again?" Erica said as she moved back into her space.

Chloe ignored the comment. She didn't want to bring Lila into this. In fact, she didn't want to have another conversation about Lila ever again. They'd been over it a thousand times, and the words that came out of Shay's mouth were always the same…*I'm sorry. Someone made me feel beautiful and wanted while you were off getting the same thing from Erica. I lost sight of what we have. I was stupid, and I fucked up.* Both were true, but Chloe couldn't just simply forgive and forget. Not yet anyway.

"I'm going to get more wine." *A lot of wine.* She brushed past Erica and headed to the makeshift bar set up on the counter in the corner of the kitchen. A drop or two of merlot splashed into her glass as she upended the bottle. She set it down, picked up another, and searched for the wine opener.

Jackson plucked the bottle from her hand. "I've got it." He scored around the top of the bottle and ripped the foil from it. "This is a new one. I think you'll like it." After he pulled the cork, he poured a small amount into her glass.

She drank it down, nodded, and then held out her glass for more. "Nice." She didn't care about taste at this point. She just wanted something to deaden the pain filling her heart.

Erica had wandered across the room and seemed to be having an intense conversation with another couple.

"Is that really who you want?" Jackson asked. He'd made it very clear what he thought about Erica and the way she'd exploited her feelings after she'd found out about Shay's infidelity.

"Jack, can we just leave it alone for now? I've had enough turmoil for tonight." She stared at the small amount of wine left in her glass as she swirled it. "Why didn't you tell Whitney about her?"

"Because I don't like her, and I didn't think you'd bring her."

"Don't hold back on my account."

"I won't." He filled her glass again. "Last one. I'm cutting you off until you eat something."

She zoomed in on Shay across the room, felt the flutter in her stomach, and turned back to Jackson. "I need to go. I'm not even sure why I came."

"You just got here. Have some food." He took her to the buffet table in the dining room and handed her a plate. The spread was impressive: sliced chicken breast stuffed with spinach and cheese, sautéed shredded vegetables, spicy Parmesan green beans and kale, and herb-infused mashed potatoes, among other salads and small dishes. She slapped a couple of heaping spoonfuls of potatoes onto her plate, the only thing she could stomach. She was anything but hungry after seeing Shay. Dressed in denim skinny jeans, a pink button-down shirt, and distressed-blue, laceless slip-ons, she was still the most beautiful woman she'd ever seen. She hated herself for still thinking that.

Jackson smiled. "I made those just for you."

A fork magically appeared on her plate, and he whooshed her over to an empty spot on the couch. He collected their drinks and perched on the arm of the couch next to her.

"You don't have to sit here with me. I'll be fine."

"Oh, but I do." He scanned the room. "I need you to keep me company. You're my only friend here." He pulled his brows together. "Why else would I invite you?" he asked with a wink.

"Besides your wife, and that I'm your sister?"

"I guess that's true. Now eat."

The mashed potatoes were perfection, as always, and she surprised herself by devouring the whole plateful. She'd excused herself to go to the bathroom and spent several minutes staring at herself in the mirror. She hardly recognized herself bcause her eyes were sullen with dark circles below them, the vibrancy she remembered had left them long ago. That wasn't surprising, considering the amount of sleep she wasn't getting. Jackson had been deep in conversation with another group of people when she'd returned to the living room. She was ready to go. She'd been ready an hour ago, but Erica was still off mingling with other guests. She headed to the balcony to get some air.

"I was hoping I'd see you here." The familiar voice filled her ears as she stared out into the night sky, and she shuddered. *Shay.*

She didn't turn around. "And I was hoping you wouldn't come."

"I wasn't expecting you to move your things out so soon." Shay's voice faltered. "I had to see you. If only to say—"

"You're sorry? Again?" She spun around and narrowed her eyes. Choked down the pain expanding in her heart.

"I *am* sorry, Chloe. I don't know what else to say. What can I do to fix this?"

"Nothing. Just leave me alone."

She moved around Shay and headed back inside. She had to go now, and the struggle to leave was about to begin. She touched Erica on the elbow. "I'm beat. Can we go?"

"You remember Jane and Allen?" She motioned to the couple in front of her. "They have a piece of your art."

Fuck. She held out her hand and smiled. "Yes. Nice to see you again."

They exchanged niceties and asked a few questions about her current work before she said, "I'm so sorry, but I did a lot of heavy lifting today, and I'm just wiped out." She smiled. "I'd love to visit with you more. Are you coming to the next First Friday at the gallery?"

They both nodded eagerly. "Yes. We'll definitely be there."

"Okay. We'll talk more then." She turned and sped across the room. She'd grab a cab if she had to, but she was leaving now.

Erica caught up with her as she reached the door. "What are you doing? Those people love you." Her voice was louder than necessary.

"That's awesome, but I'm tired. I'm going home." She needed time to recharge. Talking to strangers physically and mentally drained her. She'd also had too much wine, and seeing Shay had pushed her over the edge.

"You're being rude." Erica pulled her lips into a scowl.

"No, she's not," Shay said, suddenly right there beside her. "I can take you home."

"Absolutely not." Chloe swayed, trying to get her balance. Shay wrapped her arm around her waist to steady her. Chloe moved out of her grasp quickly and leaned against the wall. She couldn't believe Shay was still trying after the conversation they'd just had.

Jackson appeared out of nowhere to save her, as he always did. "Do you want me to take you home?"

"God, no. This is your party, Jackson. Just call me a cab, please."

He took his phone out of his pocket, and Erica stopped him from punching in the number. "No need." Her voice softened. "I'll take her."

Conversation was sparse on the ride to the beach house, and Chloe dozed on and off. The mashed potatoes hadn't helped absorb the alcohol. They'd hit her system too late to prevent the dizzy feeling brought on by too many glasses of wine.

She'd stripped off all her clothes except her panties on the way to the bedroom, then fell into the bed. When she felt Erica slide in and press up against her back, she knew what came next, but all she wanted was sleep. When Erica's hand went to her breast and plucked at her nipple, she placed her hand on top of Erica's and stopped the motion. Her message wasn't received. Erica rolled her over and continued. She crawled on top of her and sucked the other nipple into her mouth. She wished her body wasn't so sensitive, but it was, and it reacted fully. Even though all she wanted was comfort tonight, she didn't stop her again.

❖

The next morning, Shay sat in front of the beach house gripping the steering wheel as she gathered her courage. She flipped down the visor and looked at herself in the vanity mirror. Minimal makeup as usual, but more wouldn't hide the dark circles. They made her amber eyes look dull, void of any life.

She hadn't slept much last night. Chloe had known she'd be at Jackson's party—it had been planned for over a month, and they'd been invited as a couple. She'd hoped to have an opportunity to talk to her, plead her case again. And she'd tried, but Chloe had immediately cut her off. She certainly hadn't expected her to have brought Erica, who was an extra, an outsider who didn't belong there. Yet Shay had been the one treated as an outsider, which had been incredibly hurtful. Not by Jackson or Whitney, but by Erica, and Chloe hadn't prevented it. Her usual plus-one had chosen someone else as her escort last night.

What the fuck had she been thinking when she'd gotten involved with Lila? She'd made so many mistakes over the past year, and she didn't know how to atone for them. Even if she could, she didn't know if Chloe would forgive her. If last night was any indication, she might never. This was her last shot. She wasn't willing to just walk away from what she had with Chloe without doing whatever she could to stop the divide between them.

She stood at the doorway debating whether to knock or let herself in. It was technically still *their* house. She'd socked away every extra penny she could for two years, so they could afford to buy it. The renovation hadn't been easy, but Chloe had needed an inspirational place to create her art. Shay had done everything in her power to give it to her. It would soon be Chloe's alone, unless Shay could convince her that she was worth a second chance. That *they* were worth a second chance.

The door was unlocked, so she pushed it open and walked slowly through the small entryway. "Chloe, you here?" No response. She wandered into the bedroom, thinking she might be still asleep. "I'd like to talk if you have some time."

The bed wasn't made, and she noticed a pile of clothes on the floor at the foot of it, a storage container in the corner. She picked up a few items. They were her clothes. *What the fuck?* She went to the closet and fingered through the clothes hanging in their place, recognizing them immediately.

"I wasn't expecting to see you today." Chloe's voice startled her, and she spun around.

The jolt she felt when Chloe's startling blue eyes caught her reminded her that she was nowhere near being done with her. Her hair was pulled up into a messy bun on the top of her head, and the skin peeking out from under the robe she was wearing was damp. Apparently, the hot tub they'd purchased last year was being put to good use.

"Clearly." She motioned to her clothes on the floor. "Were you just going to jam all my stuff into that container and leave it out front with the rest of the trash?"

"No. I—"

"We were going to have them delivered to you." Erica appeared out of nowhere and was standing in the doorway wearing a skimpy bikini while dabbing herself with a beach towel.

Shay's neck heated, and the room shrank. Her ears rang, and she couldn't catch her breath as her eyes flashed from Chloe to Erica and back again. "Are you fucking kidding me?"

"It's not what you think."

"Oh yeah? Because it looks exactly like what I've been saying all along." She turned her focus on Erica. "You certainly move quickly."

"Jesus, Shay. We decided to split. Didn't we? I wasn't alone in that conversation, was I?" Chloe reached for her and she backed away. "I'm sure Lila will move in to the apartment to take my place just as quickly, if she hasn't already."

"She won't move in. That was never the plan. I never in a million years thought she would replace you." Her heart clenched. *No one could ever do that.* "Apparently you didn't have the same sentiment about me." She pressed her fingers to her forehead. "I've been such an idiot. I actually came here to ask you to reconsider for the billionth time. To forgive me for the awful things I've done." She glanced at Erica. "Now I can see we're even." She pushed past her and raced out the door to her car, stopping only to yank off her wedding ring and slap it onto the entryway table.

She knew she wasn't being rational, but she couldn't believe this was happening after all they'd been through. That Chloe could remove her from her life so easily—from her heart. Tears streamed down her cheeks as she fired the engine and took off down the street. The satisfied look on Erica's face was burned into her mind. She'd never been so humiliated, and it was her own fault. Trusting Chloe when she'd told her nothing was going on between her and Erica had been a huge mistake. For Chloe to bring Erica to the beach house Shay had bought for her, that they'd redesigned together, was so totally wrong.

Her mind was still whirling as the car spun and then came to a stop in the middle of the intersection. The light was green. She hadn't seen it change to red, only felt the impact of the other car when it crashed into her. She gripped the steering wheel. She was okay. Then she heard the loud, blaring horn. She looked to her side and saw the dump truck speeding toward her, smoke billowing from the wheel wells. The smell of burned rubber filled her nostrils. She couldn't move.

Chapter Two

When Chloe received the call from the hospital, she'd thought it was just a minor accident, possibly whiplash at the most. She'd had no idea how badly Shay had been hurt until she arrived. The nurses immediately pushed paperwork in front of her that required signatures. Then one of them spouted questions at her about drug allergies and current medications.

Her mind spun. "No. She's not taking anything. Ibuprofen, maybe, for headaches."

"Allergies?" the nurse asked again.

She closed her eyes and tried to concentrate. "Penicillin, I think."

"That was on the card in her wallet. Anything else?" The nurse was persistent.

"No. Not that I know of. She's never had any major sickness or accidents that she's told me about."

The clipboard rattled as the nurse slid it across the counter to another one, who immediately typed the information into the computer. "Come with me." She led her to a secluded waiting room, where various people were sleeping in recliners or watching TV. "The doctor will come talk to you when the surgery is done."

Surgery. The word echoed in her head. "What? Can't I see her first?"

"Her leg is broken, and they're going to repair it. She's already on her way to the OR."

"Repair? What does that mean?"

"Possibly a plate or rod and compression screws. They won't know until they get in there."

Oh my God. She felt like vomiting.

The nurse must have noticed because she went to the water machine, filled a cup, and brought it to her. "She'll be fine. They do these all the time."

She nodded as she took the cup and sipped the cool water. She poured a little into her hand and rubbed it across her neck, which seemed to help the nausea.

It felt like a full day had slipped by as Chloe sat waiting for the surgeon to come through the doors and tell her how the surgery had gone. When he finally had, she'd waited another hour before the nurse took her back to see Shay. Chloe thought she was going to pass out when she saw the cut on her forehead and the bruise on her cheek. She'd sucked in a deep breath and clutched the bed rail as they went up to her room in the elevator.

Now she sat next to Shay's hospital bed watching her chest rise and fall in sync with the breathing machine. Relief had flooded through her when, a little over three hours ago, the doctor had told her everything had gone as expected and she would be coming out of the anesthesia soon. Not long after that, the nurse had come to get her and taken her back to be with Shay as they moved her to her room. On the way, Shay's eyes had fluttered open, and she'd made contact with her. She'd held Shay's hand, letting her know she was here. She was going to be okay. Shay was broken but still alive. Chloe had never been so relieved as she was at that moment.

Two months ago, Chloe's world had exploded. One act that she'd wished she'd never discovered had decimated her whole relationship with Shay. It had pushed her into moving forward toward a new uncertain future with Erica, away from all the hurt she'd experienced with Shay. And now it had happened again. One careless action on her part had landed Shay in intensive care and thrown her life into chaos again.

The discussion they'd had a few days earlier whirled through her mind. It was more of a shouting match than a conversation. Everything that had happened over the past six months had come roaring back. The suggestive texts, the visions of Shay and Lila, and the lack of connection that had developed between them were at the forefront of her thoughts. She remembered it vividly and couldn't possibly have tamed her temper. She'd poured it all out, hit Shay with both barrels, and Shay had done the same.

"It was a mistake."

"One time is a mistake. You've been fucking her for months."

"That's all it was. I swear."

Chloe shivered as the vision of Shay and Lila together in her office shot into her mind. "Fucking every chance you got." Her head throbbed. "Fucking while I was downstairs waiting for you in the car." Her voice faltered as she hauled in a deep breath. She held her tears. This was not going to turn into a pity party.

They'd been on the way to a gallery event, and Shay had said she'd needed to pick up her laptop from the office so she could finish some work later. After twenty minutes of waiting, Chloe had begun to worry and had gone into the building after her. The biggest mistake of her life.

"I'm so sorry." Shay said.

"About the affair or that I caught you?"

"I didn't know she was there."

"But you took full advantage of the fact that she was." The vision of Shay pushed up against the wall with Lila's mouth on hers and her hand down her pants filled her thoughts. She hadn't been able to erase it. Didn't know if she ever could.

"No. That was all her. Everything was all her." Shay rubbed her forehead as tears streamed down her face. "She convinced me that you were having an affair, that all the nights you spent at the gallery without me were with someone else."

"Did you ever think of talking to me about it?" When had that gotten so difficult?

"I admit not talking to you was a huge mistake. She convinced me that you were moving on with your career and I wasn't good enough for you anymore."

"That's ridiculous." She lowered her voice and paced the apartment. "If anything, I needed you more."

"I'm still here." Shay moved closer, cupped her face in her hands.

Chloe swayed into her, and the tears rushed from her eyes. She knew she was weak. Shay had been the only woman she'd completely trusted, and they had never had any walls or borders between them. She'd loved her unconditionally.

Shay's phone chimed, and she knew it was Lila. "And so is she." She grabbed her bag and took off out the door.

Chloe hadn't gone to the gallery event that night. She'd gone to the beach house instead and spent the next few hours sitting in the sand sobbing and staring at the ocean waves. The vacant beach lit only by a sliver of the moon made the loneliness hit her square in the chest. The love of her life had found someone else to fill her existence.

She hadn't returned to their apartment after that. She'd gone to Jackson and Whitney's apartment. They'd put her in the guest room and told her she could stay as long as she wanted. She'd successfully avoided Shay for days, until she'd finally found her at Jackson's place. They'd talked, but that hadn't done any good. Shay's reasons for the affair were ridiculous, and even if they *had* made sense, the hurt was still enormously real. Many more conversations had followed after that, and Shay's insistence on blaming everything on Lila had been the breaking point. That's when Chloe had decided to move permanently to the beach house in Clearwater and leave Shay behind at the apartment in Tampa.

It wasn't like she'd been innocent in the whole disaster. Chloe had been spending more and more time at the gallery, and the banter between her and Erica had gone way too far, but Chloe had never intended to do anything more than flirt. Shay had been the one to stray. Chloe had been devastated, emotionally wrecked when she found out about Shay's affair. She still was, and she didn't know how to get over it—whether she even wanted to.

When she'd gone to the gallery the next night, Erica was there. She'd been concerned that she hadn't shown up for the event the night before and could tell something was wrong. Erica was compassionate, understanding, and loving that night. No wonder she'd fallen into her arms a month later. She'd needed to be held, understood, comforted, and Erica had assumed the role perfectly.

❖

Chloe had just begun to doze off in the chair when she heard a commotion in the hallway. The door flew open, and Shay's parents rushed into the room, followed closely by a nurse.

"Only two people can be in here at a time."

"We're her parents. We belong here." Shay's mother, Mary, was the type of woman who could give you a look and everyone would stop talking. *Not this girl.*

"That may be so, but you weren't listed on the emergency card in her wallet."

Shay's mother halted and looked at Shay before she veered her stare to Chloe. "I suppose you're listed on there?"

Chloe nodded. Thank God for Shay's obsessive-compulsive disorder. She'd downloaded an emergency-contact card template from the American Red Cross and created one for each of them. She'd listed them each as one another's main contact, with all their numbers, and added Chloe's parents to them both. After that she'd had them laminated and insisted Chloe keep hers in her wallet, where it still remained.

Chloe had contacted Mary and Fred to let them know about the accident. It might not have been what Shay wanted, since she didn't have the same loving relationship Chloe had with her parents, but even so, she thought they should know their daughter had been hurt.

"I'll step out." Fred dipped his chin at Chloe, then turned to the nurse. "Can you update me on her condition?"

The nurse nodded and led him out the door. As they stood there, Mary continued to stare at Shay as though afraid to touch her. The resemblance was clear, especially the sandy-blond hair color and brown eyes. However, Mary's eyes were cold, even hard, not filled with the compassion usually present in Shay's. Chloe had seen that similar look only once in Shay's eyes, right before she'd left the beach house this morning. Her heart clenched. This was her fault.

"How did this happen?" Mary's voice pulled her out of her thoughts, demanding her attention.

She swiped a tear from her eye. "Her car was T-boned in an intersection."

Mary's expression didn't change. "Someone ran a red light?"

"Seems that way."

Unchanged, Mary moved closer and examined the bruises on Shay's face. "Have you contacted her insurance?"

"Really? That's what you're thinking about right now?" Shay had told Chloe many times how cold her mother was, but she hadn't been around her enough to experience her frigidness.

Mary squared her shoulders. "Well, someone's going to have to pay for all this, as well as her rehab if she wakes up," she said, her voice flat, emotionless.

If she wakes up? Chloe bolted out of the chair, went to the side of the bed, and took Shay's hand. "She *will* wake up." The thought that she wouldn't hadn't entered her mind.

"One can only hope." Mary's voice hadn't changed at all. She was the same cold, unfeeling mother Shay had described to her.

Chloe restrained herself from barreling into her and shoving her out the door. "Don't worry. I'll take care of everything." *You can march your ass right back out of here and never look back.*

"That won't be necessary. We'll take her home with us. That's where she belongs."

"No. You will not." The back of Chloe's neck heated, and her heart raced. "In fact, I think you should go now." She wouldn't let Mary take her home. She would never put Shay back into the hands of someone who didn't understand her, who had tried to kill her spirit and demeaned her so much she had no confidence at all. Shay wouldn't be able to bear that fate. Neither of them would.

Mary had narrowed her eyes and opened her mouth to say something when Fred poked his head just inside the door. "Mary, can I have a minute with her?"

Mary blew out a breath and reluctantly left the room as Fred entered. He immediately went to Shay's bedside, took her hand, and kissed her on the cheek, something you would expect from any good parent. Chloe watched the tears well in his eyes and wondered how two people so different had managed to stay married this long. She couldn't imagine the shit he had to put up with from Mary. She'd never had to experience such treatment with Shay. Their life had been perfect up until six months ago, and then it had exploded so quickly, she hadn't had time to even comprehend how things were changing.

"The nurse said her prognosis looks good. She'll have some recovery ahead of her once she wakes up." He motioned to her broken leg. "Walking and anything she does with her left leg will be a challenge. They want to start physical therapy right away." He smiled slightly. "Thankfully she's resilient, like me."

Shay had undergone surgery immediately to put in an internal plate and screws to properly align her broken femur. Fortunately the impact had been to the passenger side of the car, and she'd injured her head when it whipped back against the driver's door window.

"I know you'll take care of her."

Apparently, Shay hadn't told him the news. "I'll make sure she gets the right care." She didn't want to be Shay's caregiver, but she had no choice. Fred was a good father, Shay had told her about him, but her mother certainly didn't mirror the same values as he or Shay did. Moments of disapproval and efforts to recondition her into the person her mother thought she should be had riddled her entire adolescence.

Shay had been strong, but that strength hadn't come without pain. It hurt Chloe to think of what she'd been through because of her mother's refusal to accept her as she was—a sweet, beautiful woman who happened to love women. Thankfully, the beautiful woman Chloe had fallen in love with had persevered. She wasn't going to be in Shay's life permanently anymore, but she still wanted to be there when she woke up. She would never consider leaving Shay in her mother's care to recover, even if it meant putting her life with Erica, whatever that was, on hold.

CHAPTER THREE

Jackson rushed into the hospital room, set his cup on the bedside table, and took Chloe into his arms. The warmth and love he gave her made half her worries fade away immediately. Being here alone had her mind spinning up all kinds of ridiculous scenarios.

He put his hands on her shoulders and looked at her. "Why didn't you call me sooner?"

"I didn't see any sense in you being up here all night. There was nothing you could do."

"Bullshit. I could've kept you company. Got you coffee. Rubbed your feet. All the things a big brother does."

She chuckled at his humor. "Yes. You could've done all that."

"Well, I'm here now." He picked up the Starbucks cup from the bedside table and handed it to her. "Tell me what happened."

She sank down into the recliner. "A truck hit her car in an intersection. The whole thing was my fault." Chloe closed her eyes, reliving the event that had sent her on the road.

Jackson slid into the chair next to her. "The word 'accident' indicates that it wasn't your fault."

"She came to the beach house yesterday." She hesitated as she took a sip of coffee and let the warmth run from her mouth to her belly and settle in.

"You had another fight?" he asked.

She nodded. "Erica was there." Her stomach rumbled. She hadn't had anything to eat since Shay had left the beach house yesterday. The whole incident had made her appetite vanish.

"Oh. Now I see what you're saying." He took in a breath. "She couldn't have thought you weren't going to move on."

"I don't know what she thought, but I didn't want her to find out about my relation...whatever it is I have with Erica that way." She shook her head. "Not the way I found out about her and Lila. I wanted to tell her."

"She walked in on you having sex?" His voice rose, and an eyebrow flew up.

"No. Nothing like that. Erica moved some of her clothes in and had thrown Shay's in a pile on the chair."

Both his eyebrows rose this time. "You let Erica move in?"

She shrugged. "I didn't *let her*. She just kind of did."

"That was pretty presumptuous."

She nodded. "It was."

"Did you tell her it was?"

"Kind of, but not really. I guess." She'd never been good at laying down the law with anyone, let alone someone with as strong a personality as Erica.

The ICU nurse came in, checked the level of the IV medication, and left just as silently as she'd arrived.

Jackson motioned with his chin to Shay. "How's she doing?"

"The doctor says everything looks good, but they're keeping her in a medically induced coma to protect her brain from swelling. They think she hit her head on the window during the impact."

"What does that mean?"

"They're keeping her on a ventilator and in a deep, unconscious state to give her brain time to heal. She has an injury that hasn't responded to other medication."

The look on his face mirrored her thoughts. It was serious. "Is that unusual?"

"They act like it's standard procedure." She walked over to the bed and took Shay's hand. "The doctor said they should be able to bring her out of it in a few days." She stared at the cut and bruises on the left side of her head. "Hopefully, everything will be okay."

"I'm sure it will. You just need to be positive."

"I'm trying, Jackson. It's just not easy. There's been so much shit between us lately that I haven't been able to get past." She turned and fell into his arms. "If she doesn't recover from this, she'll never know how sorry I am." Or what an ass she'd been, not believing her, insisting she was lying about everything. So many things in her mind were uncertain now. Maybe it *was* all Lila. Maybe she'd seduced her when she was vulnerable. That wasn't impossible since the same thing had happened to her with Erica.

"When she wakes up, you can tell her everything. She's going to be all right."

Chloe didn't want anything in the world more than for Shay to come out of this unscathed, but she might not. She had no idea what she would do if she didn't.

Another nurse came through the door. "Do you mind stepping out for a few minutes? I need to give her a bath."

Jackson stood up and offered her his hand. "How about we go down to the cafeteria and get some food."

Chloe didn't move.

He took her hand from the bed rail and tugged her forward. "Come on. What good are you to her if you get sick?"

He was right. She needed to eat something, even if her appetite was gone. She reluctantly followed him out the door.

Chloe was only going to get a cup of soup. It was her go-to food when nothing sounded good, but Jackson pushed her to try a turkey sandwich as well. Now that she was eating it, she was glad he had. It had settled her stomach and didn't taste half bad. Hospital food seemed to have improved since the last time she'd been there as a kid when her mom was admitted for minor surgery. Or maybe she'd changed.

"So, I'm going to pick up some clothes for you at the beach house. Do you want me to take some of your things back to the apartment?"

She drew her brows together. "I'm not moving back in there."

"I know, but since you need to be here, it's much more convenient than driving to the beach."

"I guess you're right. It is a lot closer."

"Is there anything you'd like me to pick up at the apartment for Shay?"

"Oh my God, Ginger." She'd totally forgotten about their cat. "She's probably starving."

Jackson covered her hand with his. "Don't worry. I'll get the cat and take her to my place. It's only been a day. I'm sure she's fine. She's resilient and resourceful, like me." He grinned.

She laughed. "She's probably already eaten all the Cheerios in the pantry." Their three-year-old calico had learned how to open the cabinets and doors in the apartment. They'd had to make sure she always had food in her dish to prevent her from scavenging daily.

"And the Fruit Loops."

"Yes. Those too." Fruit Loops were too sweet for Chloe, but they were Shay's favorite.

"She's probably riding out the sugar high as we speak." He stood and picked up both their trays. "I'll walk you back upstairs, and then I'll go get her."

❖

Chloe's mind had wandered from the comedy show she'd been watching on the TV bolted to the wall of Shay's hospital room. The volume was low, and she was so tired she was having trouble keeping up with the captions on the bottom of the screen. The words just didn't have the same zing when you couldn't hear the feeling in them. The shows weren't as funny when you had no one to laugh about them with either. It had been another long night of insomnia sleeping in the recliner next to Shay's hospital bed.

She hoped the doctor would be in soon. The haze of worry and sadness she was stuck in was growing unbearable. Jackson had called a few times. Chloe's parents had checked in as well. Thankfully, Shay's parents hadn't been back to press the matter of taking her home with them. She would ignore many battles with them at this point—visitation and status information—but she refused to lose a battle about her after-hospital care. She still didn't know if she could handle it, but she wasn't willing to go with the alternative.

"Chloe?" Her mother's voice sang into the room as she opened the door.

She pushed forward in the recliner and scrubbed her face with her hands. "Hi, Mom." She smiled as her dad followed her in. "Dad."

"How are you doing, honey?"

"I'm fine. Did you find out anything about Shay?"

"Your father talked to her doctor, and he agrees this is the best treatment," her mother said as she crossed the room.

She looked at her father. "How long will they keep her like this?"

"A couple more days, max." He smiled slightly. "The prognosis looks good."

Relief washed over her. When it came to medicine, her dad didn't say anything that wasn't true.

Her mother took Shay's wrist, checked her pulse, and laid it back on the bed. "We're going to have her moved to a better room where she has dedicated care."

Just the mention of that change had her on her feet standing next to her mother. "Why? Is there something you're not telling me?"

"Of course not. We're doing it because we have the power to, and we want her to have the best care. She's our daughter-in-law." Her mother wrapped her hand around her shoulder and squeezed. Having a cardiothoracic surgeon for a father and a psychologist for a mother had its perks.

"Right." She hadn't told her parents about any of the trouble they'd been having or about her decision to move out. From the start of their relationship, they'd taken Shay in and loved her like she was their own. She hadn't wanted to disappoint them until she knew the break was a done deal, and she hadn't had enough time to decide that yet.

Once the staff was called into action, the move happened swiftly. Chloe hadn't had to do a thing except grab her bag and follow the crew of nurses and orderlies to the room. Shay had been moved to the VIP wing of the hospital that contained ten deluxe suites with the amenities of home and spectacular views. Furnished with a padded headboard and marble-topped bedside tables, this one seemed more like a five-star hotel suite than a hospital room.

Only the constant beep of the machines reminded her where they were. She just wanted Shay to wake up, so they could go back home. *Home.* Which home? The apartment or the beach? She thought the beach would be a more soothing atmosphere but didn't know if Shay would agree to stay there after what had happened before the accident. In fact, she didn't even know if Shay would allow her to care for her at all.

Her phone chirped, and she struggled to locate it. She finally found it in the bottom of her bag. She'd tossed it there last night after reading the gazzillionth text from Erica. The woman had a heart of stone. She'd wanted her to come home last night, but she wasn't leaving Shay alone. She'd heard enough horror stories about bad things that had happened to patients left alone in hospitals. She wouldn't abandon Shay to wake up in a strange place with strange people. Just the thought horrified her.

She looked at the screen. Multiple texts from Erica and one from Jackson. She skipped Erica's and opened Jackson's.

Picked up your clothes and got Ginger situated. I'm on my way back. Picking up food. What do you want?

Nothing for me. I'm not hungry.

Okay. Then I'll pick.

No Thai.

That would stink up the whole room, and if she happened to feel like eating anything when he got here, spicy wouldn't sit well on her stomach.

"I'm back," he sang as he pushed through the door, hands full of food and drinks. "Sorry it took so long. Traffic was hell, and then I had to find you."

She jumped up and pushed various items on the coffee table in front of the couch aside. "I forgot to tell you we moved."

"Into the fancy wing. You must rate somehow." He dropped the bag onto the table and handed her a drink. "Unsweet tea, right?"

She nodded and took the drink before she sat on the couch while Jackson unpacked the sandwiches and a bowl of her favorite potato soup from Panera Bread. He took off the lid and slid it across to her. It actually smelled really good, and her stomach growled loudly.

He laughed as he fished a plastic spoon out of the bag and handed it to her. "I knew that would get you."

And it did. She shoveled multiple spoonfuls into her mouth before she spoke again. "Thanks, Jackie. I didn't realize how hungry I was."

"I also got you that turkey-avocado sandwich you like." He took it out of the bag along with his and set it in front of her.

Her stomach rumbled at the thought of eating the sandwich. The mixed emotions she'd been experiencing over the past couple of days had kept her gut unsettled. She hadn't been able to eat much since the accident. "I'm not sure I can handle more than this right now."

"No worries. We'll put it in the fridge for later."

She probably wouldn't eat it, but he'd leave it just in case. "Have I told you lately what an awesome brother you are?"

"You don't have to tell me. I already know." He winked at her and then took a huge bite of his sandwich. "So, what are you gonna do, kid?" He reverted to what he always called her when they were talking about something serious. She'd never outgrow being his little sister.

"I honestly don't know." She took in a deep breath. "She may hate me when she wakes up, and I won't have an option."

"And if she doesn't?" he said around the bite of sandwich in his mouth.

She contemplated the question they'd been dancing around for the past couple of days. "Then I'll take her home and help her while she recuperates."

A stray piece of avocado that had fallen from his sandwich caught his attention. He picked it up and placed it between the turkey and bread as he seemed to gather his thoughts. "Do you think you can do that after all that's happened?"

She shrugged. "It'll be a challenge, but she doesn't have anyone besides her parents, and I'm not letting that happen."

"I'll help in any way I can." He wadded up the paper from his sandwich and tossed it into the bag on the coffee table.

She smiled softly. "I know. Thanks." Her brother was a huge goofball, but when it came to taking care of family, he was always there. No one could ask for a better big brother.

He picked up the remote and clicked on the TV. "Mind if I watch the game?"

"Sure. Whatever." The hard conversation was over. She knew he'd been wanting to know since the accident. He wasn't happy when he found out she and Shay were splitting and even more unhappy when he found out why. She'd asked him to stay out of it, and he had for the most part. She couldn't blame him for being curious about her next move.

They sat in silence as she finished the whole bowl of soup and then relaxed into the couch. She could barely keep her eyes open. Last night had been rough. She'd woken up every time someone had come into the room, which was about every hour.

When she woke up again, the TV was off, and the table was clear, except for a small, five-by-eight leather book. On top of it she found a note from Jackson.

Going home to check on Ginger. Be back later with Whitney. Text if you need anything. Found a stack of these in Shay's closet while I was searching for Ginger. This looks like #1 for you two. You should read it.

CHAPTER FOUR

Jackson was so sweet, and Chloe knew she didn't have time to worry about anything but Shay right now. But she hadn't expected him to find the journals. She knew they were there, and another stack remained in the closet at the beach house as well. She'd never felt the need to invade Shay's privacy to glimpse her thoughts or see what she might have written about her. Especially during the past few months.

Chloe stared at the leather-bound book in her lap, afraid to open it, afraid of what she might find inside. It wasn't really a book. It was a ledger of her daily activities. Shay was so analytical it was unreal, but Chloe had learned to accept and come to love that trait in her. When she'd first found out that Shay kept a journal, she was surprised. She'd thought that most people who kept them did so because they had no one to talk to. Maybe that had been the case for Shay before they'd met, but they'd been together for the better part of the past five years. Chloe thought they'd communicated well through most of it, except the last six months or so, when neither one of them had confided their feelings of loneliness to the other. Why hadn't Shay just talked to her? Why hadn't *she* just talked to Shay?

Between the leather bindings were Shay's innermost thoughts—writings from the soul, perhaps even confessions. The journal was staring back at her, begging her to open it, turn the pages, and discover things about Shay she'd never known and possibly some she'd never known about herself as well. She opened the cover and read the date, which was June 23, close to five years ago. The day they met. Her heartbeat raced as she read the first line.

> *Now I believe in love at first sight...*
> *The girl of my dreams stepped into my life tonight. I don't know*

how or when, but there will be something between us, and whatever it is, I'm positive it will be spectacular. She's an artist. Her name is Chloe, a beautiful name, and it fits her perfectly. She doesn't look at all like her brother, Jackson. Her hair is raven black, and her blue eyes were enough to mesmerize me the moment she looked at me. When I touched her arm, her porcelain skin felt creamy-soft. She looked as though she'd never spent a day in the sun. Tonight, my life changed in just one moment. To think that I almost didn't go to the wedding, and then, once I got there, I debated about leaving early. Thank God I didn't.

When the reception got too loud, I walked down the steps to the beach. I was sitting in the sand watching the waves crash into the shore when I first saw her. She strolled by with her friends, red dress pulled up in one hand off the ground, strappy, silver shoes dangling from her fingers in the other. Legs to die for, she was simply gorgeous. Too gorgeous for me to think she'd ever be interested in someone like me. I watched her stroll down the beach away from me, stopping momentarily and squealing when the icy ocean water crashed across her feet. She glanced back over her shoulder but didn't seem to notice me until she and her friends were on their way back. My eyes were glued to the water when she stopped and said hi. I was so nervous, I'm not even sure I answered. She asked me what I was doing on the beach all alone. I managed to tell her I was enjoying the view and the sound of the waves, which had been totally drowned out by the sound of my heartbeat pounding in my ears. I love the serenity of the ocean. It helps me stay at peace with myself. Chloe kept eye contact for longer than I was comfortable with, and then she suddenly turned to her friends and told them to go on without her, that she'd be up in a bit.

My heart pounded faster when she sat in the sand next to me. I had no idea what was coming next, but she didn't say a word, just stared out at the ocean. We watched the sunset together, and when the stars came out, Chloe whispered, "Thank you for enjoying that gorgeous sunset with me. You made it so much more special," and then she stood up.

My tongue doubled in size, and anything that spilled out of my mouth seemed primitive. Chloe leaned forward, her brows furrowed as she tried to interpret what I'd said. Then she smiled slowly and offered me her hand. She was too gracious to make me repeat what I had barely managed to choke out.

My hand tingled as she took it and led me up the beach and inside to the reception. The warmth of her hand spread throughout me, and I felt things I'd never felt before. We found a table in the corner, where we talked for the rest of the night about anything and everything. All I could see were her beautiful blue eyes and gorgeous smile. Her laugh penetrated my very core, and I knew right then if anything ever came of our chance meeting, I was going to fall hard for her.

She stayed with me for the rest of the reception, talking about art, culture, and so many other things. By the time the night was over, I felt like I'd known her forever. Before we left, she sought out her parents and introduced me to them as an old friend. Oddly enough, after only a few hours with her, that's the way I felt. The look she gave me made me shudder as though an invisible pulse of electricity was hovering between us, and there was exactly that. I walked her to her car, and as I opened the door for her, I wondered if I should chance a kiss on the cheek, but I didn't have the guts. While I was letting my nerves get the best of me, she hovered closer and brushed my cheek with a kiss that was gentle and warm. I breathed her in, a mixture of sea air and spice that's still with me now. I can't describe the incredible feeling I had tonight, but I know it's something I've never felt before.

Chloe had never forgotten it either. She remembered the night like it had happened only yesterday. She'd noticed her, all right. It wasn't by chance that she'd come across Shay sitting on the beach that night. She'd seen her arrive and had been stealing glimpses of her all evening. Shay had spent most of her time with people whom her brother, Jackson, had invited from work. She couldn't imagine why he hadn't told her about Shay before. She'd managed to pull him away for a few minutes and fire questions at him about her. He'd given her minimal information before his attention had returned to his bride, Whitney. But it was enough to start a conversation, if she had the nerve. Shay was new to his insurance company, an actuary just like him. He'd said she seemed to know her stuff and was great with numbers. Who knew an actuary could be so beautiful? Her brother was a horrible wingman. He didn't know if she was gay or even if she was single. She'd shown up solo, and Chloe had witnessed her refuse to dance with her coworkers more than once. She'd thought her odds were good.

She'd watched her leave the reception and head down to the beach. Shay had descended the steps leisurely and paused at the bottom to glance at the ocean before she'd stepped into the sand, moved to her right, and walked out of Chloe's view. Dressed in a black dress that accentuated her thin, slight figure, Shay was a gorgeous sight, someone Chloe knew she had to meet. She couldn't help herself. She'd immediately rounded up two of her best friends from college and made them come with her to the beach.

They'd made one pass in front of Shay, who hadn't looked up. So, with the help of her friends as they turned and walked back up the beach, she worked up enough nerve to talk to her. Then she'd done something totally out of character. She'd made the first move. She'd sent her friends on their way and sat down next to her.

Conversation had been sparse. They'd only spoken a handful of words to each other. No meaningless conversation about the weather, the waves, or anything else. They'd just sat and enjoyed the sunset together. Any other time she would've been extremely uncomfortable sitting in silence with someone, especially a stranger. She remembered glancing sideways and catching Shay's sandy-blond, shoulder-length hair as it flew up and scattered with the wind. The way the sunset reflected on Shay's face and in her amber eyes was stunning. She'd never seen such a gorgeous sight.

Later, after they'd rejoined the reception, their conversation started, and it hadn't stopped until the party was over. The chemistry between them had been electric from the very beginning. She'd wanted to spend the rest of the night with her, would've if she'd asked. Instead she'd let Shay walk with her to her car, brushed her cheek lightly with her lips, and held back on the first kiss that eventually changed her life.

She'd thought about Shay for days after the wedding until she'd finally gained the courage to drop by Jackson's office and pretend to pick up something, anything, just to run into her. She hadn't had her phone at the reception, so she hadn't gotten Shay's number. She would've absolutely died if she'd had to wait another week for Jackson to get back from his honeymoon before she could see her. That day she went to his office, she had, indeed, run into Shay. The encounter was a little awkward at first, but they'd recovered quickly. She'd gotten Shay's number, and they'd also had lunch that day. Not a day had passed since then that they hadn't talked…until recently. How had they traveled so far from a moment that had affected them both so deeply?

CHAPTER FIVE

When Chloe woke, Shay's mother, Mary, was sitting on the couch thumbing through Shay's journal. She bolted out of the chair and snatched it from her hand. "What do you think you're doing? That's personal."

"It was on the floor. I picked it up."

"And then decided to invade Shay's privacy." The woman had no boundaries.

"Seems you have too." Mary twisted her lip into a smirk.

"She's my wife."

"She's my daughter." The fuck-you tone in Mary's voice told Chloe she was in for a fight.

"You lost all parental rights when you didn't support her."

"I supported her in everything." Mary's voice rose sharply before she took in a breath and said softly, "But not the things that went against my beliefs. I could never do that."

"No, but you expected her to conform to them. Shay told me all about the so-called summer camps you sent her to trying to make her into someone she isn't." Just the thought made her blood boil.

"You have no idea what you're talking about." Mary denied her callous actions as though they had never occurred, but Chloe knew better.

"I know that's not something a loving mother does. Do you even love her?"

"Of course I love her."

"Did you ever tell her that? Or were you too busy trying to change her?"

Mary narrowed her eyes. "Being married to you has kept her away from me more than I'd like."

At least she'd acknowledged that they were married. "Her choice, not mine."

"I'd like to take her home with me and work on that."

"Absolutely not. If she decides to see you during her recovery, you can come see her at our house." *Our house.* The words had come out so naturally, like nothing had changed between them. She guessed her need to protect Shay from going back to a home void of unconditional love was affecting her.

"Her recovery is going to take some time, which will take your focus from your art. It would benefit us both if she comes home with me." Mary stood up. "Think about it."

"You're not listening, Mary. I said no. Shay is much more important to me than any piece of art." The funny thing was, it was true. Even after everything that had happened between them, she felt her words deep in her heart. She could never let her go back to that environment, whether they were together or not. No. She would make sure Shay got the care she needed while she recovered. After that, she had no idea what would happen.

❖

The sky was dark and overcast. As Chloe stared out the window, she wondered if a storm was coming in off the ocean. She knew it was at least twenty degrees hotter outside than it was in the hospital. The clouds were deceiving. She opened the weather app on her phone and watched red, yellow, and green radar motion travel across the screen. A storm was indeed on its way.

When she turned to check on Shay, she was startled to see Lila standing next to the bed.

"What are you doing here?" She rushed across the room. "And how did you get past the nurses' station?" A nurse was stationed just inside the double doors of the wing. They didn't let just anyone past that point.

"When I got word about the accident, I drove back immediately." She seemed to ignore the second question.

Drove back? From where? Wasn't she waiting for her somewhere yesterday? Their apartment, her apartment? Millions of questions swam in her head. Had Shay really stopped seeing her? Had she been telling the truth when she came to the beach house? "She said she was done with you." Chloe had to know if it was true.

"She also said you were done with her." She rolled her eyes. "You think she's analytical, unemotional, and boring."

"I've never, *ever* thought that at all." Were those Lila's words or Shay's? Had she ever done anything to make Shay think she was unemotional or boring? Chloe shook her head as the back of her neck heated. No, she hadn't. "She's still my wife and my responsibility."

"So, you're not?" Lila took Shay's hand in hers. "Done with her?"

She saw sadness in Lila's eyes, something she hadn't expected to have to deal with. Something she didn't *want* to deal with. She shrugged off the compassion that threatened to overshadow her anger. "What happens between me and Shay is none of your business."

"Oh, but I think it is now." Her eyes hardened. "Last I heard, you permanently moved out of the apartment to that beautiful place she bought on the beach."

Who the fuck does she think she is? "We bought that together." She gripped the side rail of the bed to steady herself. It had been a surprise, and Shay had made the down payment, but they'd made the payments together.

Lila glanced up at her for a moment and raised an eyebrow. "Right. She worked sixty hours a week while you played at your gallery, but you bought it *together*." Her gaze went back to Shay, and she stroked the back of Shay's hand with her thumb.

Jealousy flooded her as she watched Lila caress her hand. "You should go." She forced herself not to round the bed and physically remove Lila from the room. "Now."

Lila gently placed Shay's hand back onto the bed and went to the door before glancing back. "Just so you know. Whether or not your marriage is finished, *I'm not* done with her." She pulled the door open and was gone.

She turned back to the window, grabbed the windowsill, and let the tears flow. She would certainly have more than one storm in her future.

❖

The hospital was quiet for the time being. The nurses had been in and out several times throughout the day, checking Shay's IV and vitals. She hadn't turned the TV back on since the last nurse had left about ten minutes ago after delivering an elegant rolling table with dinner. Although the shrimp fettuccine looked delicious, she still didn't have an appetite. The nurse had urged her to spend some time in the other room of the suite, which had a larger TV and more comfortable furniture. She'd appreciated the suggestion but remained sitting in the recliner next to Shay's bed, staring out the window. It was a beautiful view that Shay would enjoy if she were awake. She was very grateful for the care Shay was getting and thankful her parents had been able to arrange it. They were both on the hospital board and were willing to pay any extra cost incurred.

The door pushed open, breaking her thoughts. "Hey, how's she doing?" Jackson stepped into the room and handed her one of the coffee cups in his hands before he wrapped his free arm around her and squeezed.

"Thanks, but I really don't need any more caffeine." She set it on the bedside table. "I haven't slept much at all."

He swiped it back up, handed it to her, and lifted his cup. "It's a special blend of decaf. I think you'll like it." He took a drink and smiled.

She gave in like she always did with her brother and took a small sip. When the sweet nectar of fermented grapes filled her mouth, she almost choked. "Wine?"

He shrugged "I thought you might need something to take the edge off." He held his up and winked. "Cheers."

"Oh my God, Jackson. You don't know how much I need this. I've had the day from hell." She snuggled under his arm and squeezed him. Jackson was the most awesome brother a girl could ask for—a rule-breaker with all the right intentions, who also had the smarts to stay out of trouble.

He pointed his cup toward Shay. "Everything okay with her?"

"Yeah. No change there." She took another drink and let the taste wash over her. "Her mother came by again today." She held back telling him about Lila's visit.

"She still wants to take her home?"

She nodded. "Not gonna happen."

"I'm glad you're taking control of this, sis."

"I have to. That toxic environment would be hell on her."

The door opened again, and Whitney walked in. His eyes widened, and he held his finger to his lips.

"Stop." Whitney rolled her eyes. "I saw you hide the bottle. Who wears a jacket in eighty-degree weather?" She took the top off her coffee and poured what was left into the sink. "Now give me some."

He took out the bottle, pulled the cork loose, and filled her cup halfway. "What's for dinner, sis?" Jackson set his cup on the white table cloth and lifted the lid from the plate. "Shrimp fettuccine. Yum."

"Jackson. Leave that. It's for Chloe, and she needs to eat it."

"I just want a taste. She doesn't mind." He unwrapped the silverware, picked up the fork, and twirled a gob of pasta with it. "Oh my God, this is delicious," he said with a mouthful of food as he spooled another forkful of fettuccine. "You need to taste this." He held the fork in front of Chloe's mouth.

She shook her head. "I'm not hungry." She held up her cup. "I will take more wine, though."

"If you want more wine, you have to eat some pasta."

"What the fuck, Jackson." She reached for the bottle. "I'm a grown woman. I can have wine if I want it." She grabbed the bottle and plucked the cork from it.

He flattened his lips. "Yes, you can. But you need to take care of yourself so that when Shay wakes up, you have the strength to take care of her." He dropped the fork onto the plate, took the bottle from her, and poured more into her cup. "That is your plan, right?"

"You're going to care for her?" Whitney's voice rose. "What about her parents?" Apparently, she'd forgotten about Shay's family situation.

"I don't want her parents involved. At least not her mother. Shay would hate me even more for that."

Whitney glanced at Jackson, and he nodded. "It's a bad deal." He picked up the fork and held it in front of her again. "So, eat, please."

She took the bite of pasta and swallowed it. "It's cold."

He picked up the plate. "I can fix that. There's a microwave at the nurses' station." He headed for the door. "Be right back."

Whitney moved a couple of throw pillows to the corner of the couch and sank down next to them, propping her arm on top of the back. "What are you gonna do if Shay doesn't want your help?"

"I don't know. I'll cross that bridge when I come to it. But I won't abandon her. Not now. Not since I'm the reason she's here." She couldn't stop the tears she'd been holding back for the past few days.

Whitney bolted from the couch and took her into her arms. "You're not why she's here. The guy who ran the red light did this."

"Oh my God, Whit. What the hell am I going to do if she doesn't wake up?" She sobbed into Whitney's shoulder.

"She'll wake up. The doctor doesn't see any reason why she shouldn't."

"Other than the fact that her head shattered the fucking window." She pushed away and scrubbed the tears from her cheeks. "I don't care if she hates me for the rest of my life as long as she comes out of this."

"Jesus, Chloe. What happened to that glass-half-full girl I went to college with?"

"She's gone. Has been for months." She shook her head. "I'm responsible for this. All of it." Nothing was going to rid her of the guilt she felt right now. Whether it would go away after Shay regained consciousness was yet to be seen.

Jackson came back with the pasta. "Shit, that's hot." He slid it onto the table and then shook his hands. "You'd think in a ritzy place like this they'd have some hot pads."

Chloe chuckled. "Or a towel, or something."

"Shut it," he said and handed her the fork. "Now sit and eat."

She made herself eat a few bites, chugged the rest of her wine, and then forced down a few more before she dropped the fork to the plate. "That's it. No more."

He examined the plate and said, "Okay," before he picked up the fork and finished what was left.

The three of them watched the sunset through the window, and then Jackson found a movie on TV to watch, so they stayed a few more hours. Chloe couldn't keep her eyes open, but she'd been awake to hear Jackson say he'd see her tomorrow after he covered her with a blanket and kissed her forehead. He knew she wasn't leaving this hospital until they brought Shay out of this coma. She needed to make sure she was awake and okay.

CHAPTER SIX

The door opened, and the nurse stood on the threshold. "A woman out here named Erica says she's a friend of the family. Do you want us to let her in?"

Two in two days was too much for Chloe to handle. She launched out of the chair and rushed to the door. "No. I'll come out there." She went to the bed and patted Shay's hand. "I'll be right back." She didn't know if Shay could hear her, but she'd read stories of people who said they'd heard everything while they were unconscious.

She followed the nurse down the hallway and around the corner, where she found Erica chatting up the orderly at the desk.

Erica immediately rushed to her and pulled her into a hug. "I've been so worried. You haven't been answering my texts or my calls."

"My phone's dead." She was lying. She led her to the doors and pushed the button to open them. "You can't come in here." She stepped out into the hallway and then the waiting room as the door closed behind them.

"What can I do?"

"Nothing." She looked at the chairs, the door, the vending machine. Everywhere but at Erica. "You've done enough."

"You can't possibly be blaming this on me," Erica said as her hand went to her hip.

"No. It's all on me. I accept full responsibility." She should've never let Erica move her clothes in so soon. Not that she'd had a choice. She and Shay had barely separated, and the emotional wounds were still raw. And now Erica was here to claim her again, while her soul mate, the woman she'd thought she'd be with forever, was lying in a hospital bed in a medically induced coma to reduce the swelling of her brain.

"How long are you going to keep this up? Sitting by her bedside like this?" It was clear Erica wasn't happy. "I haven't seen you in days." She reached for Chloe's hand and squeezed it. "I miss you."

"I don't know." She slipped her hand away. "I can't leave her here alone." Everything she'd said was true. She had no idea what her next step would be. That would depend on whether the prognosis the doctor had given them was accurate, which they had yet to see. She planned to do everything she could to help with Shay's recovery. Even if it meant limiting herself to a few stolen moments with Erica here and there while Shay recovered. If her conscience would even let her do that. She wasn't about to let Erica make things harder for Shay or her.

"Can I get you some food? Bring you some clothes?"

She shook her head. "Jackson's taking care of that." She went into the hall and pushed the button for the doors. "I have to get back to her." She turned and left Erica standing in the waiting room. It was cruel, but Erica had been the catalyst for the accident. She'd taken liberties, done things Chloe hadn't given her permission to do, and she couldn't get past that yet.

She shouldn't have been so cold to Erica. She'd been there for her when she'd needed comfort, hadn't she? Or had she just been an opportunist who had stepped in at the right time? She'd heard so many lies over the past six months, she wasn't sure about anything anymore.

Chloe hadn't meant to spy on Shay. The fact that she'd even seen the text messages was a fluke, really. Shay had bought a new MacBook Pro and had given Chloe her old MacBook to use at the studio. No one was more surprised when the message popped up on the screen from Lila. Right after that, all the previous messages populated as well. The whole horrible discovery was burned into her memory.

"What the fuck?" she said as she read the first line of text from Lila.

Can you come over tonight? I miss you.

Shay's response appeared from the bubbles next: *I should be able to break away for a little while. Should I bring dinner?*

Lila's response made her stomach clench. *I'm only hungry for one thing. You'd better get here quick before I start without you.*

Shay wrote back, *On my way…we'll be working though.*

Lila responded with a sad-face emoji. *All work and no play makes Lila a sad girl.*

After reading the first few texts, Chloe thought she might vomit. She read a few more, ran to the bathroom, and became physically ill. They might not have been sleeping together yet, but she'd seen flirting like that before, and they were definitely moving in that direction.

Three days had passed before she could look again. Later that week, she'd closed the gallery and sat all alone in the office wondering if she wanted to know more. She didn't, but she *needed* to know more. She stayed until almost midnight reading through thousands of texts, finding out things she didn't want to and didn't know what she'd done to push Shay away. How could she derail the direction this was taking?

All this time Shay had been so jealous of Erica, yet nothing at all had gone on between them. Not that Erica hadn't tried, but Chloe loved Shay and was crushed that she didn't feel the same anymore. That night of discovery was burned into her memory.

She heard a knock on the glass in the front of the gallery and peeked around the corner of the office to get a glimpse of who in the world would be here at this time of night. It was Erica. She gave her a wave, stepped back into the office, wiped her face, and checked her reflection in the mirror. She couldn't hide her red, swollen eyes. After taking a few deep breaths to calm herself, she smoothed her skirt, walked to the front of the gallery, and opened the door.

"Hey. What are you doing here so late?"

"How did you know I was here?" She let Erica inside, relocked the door, and headed back to the office. She didn't like hanging out in the middle of the gallery when it was closed. The way the gallery was lit inside, it was like being in a fishbowl. People could easily see in, but it was difficult to see out.

"I was on my way home and saw your car."

That was a plausible excuse. Erica owned a very nice house in the upscale neighborhood bordering the arts district.

"I was just catching up on some paperwork."

"You don't look like you were doing paperwork." Erica reached over and lifted her chin. "What's going on?"

She shrugged out of her grasp. "I'm fine." She rushed into the office and slapped the laptop closed as she sat behind the desk.

"Is it money?" Erica's look of concern seemed genuine. "I'll be happy to loan you whatever you need."

She shook her head. "No. Money can't fix this."

"What is it, love?" Erica slid onto the corner of the desk. "Let me help." She lowered her chin to catch Chloe's gaze. "Please?"

She couldn't stop the tears, and they rushed from her eyes and down her cheeks. Erica was on her knees immediately, pulling her into her arms.

"Shay is having an affair." She couldn't stop the words as they tumbled out, possibly not physically but definitely emotionally.

"Oh my God." Erica squeezed her tighter. "That girl must be out of her mind to fuck around on you."

"All this time she's been accusing me of having an affair with you."

"I'd be a lucky girl if that were happening."

"I don't think so. Apparently, I'm not all that special."

"Don't ever say that. You're the most beautiful creature I know." Erica stared into her eyes, holding contact.

"You really think so?"

"I've thought so since the first moment I walked into this gallery."

That was the beginning of the decimation of her relationship with Shay. A month later she'd caught Shay and Lila together at Shay's office and couldn't go back from there.

It had been three days since Chloe had showered. She bent her head under the stream and let the warmth wash over her. Her muscles ached from sleeping in the recliner, and she seemed to have a permanent kink in her neck. She flipped the dial hotter, and the heat felt wonderful as it pulsed on her shoulders. When the nurse had come in to get Shay for an MRI, she'd given her one look and advised her to go home and change. Chloe hadn't wanted to leave, but the nurse said it would take at least an hour and she should take some time to care for herself or she wouldn't be much good to Shay when she regained consciousness. She'd sat in the empty room for a few minutes before she'd gone into the bathroom and looked in the mirror. Her reflection was alarming, if not scary. A woman she didn't recognize stared back at her, hair pushed up on one side, black mascara smudges and dark circles under her eyes. She looked like she'd been sleeping in the back of her car for weeks. She took the nurse's advice and had gone to the apartment to shower and change.

She sorted through the pieces of clothing in the closet. She hadn't made it back for the last load the other day, and unlike Erica, Shay hadn't tossed the items remaining into a pile on a chair somewhere. *Erica.* What had she been thinking, getting involved with her? They really didn't have anything in common, except that Chloe created art and Erica loved to buy it. Sure, every bit of her art that Erica bought had brought her one step closer to where she was today—to her own exclusive gallery. Erica had connections and had used them to get her noticed. Chloe hadn't even slept with her because of that, which would've made sense in so many ways. She'd just been stupid and vulnerable after she'd discovered Shay's indiscretion and had fallen into her bed looking for comfort. As soon as it was over, she'd felt so guilty, she'd left immediately and then gone straight to the beach house and cried. She hadn't understood her feelings then, and she still didn't now.

She held a sleeve from one of Shay's dress shirts in her hand, rubbed the soft cotton-blend fabric between her fingers before she pressed it to her nose, and inhaled. The scent both calmed and agitated her. So many thoughts cluttered her mind. She wished she'd never read those text messages. Never gone looking for Shay that day. Never seen what she'd seen. She didn't care what people who knew thought. She would've still been blissfully happy. Well, maybe not blissfully, but she'd still be living within her comfort zone. When had she become so weak?

She spun around, took a pair of jeans and a black tank top from the bottom drawer of the dresser, and slipped them on. The hanger flew off the rod when she tugged an oversized off-the-shoulder cotton shirt from the closet and slipped it over her head. She refused to wallow in self-pity. All she could do now was move forward.

CHAPTER SEVEN

Shay wanted the noise to stop. It was Sunday and she wanted to sleep in. Yesterday had been a glorious day. She and Chloe had spent the afternoon at the beach, which was now located just five hundred feet from the back door of their new beach house. Chloe had finally arranged her studio the way she'd wanted it and had painted for most of the morning. She'd seemed so happy when Shay had peeked in on her mid-morning to bring her a fresh cup of coffee. The huge smile had been an indication, but the long, lingering kiss had been a definite notification. They'd made love and then grabbed their boogie boards and headed for the water. Perfect day, perfect location, perfect wife. Life was good.

"Shay. Can you open your eyes for me?"

The man's voice rang though Shay's dreams, but she didn't recognize it. She tried to open her eyes, but they were so heavy. "Stop," she said, pushing the hand from her shoulder.

"That's a good sign, right?" she heard Chloe say.

"What's a good sign? That I want to sleep in?" She rubbed her eyes, felt a tug on her arm when she raised it. "I always sleep in on Sunday."

Chloe chuckled. "That's true."

She opened her eyes slightly and reached for Chloe. "Come back to bed." She grasped her arm and pulled her forward.

Chloe found her balance again. "The doctor needs to talk to you."

Doctor? Why was a doctor in their bedroom? She bolted up, felt a sharp penetrating pain all the way up her leg, and her head swam. She glanced around the room. A hotel room? Had they gone on a trip? And what the hell was attached to her arm? Why was it so cold? She sank back into the bed.

"What…" Her voice cracked. Chloe put a straw into her mouth, and she sipped some water. "Where are we?" She moved her arm to take the cup and winced.

"Shay, I'm Dr. Graves and you're in the hospital."

She opened her eyes, looked briefly at the doctor before she stared at her hand, and traced the clear tubing to the IV pole.

"Chloe." She spoke softly at first, then repeated her name anxiously. "Chloe!" She tried to shift, and pain shot down her leg.

"It's okay, I'm here." Chloe stroked the side of Shay's face before she took her hand. "Try not to move. You were in a car accident."

"I don't remember it."

"That's not unusual," the doctor said. "It's not uncommon for people to forget the whole traumatic event." He took something out of his pocket and said, "Look straight ahead." Suddenly she had a bright light in her eyes. "What's the last thing you remember?"

She looked up at Chloe and couldn't quite make out her expression. Fear, worry? She didn't know, but it seemed to be something other than relief. "We were at the beach." Chloe's expression didn't change. "You painted in your studio all morning, and then we spent the rest of the day at the beach in the water."

Chloe's eyebrows rose. "Are you sure that's all you remember?"

"Yeah." She squeezed Chloe's hand. "It was an awesome day. I'm so glad we closed early on the beach house, or we would've missed a beautiful weekend."

"It was a wonderful day." Chloe smiled softly.

Son of a bitch! Pain shot through her again as she shifted. "Something hurts really bad." Beads of sweat formed on her forehead.

"It's your leg," Chloe said and then glanced at the doctor.

He nodded. "Your femur was broken in the accident. We inserted a rod, and everything looks good."

"A rod?" The words blew out of her mouth softly.

"Secured by six screws. The femur is the largest bone in your body. It holds most of your body weight when you walk. You'll have to go through physical therapy for a few weeks, and you'll need to hold off on any sports activities for a while, but it should heal nicely." He turned to the nurse. "We need to get her scheduled for PT right away." He headed for the door and the nurse followed.

"Can I have a quick word with you?" Chloe asked.

He stopped just short of the door and turned around. Shay couldn't hear what Chloe was saying, but his brows furrowed, and he walked back to her bedside.

"Can you tell me what month it is?"

The beautiful lilies and honeysuckle they'd planted in the front yard flashed in her head, then the crispness of the beach. "May. We just closed on the beach house last month." She glanced up at Chloe, but she wasn't smiling. "Right?"

"You're a few months off." He plucked his flashlight from his pocket and flashed it in her eyes again.

She shifted forward, and her body tingled from the pain. "How many months?"

"It's March now." Chloe's voice was soft, tentative even, and the concern in her eyes was clear.

"You'll have a few things to catch up on." He smiled and patted her on the hand.

"She will remember, right?" Chloe asked.

"The memories may or may not come back." The smile on the doctor's face didn't falter.

She'd lost time. Almost a whole year. The pain in her leg increased as she blew out a breath and settled back against the mattress. "Can you give me something for this pain?"

"Sure. Nothing too strong. We need to get you back on your feet as soon as possible." He glanced at the nurse, nodded, and they both left the room.

They weren't even going to give her a day to absorb the loss. She glanced up at Chloe, who was smiling slightly, but her brows were pulled together. Clearly, the news had upset her too. She hadn't noticed at first, but Chloe looked different. Her hair was longer, straighter. Ten or eleven months' worth of growth. She reached up, took a few strands between her fingers.

"It's gotten long. I need to cut it," Chloe said.

"No. Don't. It's beautiful." Everything about Chloe was beautiful: her hair, her eyes, her smile. She was even more gorgeous than she remembered.

Chloe's cheeks reddened as she smiled, and she looked away. It seemed as though she'd never heard that compliment before.

The nurse came back with a small cup containing a pill and a Styrofoam cup full of water. "This should help take the edge off. You're scheduled for physical therapy this afternoon."

"You guys don't mess around, do you?"

"Nope. We don't want those joints to freeze up on you." She took the cup from her and walked to the door. "You'll thank me six months down the road when you have full mobility."

"Can you fill me in on what happened?" She saw the reluctance in Chloe's eyes. "Maybe just start with the accident. You look okay, so you weren't with me, right?"

Chloe shook her head. "No. I was at the beach house." She took in a deep breath and smiled. "But I can tell you what the emergency responders told me."

"Did you call my parents?"

Chloe nodded. "Considering your condition, I felt I should."

"Have they been here at all?"

Chloe nodded again. "A couple of times. Your dad's downstairs getting coffee. And I think your mother is hoping you've forgotten you're a lesbian," Chloe said with a chuckle.

She reached for Chloe's hand. "Definitely not the case. I'm still hopelessly in love with this gorgeous woman who picked me up on the beach at her brother's wedding."

"I didn't pick you up. We just ran into each other."

"Hmm, that's not the way I remember it."

"We'll have to table that discussion for another time." Chloe's voice was low and soft, the way it got when she was unsure of herself. "Your dad should be back soon." Chloe squeezed her hand. "I'm so glad you're awake. I was worried about you."

"How long have I been out?"

"Just a few days."

"The whole waiting thing must have been tough. Are you okay?"

The door pushed open before Chloe could answer, and Shay's father came in.

"Princess, you're awake." The excitement in his voice was clear. "We've been so worried." He looked at Chloe.

"She doesn't remember the accident," Chloe said.

Her father patted her hand. "You just relax, honey. It will all come back to you soon."

"It's possible she may not remember."

Shay's dad cut her off. "We can discuss her recovery in more detail with the doctor later."

❖

Chloe sat silently, staring at the journal on the table in front of her as she waited for Jackson to arrive. She'd called him, and he'd agreed to meet her at the pancake house across from the hospital. It hadn't taken Shay long to fall asleep after Chloe had given her the facts she knew about the accident. She'd purposely not told her why she'd been at that intersection at that time or what had driven her to be distracted and not see the car speeding through the red light. None of it had come back to her, and that was probably a good thing at this point.

Shay had sat frozen for some time, amazed and a bit disturbed that she couldn't remember anything about it and seemed sad to learn that her Kona Blue Mustang convertible, her only real indulgence, had been totaled. That was the least of Chloe's worries. She had no idea how she was going to tell Shay about the last six months, especially how abruptly their relationship had come to an end, and *why*.

A calmness had enveloped her now that Shay was sleeping. She was alive and okay. Her heart had thumped wildly when she saw Shay's eyes flutter open. She'd been so relieved she hadn't thought anything else could go wrong. They'd finally reduced the medication they'd been giving her to induce the coma. Whatever swelling had existed in her brain had gone down, and the doctor was optimistic about her recovery. He'd said it had been minimal, which was beneficial.

Clear horror had shown in Shay's eyes. Her gaze had darted around the room and then finally settled on Chloe. A wisp of a smile had come and then left her lips, and she'd tried to speak. Chloe had picked up the water glass from the table, slipped the straw between Shay's lips, and let her drink.

The sound she'd made when she'd tried to move had been horrifying, and the confusion was evident in her voice when Shay finally realized she was in the hospital. The look in her eyes when the doctor mentioned the accident and her broken leg had been nothing short of panic.

Chloe had been relieved and terrified all at once. Shay was awake, but how would she react to her? Would Shay blame her for the accident or, even worse, hate her for moving on? But then the last thing she'd remembered turned out to be a day on the beach so many months ago. Chloe remembered the day clearly. It *was* beautiful, the first time in weeks that everything had felt right between the two of them. They hadn't had any work or events, absolutely no obligations, and they'd thoroughly enjoyed each other.

A whirlwind of thoughts filled Chloe's mind, and she felt dizzy. The love of her life had wiped every scrap of the last year from her memory. Good and bad. Had it been that inconsequential? Had she been that unimportant? An odd jumble of emotions flooded her— relief, happiness, joy, sadness. She couldn't even begin to interpret her feelings in that moment. Clearly she still loved Shay with all her heart. What happened next would be the struggle. How could she reconcile her immense love for Shay with the pain of betrayal in her heart?

She saw Jackson pull into the parking lot through the window and watched him park. He seemed to be taking an excessive amount of time getting inside. She saw him approach the door with his phone glued to his ear, probably talking to Whitney. In that marriage, one of them never did anything without telling the other. Once he was inside and seated, the waitress came over and took their order. Chloe didn't have much of an appetite, so she ordered French fries, and Jackson got pancakes. Since he was a kid, breakfast for dinner had always been one of his favorites.

They'd been sitting there for close to ten minutes, and she'd barely said a word to him. She had no idea where to start.

"Are you gonna tell me what's going on in that head of yours?"

"She doesn't remember anything that happened. Not her affair, not the separation. None of it. I don't know what to do."

"Why can't you start again?" Jackson picked up Shay's journal, thumbed through it, and paused to read an entry. "There's some pretty strong stuff in here."

"I'm aware." That didn't make the situation any easier.

The waitress brought their order, and he set the journal on the table. "Do you regret falling in love with her the first time? Would you do it all again?" he asked as he buttered and syruped his pancakes.

"No. I don't regret any of that. Would I do it again?" She blew out a slow breath. "I might."

He stuffed a bite of pancake into his mouth and chewed before he spoke again. "That's good enough for me. What are you waiting for? Make it work this time." Chloe glanced up at Jackson and saw a slow smile creep across his face. "Fall in love with her again." He tapped the journal with his index finger. "Be open to the second chance you've been given. Not necessarily the same as it was before, maybe something new."

"You don't understand. I never really fell out of love with her." She closed her eyes and took in a deep breath. "We did so many wonderful things together. It was a courtship most people only dream about, and it didn't change after we were married. Well, until this last year." She closed her eyes and took in a deep breath, trying to ignore the pain stabbing her heart. "My life was perfect until I fucked it up. I thought everything would always stay the same, but Shay got busy, preoccupied with life. No, she was trying to make our life better, and I acted like a spoiled princess who wasn't getting enough attention."

"Then you found out about Lila." He talked through the food in his mouth. "And Erica gave you the attention you needed, and you fell right into it." He took a gulp of coffee and relaxed against his chair.

"I don't want to think about Lila or Erica." She really wanted to blame it on them, but she couldn't. They hadn't poked the holes in the dam. They'd only loosened the corks.

"I didn't say it would be easy." Jackson eyed the journal. "But you have this." He picked it up, thumbed through it again. "Use it."

"What do you mean?"

"Everything you need to know is right in here." He dropped it onto the table and pushed it in front of her. "Keep reading it. Whether you know it or not, there are clearly things in here *you* need to remember." He got up, took two twenties from his pocket, and dropped them onto the check tray. He waved her off when she started to protest. "My treat today. You get the next one." He kissed her on the cheek. "Just remember she's not innocent in this whole mess."

❖

It wasn't long before Dr. Graves had the nurse bring Chloe from the waiting room to his office. She'd set up an appointment for this morning to visit with him about Shay's memory loss and to find out when she would be discharged. After they'd exchanged niceties, she'd taken a seat in one of the leather chairs in front of his desk, and he began to fill her in on the details as he flipped through her chart.

"We need to keep her for a few more days, possibly a week to get therapy for her leg on schedule. After that, she'll need to continue therapy for a few months." He continued to read his notes. "You can do that outpatient here at the hospital and at home as she regains her mobility."

"What about her memory?" She leaned forward in her chair. "When will that come back?"

"When a patient has a traumatic brain injury, also known as a TBI, we can expect a variety of outcomes. It's very common for the brain to conceal unwanted events from the conscious mind, including the event that caused the trauma. The brain injury can affect cognitive functions such as attention span, learning, information processing, and both short- and long-term memory. Some patients have issues remembering to remember as well. Shay seems to have lost a chunk of memory, which isn't uncommon. Whether it will come back or not remains to be seen."

"What can I do to help her?"

"Be flexible and patient. She may remember all of it, some of it, or none of it." He didn't seem concerned as he relaxed in his chair and spoke matter-of-factly.

"Should I help her? I mean, tell her things that happened?"

"That's up to you. I wouldn't share anything that might cause her more stress." Dr. Graves pulled his brows together. "I've seen cases where that kind of information has been a detriment."

They'd definitely had a tumultuous year. "So, don't tell her the bad things?"

"Correct. She may have blocked those memories because they were too difficult."

A knot formed in her stomach and immediately leapt to her throat. *She doesn't remember any of it.* Had Shay rejected everything that had happened between them over the past year? Had Chloe's actions pushed her into the affair? She could hardly bear the ache within her.

She shot up out of her chair and thanked the doctor. He gave her a strange look, said he would be available if she needed more information, and walked her to the door. He must have thought she was crazy, but she had to get out of there. She rushed to the elevator and punched the button for the lobby several times. The ride down was a blur, and when the doors opened, she pushed past a few waiting people, headed directly outside, and sucked in a huge breath of fresh air. She didn't know where she was going from here, but it wasn't into her current relationship with Erica. She had more questions than answers at this point.

As she sat on the bench in front of the hospital watching people come and go, Chloe slowly decided that Shay was coming home with her when she was released. She'd known that was the only choice from the beginning but hadn't cemented it in her mind yet. Her first thought had been *this can't be happening.* But now she knew what she had to do and that it would be the best for both of them.

She needed a plan. Shay always said they should have a plan when something unexpected happened. She took a piece of paper from her purse and started creating a checklist, talking out loud to herself as she wrote. "Where will we go from the hospital? The apartment or the beach house? Is it accessible?" She scratched out the apartment. "Definitely not the apartment. Getting in and out would be difficult there. With a driveway and just one story to navigate, the beach house would be much easier." It would also be so much easier for Chloe to maintain Shay's care along with her art-gallery business. After moving in, they'd set up an office there as well. "Where will she sleep? Where will *I* sleep?"

She let her hands fall to her lap, paper and pen clenched in each one. How was she going to manage the sleeping arrangements? Shay would expect her next to her in what used to be their bed. *Fuck!* She hadn't even thought about that. "Just calm down, Chloe." She closed her eyes and took a deep breath. She could handle that, couldn't she? Being close to Shay every night for the next six months or so? Conflicted emotions flooded her, and the knot that had just begun to loosen formed in her stomach again. "Oh my God." This was going to be way harder than she'd thought.

What would she tell her about the past year? Not a thing. Absolutely nothing. Maybe she'd fill her in on the basics, but not anything bad about their relationship. That would just be double punishment for Shay, and it wouldn't do her any good. Reliving the whole mess just brought the hurt back all over again. Chloe felt that every day. Shay had already lost enough, and she refused to make her recovery any more difficult.

She only hoped she could hold it together herself. Bottling up all her emotions was challenging at best, and it would only be more difficult in the future. It seemed as though Chloe was being punished as well, and all she had done was move on with her life. Too quickly, maybe.

Chapter Eight

Chloe assessed the therapy room as they entered. It was medium sized, with wood floors spanning the space and mirrors covering several walls. Various types of equipment, including parallel bars, exercise steps, stationary bikes, and medicine balls, were grouped in different stations around the room. To her left was a half-wall finished with a large plate-glass window spanning it just short of the ceiling. The room on the other side seemed to be an office that contained a desk with a computer and several generic chairs. All the walls were white except the one across from the office, which was a deep royal blue. Several people in maroon, blue, and green scrubs were scattered around the room. A couple of them were helping patients, one was folding towels on a table against the wall, and another furiously clicked keys on the keyboard of a portable computer in a kiosk across the room. The last, dressed in maroon scrubs with a white long-sleeved shirt underneath, spun around and smiled widely.

"Hey! I'm so glad to see you up and about." She crossed the room quickly and held out her hand to Shay. "I'm Rachel Taylor, your physical therapist." She was taller than Shay by a few inches and had dark-blue eyes that sparkled as she talked. Her long, dark hair had been braided and swept to the side, Chloe guessed to keep it out of the way while she worked.

"Nice to meet you." Shay gave Rachel a strange look as she took her hand and shook it.

"Sorry. It must seem weird that I know who you are. I've been to see you a couple times while you were sleeping, making sure your leg didn't get stiff." Rachel held on to Shay's hand for a beat longer than

Chloe expected before she let go. "I heard you don't want to waste any time."

Has she been in to see Shay? Chloe didn't remember seeing her at all. A face like that she would've remembered. She must have slipped in while Chloe was out at some point.

"The sooner I get back on my feet, the better," Shay said.

"Awesome!" Rachel slapped her hands together and rubbed them up and down. "I like a girl with spirit." She glanced over at Chloe as though she were a second thought. "And you are?"

"This is my wife, Chloe," Shay said.

Rachel gave Chloe a look she couldn't quite read before she held out her hand. "Oh. Nice to meet you."

"You as well." Chloe didn't know what to think of Rachel other than she was way too cheerful for the beginning of this journey.

"You may want to step out during Shay's therapy, because it might be tough at first." The hair she had trapped in the braid at the back of her head swung around as she turned, took the handles of the wheel chair, and pushed Shay to the end of the parallel bars. "Therapy works best when family members aren't around interfering."

Interfering? She wasn't about to leave Shay in a stranger's hands until she knew what was going to happen. "I'll stay unless Shay wants me to go."

Shay smiled at her and then glanced at Rachel. "I'd like her to stay."

"Okay, then. We're going to measure your range of motion before we start. That will be our baseline and what we measure your progress against." She helped her up and put her hands on the bars. "This may be a bit painful."

Chloe could see Shay's jaw clench as she held herself up.

"That's good. Now see if you can take a step forward." Rachel said.

Shay did as Rachel instructed, gripping the rails tightly, and closing her eyes. She didn't acknowledge it, but she was hurting.

"Awesome." Rachel sprinted to the other end and then between the rails to face Shay. "Now a couple more."

Chloe's stomach twisted as she watched Shay move, her jaw clenched, redness in her cheeks, and beads of sweat forming on her forehead.

The breath whooshed out of her mouth when she stopped and said, "I need to rest."

"Okay. Just a couple more." Rachel steadied her as she wobbled back and forth.

Shay got her balance and stepped forward more until only a little over a foot of railing at the end was left.

"Almost there. You got this."

Sweat dripped down her forehead and off her nose. Chloe had to force herself to stay seated.

Shay took a deep breath in through her nose and rolled her lips. She took the last few steps before she collapsed into Rachel.

"You did it!" Rachel held her tightly.

Tears sprang from Chloe's eyes, and she shot out of her chair. As Shay leaned into Rachel, Chloe wrapped her arm around her and kissed her temple. "You okay?"

"It hurts like a motherfucker."

She rushed to get the wheelchair and push it to the end of the rails. Then she tried to get between Shay and Rachel to help her to a chair.

"I've got her," Rachel said, holding her hand up before she spoke into Shay's ear softly. "Come forward with me. Then we're going to turn to your left, and I'll help you into the chair. Okay?"

Shay nodded and moved with her until she was seated. Rachel immediately grabbed a towel from the stack and blotted Shay's face before she squatted down next to her. "You did great." Her smile was broad and beautiful.

Shay's eyebrows rose. "Yeah?"

"Yeah," Rachel said softly. She held eye contact until Shay smiled and looked up at Chloe.

"I did great."

"Yes, you did." Chloe swiped the tears from her eyes. "Can I take her back to her room now?"

Rachel's focus didn't move from Shay. "Yep. I'll see you tomorrow. Same time." She patted her hand.

Shay's lunch was waiting for her when they got back to the room. After Chloe situated Shay in bed and she'd eaten, it didn't take long for Shay to fall asleep. Chloe took the opportunity to head back to the Physical Therapy Department. She was going to have a word with

Rachel Taylor. She'd pushed her hard, harder than necessary for her first day.

When she opened the door and entered the physical therapy room, Rachel wasn't anywhere in sight. She asked the nearest person dressed in scrubs, who'd pointed her to the office. She could see Rachel through the window sitting behind the desk typing at the computer just as furiously as she had been earlier.

Rachel jumped when Chloe pushed open the door and said, "What the hell was that?"

"That? You mean Shay's therapy?" Rachel's eyebrow rose.

"You saw how much it hurt, yet you kept pushing her." Shay's pained look shot through her again, making her stomach revolt.

"If I let her stop every time she says it hurts, she'll never walk normally again." Rachel sat back in her chair and crossed her arms. "You want that for her, right?"

"Of course I want that." She shook her head. "But it was her first day."

"First days are hard, and it's not going to get easier until after the first week or so. That's why we discourage family members from being in the therapy room."

"I'm not going to stop coming."

"Then you'll need to keep your mouth shut." Rachel's voice was firm.

"Just who the fuck do you think you are?" She'd never had any medical professional speak to her this way before.

"I'm the person who's going to prevent your wife from having pain in her leg for the rest of her life." She clicked a few keys on the computer and then turned the screen around. "Do you see this fracture?"

Chloe's breath caught in her chest. She hadn't seen the X-ray before. The rod and screws that had been inserted were clearly visible. She sank into the chair in front of the desk.

"That's what she has to overcome." Rachel clicked a few more keys, and the screen changed to her chart.

Chloe read the notes.

There are visible impairments in range of motion, knee extensor, and hip strength, as well as gait. Focus on immediate weight-bearing and early progression of strengthening to address the observed impairments. Outcomes expected with improved impairments, patient should be able to return to normal activities within three to six months.

"Three to six months?" Her neck heated, and the tingling sensation that accompanied her anxiety took over her body. She hadn't even thought about how long it would take for Shay to get back on her feet. This process would require much more patience that she realized. Three months minimum of living together again.

Rachel flipped the screen back around. "That's a great prognosis, considering almost half of the patients treated for a leg fracture have some residual disability twelve months after the injury, and up to twenty percent of patients treated surgically are unable to return to work three years after the injury."

"That's not going to be Shay." She sucked in a deep breath.

"Not if I can help it."

"I want her to be fully functional."

"Then we're in agreement. You stay out of therapy, and I'll get her walking again."

"Oh, I'm still coming to therapy with her, but I'll back off." Chloe pushed out of the chair and went to the door.

Rachel let out a quick breath and shook her head. "If you get out of line, just once, I'll have you removed."

Chloe didn't take kindly to threats, especially when it came to the care of someone she loved. "If I get out of line, it will be for good reason, and I'll have *you* taken off her case." She pulled the door open, closed it gently behind her, and headed for the elevator. She had to get out of this place for a while.

❖

When Shay opened her eyes, the room was empty. She was thankful for the silence. The physical therapy session had been tough, more painful than she could've ever imagined. She'd wanted to quit as soon as she'd let her weight fall on her leg and the pain had shot through her like a searing-hot branding iron. The bars weren't that long, fifteen feet maybe, but that was fourteen more feet than she'd wanted to handle at that point. When Rachel had pushed her, the only thing keeping her going was her faith in her, along with her beautiful smile. Rachel had the expertise and she had to trust her, whether it hurt or not.

Trying to keep her mind off the pain radiating in her leg, Shay flipped on the TV and found a comedy to keep her mind occupied. Just about then, the door pushed open and Rachel came in with the same dazzling smile plastered across her face as earlier.

"How's the leg feel?" Rachel asked as she clicked the button and let the bed rail slide down.

"Hurts."

Rachel quirked her lip up to one side. "Still on the scale of motherfucker?"

She chuckled. Her torturess seemed to have a sense of humor. "Down a notch to son-of-a-bitch."

Rachel smiled widely, apparently appreciating her humor. "I'm sorry about that, but if you want to get full motion back, we need to be aggressive." She pulled the blanket from her legs.

"Okay," Shay said.

"Does it bother you to have your wife watch?" Rachel assessed her undamaged leg before focusing on the two three-inch incisions on the thigh of her broken leg—one incision on the upper part of her leg, the other closer to her knee on the inside.

"No. I want her here. I need her strength."

Rachel drew her eyebrows together. "She wasn't very strong today."

"She'll get better. If not, she'll cry, and I'll be stronger because of it." It had been hard to see Chloe cry, but it had made her want to succeed even more. Seeing Chloe unhappy was one of the things she hated most in life.

"That's certainly a unique way of thinking." Rachel moved to the bottom of the bed and flattened her hand on the bottom of her foot. "Push for me."

She did, and a shot of pain coursed through her. "Back to motherfucker."

Rachel grinned again. "Yep. It's gonna hit MF on the scale a lot at first. It'll get better in a week or two. The incisions are healing nicely." She pulled the blanket up around her. "If your wife becomes a hindrance rather than a benefit to your recovery, I'll ban her from your sessions. Understood?" The words tumbled out of Rachel's mouth matter-of-factly, but Shay knew she was dead serious.

"Understood."

Rachel went to the door and opened it before glancing back with a smile. "I'll see you tomorrow, then."

"I'll be ready." She wanted to get out of this place and back to her own bed as soon as possible. The warmth of Chloe's arms was all she dreamed about, all that would get her through this.

CHAPTER NINE

Somehow Chloe had made it to the parking lot, found her car, and driven on autopilot to the apartment. She needed a shower and a whole lot of coffee to make it through the rest of the day. She grabbed a towel from the hall cabinet and threw it over the top of the shower door before she stepped inside and let the hot water run over her face. This seemed to be the only place she had any peace and quiet to think anymore, the only time she was truly alone.

The beach house was no longer a safe haven because she was afraid of running into Erica. She had no idea how she was going to handle her, hadn't even begun to figure out how to explain the situation to her. Erica would hate her decision and try her best to convince Chloe that it was a bad one. But she'd made up her mind that anything with Erica was off the table until Shay recovered and was well enough to take care of herself…or until her memory came back.

The phone was on its fourth ring by the time Chloe heard it. She didn't know how long she'd been asleep. After the shower, she'd wrapped herself in a towel, lain on the bed, and closed her eyes. Pure exhaustion had taken over. Still in a drowsy fog, she picked up the phone to see four missed calls from her mother on the screen. Thinking the worst, that something had happened to Shay, she immediately called her back.

"Hi, Mom. Is Shay all right?"

"As far as I know, she's fine. Where are you? You're not with her?"

She swiped at her eyes to clear the fog. "I'm at the apartment. I came home to shower and guess I fell asleep."

"Good. You need some rest. You're looking a little ragged."

"Thanks, Mom. Just what I wanted to hear." Her mom had a way of always making her feel worse than she already felt.

"I didn't mean it that way. I'm just worried that you're not taking care of yourself."

"It's kind of hard with Shay in the hospital. She started physical therapy today, and it wasn't pretty. The doctor and her therapist both agree that the sooner she gets mobile, the sooner she'll be able to come home."

"I know that's hard, but I have to agree. Speaking of home. Shay's mother called me. She wants to take her to her house when she's released."

"I hope you told her no. She's going home with me."

"With everything that's happening with your art career, it might not be a bad idea for her to stay with her parents."

"No. Absolutely not. I'm not letting Shay go back into that environment."

"It can't be that bad. They're her parents. Besides, are you going to have the time to care for her?"

"It is that bad, and I'll make time." She refused to go into detail with her mother over the phone. All she needed to know was that Shay was coming with her. Why she was questioning it was a mystery. "You love her like she's your own daughter. Why would you even think to send her home with them?"

"We *do* love her. She's *certainly* grounded you. I wasn't quite sure where you were going with your life until you met her." Her mother's voice was a little light for the passive-aggressive statement.

Shay shook her head. "Well, thanks for the confidence, Mom." The line was silent for a moment as a flash of heat rushed her neck, her anxiety kicking in at full force. Living up to her parents' expectations had always sent her stress level over the top.

"I didn't mean to make you feel bad, but you have to admit you were pretty wild for a while. I had some sleepless nights worrying about you." Her mother was right. Before she'd met Shay, she'd been with several women who'd had no boundaries. They'd partied hard and spent lots of money. Her money. Unfortunately, some of their habits had remained with her after they'd split up. Shay had changed all that.

"I'm sorry, Mom. That part of my life is over." She was thankful to Shay for giving her a place where she felt safe to be who she was and who wanted her for more than just her trust fund, which had been almost drained.

"Okay, then. How can we help? Do you want to bring her here to our house, there, the beach house?"

"The beach house. When she's ready to leave the hospital." She went into the bathroom and looked at her hair, which had been smashed on one side, and scrunched it with her fingers. "I can care for her and still have access to my studio to paint."

"That was sweet of her to set all that up for you," her mother said.

"Yes. It was." Incredibly sweet, and she'd repaid her by getting so wrapped up in her art that she'd ignored Shay's needs. Could she have been any more ungrateful? "Listen, Mom. I need to get dressed and go back to the hospital. Shay's probably wondering where I am."

"Okay, love. Check in with me later and let me know if you need anything."

"Will do. I love you."

"I love you too, honey."

She touched the red button, flopped down onto the bed, and stared at the ceiling. Her life had been a figurative train wreck before she'd met Shay, and now she seemed to be right back where she'd started. She didn't know how she would get all the pieces back on track, or if she even could manage it at this point.

As she gathered the things she'd picked out to take to Shay, she realized she didn't have anything appropriate for physical therapy, so she'd have to stop at the mall on the way and pick up a few outfits. She stuffed a few usable items into her canvas bag, and when Shay's journal spilled out, she picked it up, laid back on the bed, and opened it to the spot where she'd left off. After the phone call with her mother, she needed something to make her feel good about herself, and so far, Shay's journals had reminded her of a happier time in her life.

Our first time...

We made love last night, my first time. The intimacy and the connection we shared took me to a magical place I've never been before. Her hands—her mouth. Sweet Lord, she knows how to use them. She took me there again and again, touched me in ways I've never even imagined. She was so beautiful—is so beautiful. Her curves and swells are all perfect, and she has the softest skin, I can still feel my hands gliding across her stomach. I could've touched her for hours. I think I did, although it only feels like a few moments. Her scent, her taste are incredible. I couldn't get enough of her. Feeling her tremble beneath me as I pushed her over the edge is something I'll never forget. I want to do it a thousand times more. Loving her is the most exquisite gift I'll ever receive.

Chloe let the journal fall to her chest. She hadn't realized she was Shay's first. *Just how old was she? How many women did she date before me? Was I really that special?*

She remembered the night clearly. They'd gone to the movies to see some romantic comedy and then back to Chloe's place afterward. The movie was funny and had a happy ending, the kind she liked. The movie theater was packed, and she remembered that during the whole movie, all she'd wanted to do was go home so she could be alone with Shay.

Apparently, Shay had wanted that as well. They'd barely stepped inside, and Chloe was pulled into the most erotic kiss she'd ever had. Shay had seemed to know exactly what she was doing. The thought never crossed Chloe's mind that she was a virgin. She'd found every erogenous zone and played it perfectly. Just thinking about it had her ridiculously wet. Chloe had been with several women before, but none that took their time, touched her the way Shay had. She never knew sex could be so wonderful when you connected emotionally as well. It was Shay who had made that connection with her. Shay had taken her heart that night and kept it safe until now.

Anger bubbled inside. *How could Shay have ruined everything we had together?*

CHAPTER TEN

Chloe catapulted out of the chair when she read the message from Erica. *I'm in the waiting room.*

She quickly typed, *Which waiting room?*

The one right down the hall. They wouldn't let me come to the room.

I'll be right there.

Hospital security was good. There was that at least. She went to her purse on the dresser. "I'm going to get a soda. You want one?"

"Yeah. Whatever you get."

She clenched the five-dollar bill as she glanced back at Shay. "I'll be right back." Her heartbeat doubled as she sped out of the room, down the hallway, and into the waiting room.

Erica was waiting just inside the door and pulled her into her arms. "It's so good to see your face."

"I told you to stay away from here."

Erica's forehead creased as she pulled her eyebrows together. "Then answer my phone calls."

"Listen, it's been really busy here, and I'm totally stressed by this whole situation." Chloe rubbed the back of her neck.

"Then come home and relax." Erica stroked her arm.

"I can't. I have to be here with Shay. She needs me."

"*I* need you." Erica moved closer.

"Erica, she has no idea what's going on. She doesn't remember the past year." Chloe couldn't believe she didn't get it.

"Then tell her." Erica was clearly irritated now.

"I can't do that. Not now. She'd be devastated."

"You have got to be kidding. You're going to go through this all over again?"

"If I have to. Yes." She took Erica by the arm. "Now you have to leave."

Erica resisted as she tried to move her to the door. "I'm not leaving until you promise to spend some time with me."

It was clear that Erica wouldn't budge until she agreed. She let out a heavy breath. "Okay. I'll break away this evening and come see you." She'd have to tell Shay she was going to check on the gallery or shower or something. She'd figure that out later. Right now, she just needed to get Erica out of there.

The soda machine clanged as a can dropped to the bottom, and Chloe looked over to see Rachel taking in the show that she and Erica were so recklessly putting on as she plucked the soda from the machine. *Fuck.* Just one more thing to deal with. She took Erica's hand and led her out of the waiting room and to the elevator.

"Who's that?"

"No one." She focused back on Erica. "I'll walk you out." She went with her to the elevator and punched the button several times. "I'll call you when I get free." At this point, she would promise Erica anything to get rid of her, but she had no plans to call her.

"Okay." Erica smiled and gave her a quick peck on the cheek before she boarded the elevator.

As soon as the doors closed, she spun around and walked back to the waiting room where Rachel was seated in the corner talking to someone. "Do you have a minute?" Chloe asked.

Rachel held up a finger. "I'm just finishing here. If you'd like to wait in the hall, I'll be right out."

Chloe fed the five-dollar bill into the machine and chose a couple of sodas before she turned, left the room, and leaned up against the wall while she waited. After a few minutes, the door opened, and Rachel came out. She could tell by Rachel's expression that she'd heard the whole conversation with Erica.

"What did you need?"

"I need you to keep that conversation to yourself."

"You mean the conversation with the woman you're apparently seeing on the side?"

"Yes." Everything she said was absolutely true, just not in the same context. She wasn't about to justify or explain her actions to a total stranger who knew nothing about her relationship with Shay.

"Okay. But *only* because it might adversely impact Shay's recovery." She quirked up an eyebrow. "Can't say I understand why you'd step out on your wife. From what I've seen, she seems to be a wonderful girl all around."

"Well, everything's not always as it seems." She turned and hurried back down the hall to Shay's room. Any explanation she would give Rachel at this point would be pointless since she had no idea who or what was in Shay's future, or hers for that matter.

It had been a grueling week of physical therapy for Shay. Chloe had cried more than once watching her struggle, and that seemed to make her even more determined. Each time Rachel had told her to try harder or take one more step, Chloe had wanted to shove her out of the way, take Shay into her arms, and soothe her. She'd actually bolted across the room at one point and been met by Rachel's narrowed, piercing eyes, letting her know she was on the verge of being ejected from the room. Shay had waved her off, and she'd returned to her chair against the wall at the side of the room.

She guessed Shay hadn't been happy with her interference either. She'd been short with her when they'd gotten back to the room and had told her she needed some alone time. She even suggested she call Jackson and go get something to eat with him, to just do something away from the hospital for a few hours. She'd followed Shay's advice and was now on her third glass of merlot, wallowing in a pool of self-pity.

"She pushes her so hard, Jackson. I don't know if I can take it any longer."

"You don't have to be there, do you? I mean, has Shay asked you to go with her?"

She shook her head. "Not technically, but I thought I should be there to watch out for her."

"Maybe you should skip a few sessions. You know, let her handle it herself. It might be hard for her to see how it impacts you, for you to see her in such a weak state." Jackson was good about helping her see things clearer.

"You think?" Chloe could certainly use a break from her anxiety caused by watching her endure so much pain. The vision of her holding on to Rachel flashed through her head. "I don't like her therapist. She's a real bitch."

He shrugged. "You don't have to like her as long as she gets Shay on her feet again."

"True. And now she thinks I'm cheating on my wife."

Wine spilled from his mouth as he choked. "How did that happen?" He quickly blotted the red dots from the tablecloth with a napkin.

"Erica showed up at the hospital earlier, and Rachel overheard us talking."

"And that bothers you?"

"Hell yes, it bothers me. I may have been absent, but I didn't cheat." The words came out louder than expected. A few other people looked her way, so she smiled and relaxed into her chair.

"What do you care what she thinks? You know the truth."

"I'm not that person, Jackson, and I don't want her saying anything to Shay." Chloe shook her head and looked at her hands as she smoothed the tablecloth in front of her. "I'm afraid she'll make her hate me."

"You still love her." It wasn't a question. He said it with a smile on his face and a tone in his voice as though he could see things in her soul she hadn't wanted to recognize yet.

"I'll always love her. That'll never change." She swirled her glass and stared into it, watching the legs of wine move slowly down into the pool at the bottom. "That night we met, at your wedding reception, all I could think was 'please don't be in love with someone else.'" She glanced at Jackson, looking for some kind of understanding in his eyes. "I could handle it if she was involved with someone, but love I couldn't overcome."

"Lucky for you, she wasn't in either."

She set her glass on the table and scrubbed her face with her hands. "I don't know if it was fate, karma, or something else, but she appeared from nowhere and changed my life."

"Hell yes, she did. You were on a downward spiral."

"I was a fucking mess." She chuckled. "She was so sweet and naive.

Every time I did anything for her, she was ridiculously embarrassed and acted like it was too much." She smiled. "She loved me for me, not for things or money. Just me. I was blown away by her innocence. I fell completely in love with all of her without her even trying. I'm not sure I can get back to that place again."

"Do you want to try?" Jackson was analytical, just like Shay. He could break everything down and reach the heart of anything. He was her go-to person for sorting things out.

"I don't know. So much has happened. Other people are involved now."

"I understand. It's not like you didn't move on, but you're not committed to Erica." He rolled his eyes and gave her a look like that would be the craziest thing in the world.

"No. I'm not committed, and I can't put all the blame on Shay. I didn't know what I had," she said softly. "Or maybe I did, but I forgot. I neglected her…and then there was the accident."

"You have to stop punishing yourself for that, and you have to forgive her if you're ever going to get past it."

"I'm trying, Jackson. But it's not that easy. When I found her with Lila…in that one moment, I was devastated. The huge crater in my heart hasn't had time to heal, and when she remembers, I'm afraid it'll split wide open again."

"*If* she remembers." He raised his eyebrows and gave her a tight smile.

"It can't remain a secret forever. Someone's bound to tell her we'd split up. I'm surprised Lila hasn't been back to see her."

"So, you deal with that when it happens. Lila's an opportunist. I doubt you'll see more of her." He said it like he knew her well.

"She's more involved than you think. At least that's what she told me."

"She's working at a different office now, far enough away to keep her out of your business." He blew out a quick breath. "And mine."

"Really? Where? When did that happen?"

"Atlanta. I'm not sure exactly when, but it was before the accident." He tugged on his lip with his teeth and looked at the ceiling. "As soon as Shay was made chief actuary, she made it happen."

"Shay made it happen?" *Why would she send her away?*

He nodded. "She knew she'd made a mistake. A lot of people were upset by her choice, and I was plenty pissed as well. I would've loved to have been offered that opportunity. I followed her there to advance, not to be passed over by a girl she was fucking." He took in a deep breath. "But I squashed the rumors and kept my mouth shut because I love my sister."

"Fuck. How did we get into this mess?"

"Clean it up. Fix it. The ball's clearly in your court." He drank the rest of his wine and poured them both another glass.

"You make it sound so easy."

"It is, if that's what you want."

Was it that simple? Could she just forget about the past six months of pain she'd been through? Erase the betrayal she'd felt? God, she wished she could, right here at this moment, but she just wasn't there yet.

When Chloe got back to the hospital, she didn't expect to find that Shay had company, and honestly, after the amount of wine she'd had, she wasn't in the mood for it. Rachel was lounging with her feet up in the recliner where Chloe usually sat, a bowl of popcorn in her lap. They were watching a movie and seemed to be having an awesome time. A wave of heat coursed through her, and she had to physically force herself not to bolt across the room and yank Rachel out of the chair.

"Hey. We're watching that new comedy you were talking about," Shay said.

"I see that." She let the bag of clothes she'd picked up while she was out drop to the floor next to the dresser. "If you'd let me know, I could've come back sooner."

"I didn't think you'd be gone this long." Shay waved her closer. "It just started. Come sit down." Shay's mood seemed to have lightened, with no sign of the passive-aggressive girl she'd seen earlier today.

Rachel sprang forward in the recliner. "Shay said you'd be back soon, so I popped some popcorn." She got up and moved to the couch. "Want some?" She held the bowl out to her.

"No, thanks. I just ate." She'd mostly drunk, but even if she'd had an appetite, the cozy sight she'd just walked in on would have killed it. "Do you hang out with all your patients after hours?"

"Just the ones with super-healing powers." She smiled at Shay. "She was awesome today, wasn't she?"

Shay's face lit up, and Chloe felt like she might vomit. "Yeah. Awesome." She set her purse on the table and kissed Shay on the forehead. "You okay?"

"A little sore, but a good kind of sore."

She glanced over at Rachel, who had paused the movie and was watching them intently. She didn't smile. She didn't want Rachel thinking she was okay with her hanging out with Shay while she wasn't there. Therapy was one thing, but after hours was a whole different story. She sat in the recliner, and Rachel started the movie again. For the next two hours, she paid absolutely no attention to the film. Only one thing was jangling around in her head. She was jealous—fucking, crazy, blood-boiling jealous.

❖

"Oh my God. You need to stop pushing her like this." Chloe rushed to the parallel bars.

She could see the look in Rachel's eyes. She was just about to blast her when Shay put her hand up and said, "Just back off, Chloe. I need to do this."

Back off? "Fine. I'm out of here," she said as she rushed to the door.

"Chloe, wait," Shay said, and Chloe froze with her hand on the doorknob. "I'm sorry. Why don't you go get some of my shorts, so I don't feel like such a goofball wearing these hospital scrubs when I get up again."

A mixture of hurt and anger bubbled inside her. She didn't turn around, just nodded, opened the door, and left. Even though she'd brought a bag of new clothes last night, she'd totally forgotten about them after finding Rachel in Shay's room. She had to get out of there before she said something she'd regret—to both of them.

Chloe went home and brewed a pot of coffee before she sat down at Shay's desk and turned on the laptop. She typed Rachel Taylor,

Largo Medical Center into the Google search. Several hits came up immediately, including a video and a number of very flattering pictures. The woman knew how to work a camera. Halfway through the video, she paused it, not able to tolerate Rachel's know-it-all attitude even if her words made sense. She clicked on the first one listed from the hospital and started reading. She had a very impressive bio, which included a Doctor of Physical Therapy degree. She'd graduated with honors from the University of South Florida in Tampa, had done several research studies on gait modification and mobility recovery after trauma, and was currently working on her PhD in Rehabilitation Sciences. To top it all off, she'd also earned a Foundation for Physical Therapy Service Award.

She slapped the laptop closed. *Jesus.* As if she didn't have enough to deal with already, now she had a superstar helping Shay regain her mobility. She flopped back into the chair, closed her eyes, and took a deep breath. She wanted Shay to have the very best because she would recover faster and stronger, so why did this woman bother her so much?

The vision of Shay smiling at Rachel after she'd completed her exercises for the day invaded her thoughts. If not just grateful, Shay seemed completely enamored with her. The woman was worming her way into Shay's heart, and Chloe couldn't do anything about it. Plus, Rachel had overheard her talking to Erica. Who knew what she would do with that information.

She shook her head. Why should she care? Shay's heart wasn't her concern anymore. They weren't really *together*. They'd separated. She'd moved most of her belongings to the beach house. Divorce hadn't been put on the table yet, but it was imminent. Or was it?

The Shay she'd experienced over the past few days was different, not the driven, work-obsessed Shay she'd been living with for the past six months. She wasn't the Shay who had fucked someone else. Her stomach churned, threatening to spew what little she'd eaten today. If Shay didn't remember, was she really the same person? God, this situation was too much for her brain to process right now.

❖

When Chloe got back to the hospital, Shay was in the middle of receiving a deep-tissue leg massage compliments of her physical therapist extraordinaire. Only Rachel wasn't massaging her injured leg. She was working on the perfectly good one.

"Aren't you massaging the wrong leg?"

"Already done with that one. Since Shay did so well in therapy earlier, I thought I'd treat her to the full package today." Her smile was tentative, as though she knew she was crossing a boundary. And she was.

I bet you did. "About earlier, I think I'll skip the sessions from now on." She needed some distance. Jealousy over the attention Shay was getting from her physical therapist wasn't doing either of them any good.

Shay's eyebrows rose. "What? Why? I want you there."

She shrugged. "Didn't seem like it earlier."

"I'm sorry. I was just frustrated."

"I've got things to take care of at the gallery, and Rachel seems to be taking good care of you." She glanced over at Rachel. "I'm sure she'll keep me updated on your progress, won't you?"

The way Rachel's jaw dropped open in surprise was amusing, if not downright comical. "Of course."

"Okay, then that's settled." She took the clothes she'd brought the night before out of the bag and started placing them in one of the dresser drawers. "I didn't think any of your Bermuda shorts would work for therapy, so I bought you some new Nike training shorts." She'd chosen several pairs in black, charcoal gray, light gray, and navy. "They all seem to be stretchy enough and have a large enough leg opening to get over your incisions without irritation. I also got you shirts to match. Thought you might need some color." She took out the moisture-wicking T-shirts she'd picked out to match and held up the neon-green and pink ones before she placed them with the others alongside the shorts. "You should be all set now."

"You're amazing." Shay beamed and then looked at Rachel. "Isn't she amazing?"

Rachel rolled her lips in. "Yep. Amazing. Every girl should be so lucky to have a wife like her."

The sarcasm wasn't lost on Chloe, and even though she wanted to give her a piece of her mind, she ignored the urge. The woman had no idea what she was in for if she chose to pursue Shay.

CHAPTER ELEVEN

Once Rachel had finished the deep-tissue massage, Shay had taken the heavy dose of ibuprofen she'd ordered to counteract any soreness both the therapy session and the massage would induce. Even though she got along well with Rachel and really liked her, she needed time with Chloe. She hadn't been alone with her much since she'd woken from the coma, and something seemed to be off with her. The time she'd taken to go home, shower, and pick up clothes had been longer than usual this afternoon, and Chloe hadn't smiled much since she'd gotten back. She could attribute some of her actions to the situation, but she had also been distant since Shay had been in therapy.

The two of them hadn't spent much time apart other than work before, and when they were together, they'd always found it difficult not to touch each other in some way or another. Not necessarily in a sexual way, just loving, affectionate touches. Now Chloe seemed to be avoiding any type of contact. She glanced at her in the chair as she watched the show on TV. Dressed in a flowery spring dress and a navy cardigan to cover her shoulders, she looked absolutely radiant, more so than she'd remembered. She wanted her closer, needed the warmth of her body pressed up against her like they always did while watching TV at home. The hospital bed was larger than normal, so she slowly scooted to one side and patted the empty space in the bed.

"Come sit with me?" She raised her eyebrows at Chloe when she glanced her way. Chloe seemed reluctant but then got up and sat on the side of the bed. "Will you hold me?" It felt odd having to ask something of Chloe she'd always intuitively given before. They were always on the same page with their needs. Besides the reluctance, she seemed guarded. Something was in her eyes. Fear, maybe?

"I don't want to hurt you." Chloe said.

That she understood. If their positions were reversed, she'd be scared as well. "It's okay. I'm fine." Not totally fine, but her muscles were getting stronger, and since she'd started therapy, the pain wasn't nearly as bad when she was lying down. She shifted her injured leg farther away so Chloe could slip in next to her right side. "I just need you to be close to me."

Chloe hesitated and then toed off her sandals before she crawled up next to her and turned to face her. A tear sat in the corner of her eye, threatening to spill out. "I'm so sorry this happened, Shay."

She wiped away the tear and kissed Chloe gently before she took her into her arms and let her head rest on her chest. "I'm gonna be all right." She kissed the top of Chloe's head as she tried to soothe her soft sobs. She didn't know if it was the stress of the whole situation or the relief that was making Chloe so emotional, but Shay would do everything in her power to fix whatever was worrying her.

Chloe had done so much for her in the past—buffering between her and her mom, calming her after every altercation, removing the stigma her mother had so carefully planted in her brain as a child. Without Chloe, she'd still be spending a couple of weeks a month in her counselor's office trying to figure out what was so wrong about her that she needed to change to gain the love of her mother—and actually trying to do it. She owed everything to this woman in her arms.

Warm, soft breaths brushed across her chest, and she knew Chloe was asleep just like that. All was right in her world again. It felt wonderful to have Chloe in her arms once more. Even though it had been only a few days, it seemed like forever since they'd been this close. The accident hadn't just robbed her of memories. It had stolen the very essence of Chloe from her mind.

She gently ran her fingers across Chloe's arm, indulging in the soft, creamy smoothness of her skin. The warmth she gave soothed her. Everything would be fine as long as she had Chloe beside her. Emotions bubbled inside, and heated tears streamed down her cheeks. When had she become such an emotional basket case? The accident had done more than break her leg. It had stripped her of all her walls—made her realize just how deeply she loved Chloe.

❖

Chloe rushed out of the room, down the elevator, and out of the hospital. She found her car, keyed the ignition, and turned the air on full blast. *What was I thinking?* She'd been so warm and comfortable in Shay's arms this morning. It was like she'd been catapulted back in time to when they were happy together. Then, she'd felt Shay's hands doing wonderful, ungodly things, taking her to an unexpected point of arousal, and she hadn't stopped her. She'd let Shay make love to her, stroke her fingers through her folds—bring her to the kind of earth-shattering arousal that only Shay could, and she'd enjoyed it. Her body heated as the feeling washed over her again. She had *not* expected that to happen *ever* again.

The confusion hit her hard. She still loved Shay so much more than she wanted to admit, but she hated her for what she'd done. For not trusting her—for going outside their marriage for something she valued so deeply. Sex wasn't just an act to Chloe. It was a union to be shared with the most important person in her life, and Shay had shattered that bond. She couldn't control the sob that pushed from her lungs. She pressed her head to the steering wheel and let every emotion spill out. She'd been so worried about Shay that she hadn't let herself feel anything until now.

A tap on the window jarred her back to reality. She looked up to see Rachel standing next to the car staring at her. *Fuck. Just one more thing to deal with.* She swiped the tears from her eyes before she hit the button to roll down the window.

"Are you all right?" Her concern seemed genuine.

"Just peachy." She didn't hold back her irritation.

"Anything I can do to help?" Even though Rachel seemed sincere, she wasn't going to be friends with this woman. Rachel was far from being her ally.

"Not unless you have a magical cure for memory loss." She threw the car into reverse, backed out of the parking space, and got the hell out of there.

The plastic vents clicked as she pointed all of them toward her face and let the air cool her before she glanced in the rearview to see Rachel standing there with her hands on her hips. She pulled out of the lot and just drove. What was she going to do about this development with Shay? She was going to ignore it—that's exactly what she was going to do.

When she pulled into the driveway of the beach house, she wasn't surprised to see Erica's car there. Not what she needed this morning. The woman wasn't letting up, and she wouldn't be happy when she told her she had to move her clothes out. She had to start preparing for Shay to come home. Was it home? She squeezed her eyes shut. Yes, it was their home, the home Shay had struggled to buy and they had remodeled together.

Erica was still sleeping when she peeked into the bedroom, so she went into her studio. The view of the beach was breathtaking. They'd had the corner room on the southwest of the house remodeled with plate-glass windows on both exterior sides. The extra care Shay had put into it had made her feel so loved and cherished. She'd furnished it and bought all the supplies she'd ever need for at least a year, and she'd done all this for her.

She sat in the tall studio chair next to the canvas she'd been working on last week. The blandness in the piece depressed her. It wasn't anything special, just waves and a little moonlight. Her work had suffered over the past six months since she and Shay had split, since she'd found out about Lila. She removed the painting from the easel and leaned it up against the others she'd painted that were too dark to put up for sale. She set a new canvas on the easel and tried to let her heart lead her as it used to. But nothing was there. Her mind was blank, and that was the way the canvas would remain for now.

She tried to be super quiet when she went back into the bedroom to get some clothes, but it didn't work.

"You're home." Erica rolled over and smiled.

"Yeah. I need to change and get a few things."

"Come to bed for a little while."

"I really don't have time." After what had happened this morning, Shay would be wondering where she'd gone and why she hadn't come back sooner.

"Come on. She won't miss you for an hour or two."

"I just went out for doughnuts and coffee. I hadn't planned on coming here at all." She pulled a pair of navy shorts from the drawer, then put them back and took out a pair of tan Capri pants. The hospital was too cold for shorts. She went to the closet and looked for a blouse. All her things had been scrunched to one side to make room for Erica's clothes. It was now or never. She grabbed a pink blouse from one of the hangers and turned around. "Listen, I have to get prepared for Shay to come home, so I need you to move your clothes out."

"What?" Erica bolted up in the bed and pulled her eyebrows together. "You're going to bring her here?"

"With the leg injury, it's the most accessible place. It's too difficult to navigate the apartment."

"I just moved everything in." Erica was dramatic, as usual, enunciating each word separately.

"Seriously? That's not even half your wardrobe, and it's not like you don't still have a house of your own. Plus, I never asked you to move in."

The blanket flew up as Erica tossed it back and got out of bed. "God, you're so fucking mean when you're stressed."

"I know, and I'm sorry, but you're damn right, I'm stressed. My wife was almost killed in a car accident that I'm at fault for."

"Your wife?" Erica threw her hands up. "You've been separated for six months, and now she's suddenly your wife again?"

She took in a deep breath and let it out. "You know what I mean."

Erica moved behind her and rubbed her shoulders. "Let me help relieve some of the stress." Her hands slowly went from massaging her shoulders down her back and around her waist.

Erica pressed her lips against her neck as she started to unbutton Chloe's pants, and her mind went immediately to Shay and what had happened just an hour before. *No. This is not happening.* She spun around and held her arms out between them. "Stop. I can't do this right now."

"Jesus, Chloe. It's been a week since I've even seen you naked, let alone touched you."

"I know. I'm sorry." Again with the I'm sorry, but was she really? She was so mixed up right now she didn't know if she was or not. What she really needed was some space, time to herself to figure this whole situation out. "I'll help you load your clothes."

"You certainly know how to make me feel unimportant."

"Not my intent. I just need some space."

"Fine." Erica pulled on a pair of jeans, tucked the T-shirt she'd been wearing into the waistband, and put on a white, button-down shirt.

Chloe swiped Erica's car keys from the dresser and grabbed a bundle of clothes from the closet, leaving everything on the hanger.

She'd buy more later. The less time she took getting her clothes out, the faster she'd be gone. She needed Erica out. Now.

❖

After Chloe had finished helping Erica load her clothes into her car, she went back into the house and poured herself two fingers of bourbon. What the fuck was she going to do? She didn't want either one of these women in her life right now but seemed to have no choice about one of them. She poured another couple of fingers, went into the bedroom, gathered the pile of Shay's clothes, and dropped them onto the bed. They'd been in a heap on the chair in the corner right where Erica had carelessly tossed them last week. She took a handful of hangers from the closet in the guest room and laid them on one of the pillows. If Shay would only remember her past, she wouldn't even be dealing with these feelings. Lila would be taking care of everything instead of her, although Lila hadn't been back since she'd sent her away, so who knew if she really cared about Shay or if it was just a passing fling.

She picked up a shirt, examined it, and tossed it into a pile on the floor. All Shay's clothes, except her jeans, were totally wrinkled. She was going to have to wash them all. Thankfully, they were only her casual clothes, or she'd have an enormous dry-cleaning bill to deal with along with everything else.

Shay should remember it all—the lies she'd told, the excuses she'd made for working late. Shay should have to deal with the fallout just as she did. She pushed all the remaining clothes to the floor, flopped onto the bed, and stared at the empty side of the closet. The pile of journals taunted her from the corner. She crossed the room and pulled one randomly from the pile, went back to the bed and got comfortable, and began to read.

Eclipse day...

Today was eclipse day. The moon would totally eclipse the sun, and screw me if it wasn't totally cloudy. Chloe and I had planned to meet for lunch and watch it. My camera was ready to go, and I'd bought a special lens and protective glasses. I was utterly disappointed with the weather this morning. It would be years until this event would happen again. But Chloe surprised me! She got someone to cover the gallery today and showed up at work at eight o'clock. Then she drove me 300 miles north to some random town where the sky was clear, just so I could see the eclipse, which was spectacular. When the moon kissed the sun, there wasn't much difference in the sky. But when it drifted farther across the whole of it, hiding more of the sun, the light began to fade, and shadows on the ground became more distinct. The leaves and the trees produced shadows that were an eerie shade of gray with an odd, rounded effect, and then as the moon's movement progressed, the shadows became so much sharper. We could see the individual hairs on our heads and arms. It was absolutely stunning. I captured some good time-lapse photos of the eclipse as it happened, but Chloe took the most awesome photos of the ground shadows. She's incredible. I would've never thought to do that, but the artist in her caught their uniqueness. God, I love this woman. I think I'd die without her.

The last words stuck in her head. Had Shay been that deeply in love with her? The whole experience that day had been wonderful. Chloe remembered how giddy with excitement Shay was when she'd picked her up. She'd been planning to view the eclipse for months—had it all laid out how and when they were going to do it and had actually staked out an area on the roof of their apartment building long before any of the other tenants had thought to do so.

But when Chloe knew that wasn't going to pan out, she'd switched to plan B. She'd gathered all Shay's equipment and put it in the back of her SUV, along with some blankets. They'd sat for hours on a patch of grass, in a park in some town she couldn't even remember the name of, wrapped together in a blanket, waiting and then watching as the moon moved slowly across the sun and the temperature dropped. The birds had stopped singing, and the crickets began to chirp.

The whole experience was amazing, and Shay was so beautifully animated throughout the entire afternoon. The eclipse was truly beautiful—not just the event, but the way Shay had reacted to it. Chloe had glanced at the sky occasionally but had enjoyed watching the joy in Shay's face so much more. Science excited her the same way the sunrise excited Chloe. Shay had accompanied her on more than one early morning excursion on the beach to view the sun glistening off the sea as it rose. No way was she going to let her miss the eclipse.

She closed the journal and let it fall to the bed. They'd been so in love then. But now she couldn't reconcile the feelings of betrayal and jealousy coursing through her. In one moment, she was so angry at Shay she never wanted to see her again. In the next she was ridiculously jealous of Rachel, a woman there solely to get Shay back on her feet. But Rachel seemed more invested in Shay than just her recovery. *Ack!* There it was again. That big green monster. How was she going to get through this?

CHAPTER TWELVE

Physical therapy wasn't going well that morning. Shay's head was nowhere near where it should be right now. It had been more than twenty-four hours since Chloe left, and she hadn't been able to reach her. All her calls and texts had gone unanswered.

When she'd woken with Chloe in her arms yesterday morning, she'd wanted nothing more than to be as close to her as she could. To love her, kiss her, touch her all over, no matter what kind of pain shot through her leg, and she'd done just that. She'd woken Chloe with a kiss, a deep, lingering, lazy-morning kiss, the kind of kiss that leads to so much more—only it had, yet it really hadn't. When she'd slipped her hand under Chloe's sweater and inside her bra, felt her soft warm breast in her hand, Chloe had pressed into her, wanting more.

She rolled her nipple between her fingers and trailed her other hand across her stomach and under her dress. The warm wetness she found between Chloe's legs had instantly done the same to her, which wasn't surprising since their sexual chemistry had always been off the charts. She pushed her panties aside and circled the small, hard nub with her fingers, coaxing a long, slow moan from Chloe before moving her fingers in and out slowly, deeply, letting them drag across the sweet spot she knew would push her over the edge.

Chloe nestled closer, moving with her as her fingers slid in and out, her thumb now gliding through her folds, massaging her hardened clit. It wasn't long before she clamped around her fingers and rocketed into orgasm, pressing into her hand and holding her tightly in her arms.

Then suddenly Chloe raised her head and snapped her eyes wide. She stared blindly at her, then jumped out of bed in a weird sort of panic. She just stood there staring for a few minutes, then scrubbed her face with her hands, mumbled something about coffee, and zipped out of the room.

"Hey, you're not listening." Rachel's voice rang through her thoughts. "What's going on with you today?"

"Sorry. Just a little preoccupied." Sweat dripped from Shay's nose as she turned within the bars to take the course again.

Rachel grabbed her by the waist. "Why don't we take a break?" She led her to one of the padded tables and lowered it, so she could sit. "You wanna tell me about it?"

It wasn't really something she should discuss with her physical therapist, who was just a little less than a stranger, but she had no one else. No one that wasn't related to Chloe. "It's kind of personal."

The look on Rachel's face wasn't clear. "You don't have to tell me, but whatever you do stays with me."

"Chloe has been different." She played with the zipper of her hoodie. "She slept in the bed with me night before last and yesterday morning..." She looked around the room, anywhere but at Rachel. Sharing private details of her life was unusual for her. "We were intimate, and she ran out of the room like a jackrabbit being chased by a wild dog." She let it all spill out.

"Oh," Rachel said, then hesitated. "Maybe she was worried about hurting you."

"She didn't say anything about that. She just said something about getting coffee and left. She hasn't been back since and hasn't answered any of my calls or texts."

"Yeah, that's a little weird." Rachel patted her on the thigh. "She's probably just tired. Situations like this can be very stressful."

"I guess that's possible, but I don't understand her not letting me know she's okay." She rubbed her temple. "I just wish I could remember the past year. That would at least give me a clue what's going on with her."

"Why don't we call this session for now. We can go to the cafeteria, get something to eat, and pick this back up later. You probably need a change of scenery."

"I'm not very hungry."

"I am, and they have ice cream." Rachel smiled widely.

"Chocolate?"

"And vanilla. Soft serve. You can even get a twist."

"No." She growled. "We don't ruin chocolate ice cream by lacing it with vanilla."

Rachel smiled. "Absolutely not. The ultimate sin." She crossed the room and grabbed a wheelchair. "Your chariot, my dear." She stood and shifted into the chair. "Hold on," Rachel said once they were out of the therapy room and into the hallway. She didn't waste any time getting her through the corridor, her sneaker-clad feet slapping the floor as she pushed her swiftly to the elevator.

"Should I be worried? I mean, do you have a license to drive this thing?"

Rachel chuckled. "Learner's permit, but I'm catching on fast." She punched the button for the elevator.

"I can see that. Is this like the autobahn? No speed limits?"

"Unless my boss is here, and then it's zero to two miles per hour, a snail's pace." The elevator door opened, and a few people got out. Rachel whipped the chair around and backed inside.

"You have a boss?"

"Doesn't everyone?" Rachel continued when Shay hesitated a minute too long. "You can't remember if you have one. Can you?"

She shook her head. "No."

"So, what do you do for a living?"

"I'm an actuary." She glanced up at Rachel to see if she knew what that was, and she nodded. "Last I remember I was working on a huge new product that could've put me on track for chief actuary."

"Do you have a laptop you can look at or any pictures on your phone that might spark your memory?"

"Oh my God. I keep a journal." Why hadn't she remembered that before now? "I'm not sure where they are, though." She remembered having some at both the apartment and the beach house.

"Maybe you should ask Chloe. I'm sure she'll know."

"There are a lot of things I should ask her." And she would soon. Chloe's actions yesterday morning had rattled her, and she was worried something between them had changed over the past year. Her journals were a good place to start.

The elevator doors opened. "And we're off," Rachel said as she rushed her out toward the cafeteria.

Rachel parked her at a table and then brought back the tallest soft-serve ice cream cone she'd ever seen in one hand and a regular-sized one in the other. She kept the skyscraper cone for herself and handed the normal cone to Shay.

"Uh. I'm feeling a little cheated." Her gaze darted between the two cones.

"Sorry. This wasn't my plan, but see that kid over there?" She pointed to the little boy sitting a few tables away, and he held up an identical cone. "He bet me I couldn't eat as much ice cream as him." She rushed to the counter and brought a large drink cup and a spoon to the table. "For when it gets messy." She stared at the melting monstrosity. "I don't know how I'm supposed to eat this without it melting all over me."

"Is he one of your patients?"

"Yep, but not for long. He's going home soon. Been here too long."

"Was he in an accident?"

"Nope. Birth defect. Fixing nature can be challenging, but he's done fantastic." The smile on Rachel's face was beautiful. Did she have someone at home to brighten with it? Surely, she did.

"How did you two meet?"

Shay snapped out of her thought. "I'm sorry, what?"

"You and Chloe?" She took a lick of the ice cream that had already begun dripping onto her hand.

"We were at her brother's wedding. I work with him." She pulled her eyebrows together. "At least I do as far as I can remember."

"He introduced you?"

"Not really." She went through the whole story of how they'd met on the beach, the salty scent of the ocean, the crash of the waves, the sound of Chloe's shouts of excitement as the cold water rushed over her feet. How they'd been instantly captivated by each other.

"Wow, that's quite a story."

"I know. When I met her, I was enchanted. She was so beautiful. I didn't think I had a shot." Shay warmed at the memory.

"She is beautiful," Rachel said with a smile. "So, when did she know you were the one?"

"I said something stupid and made fun of myself. She told me months later that's what hooked her."

"I can see someone easily falling for you."

Shay's cheeks warmed. "You're just being nice."

"Nope." She held up three fingers. "If you weren't already taken, I'd be in line." Rachel took one last lick of ice cream before she dropped it into the cup, and they sat quietly for a few moments, Shay not wanting to leave but not wanting to stay. She was flattered, but she was also completely in love with her wife.

"You want to see the atrium?" Rachel said, clearing the awkward moment.

"I'd love that."

"You done with that?" Rachel chuckled and glanced downward. "I have ice cream all down the front of my shirt, don't I?"

Shay nodded and laughed. "That's you and your gambling habit's fault."

"Next time I'll give you the big cone." Rachel wiped her shirt with a napkin. "Just lost the other half of the bet. Joey said I wouldn't eat the whole thing, but I didn't have breakfast this morning, so I thought I might."

Rachel shot out of her chair, cleared the table, and took the trash to the can. She stopped by and talked to Joey, who was still eating his ice cream, before she came back. "Let's get out of here. He'll be sick later if he eats the whole thing, and I don't want to be around when that happens."

"You're a troublemaker."

"Me? Never." Rachel grinned before she got behind the wheelchair and popped a wheelie as she pushed her out of the cafeteria.

Chloe pressed her fingers to her forehead as she thumbed through the magazine in her lap. Yesterday, she'd drunk more bourbon, eaten nothing, and passed out on the bed in a pile of Shay's clothes. When she woke around eleven that night, she'd seen all the calls Shay had made and the messages she'd sent, but she was in no shape to see or communicate with her or anyone else. The feelings she'd had yesterday morning when Shay had made love to her had thrown her life into a spin cycle she couldn't temper last night. She wished she had a switch in her brain to turn off all these feelings she was having, but nothing seemed to alleviate them. Not even the alcohol had helped.

This morning, after some time alone, a nice hot shower, and some advice that drunk Chloe had left for her on a notepad in the kitchen, she knew what she had to do. Shay was still her wife, and she had to take care of her no matter how she felt. The note she'd found from herself made it perfectly clear that drunk Chloe was still hopelessly in love with Shay, but sober Chloe still didn't know if she could dive right back into a relationship she'd so painstakingly detached herself from.

The laughter in the hallway returned her focus to the magazine in her lap. She glanced up when the door opened and the sound grew louder. As Rachel pushed Shay into the room, Shay was looking up at her, smiling. Then she saw Chloe and her smile faded.

"Hey, where have you been? I've been worried."

"I had some things to take care of at the gallery that took longer than I expected."

"You don't answer your messages?" Rachel's tone showed clear disapproval.

She narrowed her eyes and veered her gaze from Shay, using the only excuse she could think of. "Battery died." She checked her watch and saw that Shay's therapy session should have ended over an hour ago. "What have you two been up to? Seems like you're having a good time." *Too good a time.*

"We went down to the cafeteria and got ice cream after my session." Shay glanced back up at Rachel. "If we'd known you were here, we would've come and got you."

Rachel nodded and smiled slightly. "Definitely."

Her heart thumped. "Must have been really good ice cream. It's almost two hours past when your session ended." She wanted to stop, but she couldn't. Her jealousy wouldn't let her.

"Rach gave me a tour of the atrium, and then we just started talking."

Rachel pushed Shay next to the bed and helped her out of the chair. "Shay doesn't remember if she got that chief actuary position at work. You want to fill her in?"

Seriously? The woman was stepping way out of bounds. The nickname—Rach—Shay had called her hadn't gone unnoticed either.

Chloe raced around the bed and took Shay by the waist and helped guide her into the bed. "It was yours, hands down."

"I got it?" A huge smile swept across Shay's face.

The perpetual knot in her stomach tightened again. "Yep. You were promoted a little over a month ago. All your hard work paid off."

"I got it." Shay held her hand up for a high-five from Rachel, which she gave her immediately.

"So, you *are* the boss. Sounds like a big deal," Rachel said.

"I guess so." She smoothed the sheet across her legs. "I should probably check in, then."

"Jackson said not to worry. They're handling everything while you're out." Chloe loosened the sheet at the bottom of the bed.

"Oh." Shay seemed disappointed. "Maybe he can bring me up to speed next time he's here."

"I'm sure Chloe can call him and let him know you're curious," Rachel said.

Again with the butting in. Who did this woman think she was? She was planning to get to all that and some other things but wasn't prepared for it to happen this soon. "Sure. I'll call him and see if he can stop by later. Bring us some dinner." She glanced at Rachel. "Are you planning to stay for a while? I'll have him pick up enough for you as well." It was killing her, but she had to play nice.

"Thanks, but I have plans." Rachel's smile was less than jovial.

"I'm sure someone as successful as you has a boyfriend waiting somewhere."

"No. No one waiting for me. Just a date with friends." Rachel went to the door. "Oh, and it would be a girlfriend if someone were waiting." She seemed to purposely ignore Chloe and smile at Shay.

I fucking knew it! "We have several single friends, if you're interested?" She tried to make sure her voice was calm and even, but totally failed.

Rachel glanced from Chloe to Shay and then back again. "I appreciate the offer, but I prefer to meet women on my own terms." She pulled opened the door. "Can I have a word with you in the hall?"

"Sure." Chloe nodded and then glanced at Shay. "Be right back." She felt like she was in grade school again, being summoned by her fifth-grade teacher after she'd been caught passing notes in class.

The door had barely closed when Rachel lit into her. "I don't know what happened to you yesterday or what you did that she can't remember, but none of that matters now."

"It won't happen again." And it wouldn't. Chloe knew it was wrong not to come back sooner.

Rachel acted like she hadn't heard her and continued to talk. "You can't just disappear on her like that. She needs you. She refused to go to physical therapy this morning, and I barely got her to do thirty minutes this afternoon."

"She didn't want to go? Why?" She moved toward the door, and Rachel grabbed her by the arm.

"No. She was worried about you. Not that you're worth it. You don't just leave or look elsewhere when times get tough."

The bare skin of her arm stung as she pulled it free. "Lay off. You have no idea what you're talking about." Rachel was alluding to what she'd overheard in the waiting room and assumed Chloe was having an affair based on a small piece of a conversation.

Rachel stood back and crossed her arms. "Okay, then clue me in."

"What's between me and Shay is none of your business." She wasn't about to elaborate, and she didn't have to justify her behavior. Especially not to someone she barely knew.

Rachel took in a deep breath. "Then keep it out of this hospital and get your ass back in there and be present until she recovers."

Her jaw clenched as she ground her teeth together. "I said, it won't happen again." She spun around to the door and pulled it open.

Rachel stuck her head just inside the door and said, "You two have fun tonight." It was amazing how she'd flipped from vicious guard dog to sweet therapist in a matter of seconds.

"You too," Shay said with a grin.

Chloe's heartbeat hadn't even begun to settle when she crossed the room to Shay's bedside. "She's totally flirting with you."

Shay rolled her eyes. "No, she's not. She's just being nice." She reached out. "I have to admit, though, I kind of like that it makes you jealous."

She sat on the side of the bed, took Shay's hand, and rubbed the back of it with her thumb nervously. "I'm not jealous. I just don't like her doing fun things with you. I should be doing that." She was jealous, and, Jesus, it was eating her up. She'd thought she was way past these feelings for Shay. "I'm sorry I worried you. I'll make sure my phone is fully charged from now on." She kissed her on the forehead and propped herself up next to her in bed. Shay leaned into her and quickly went to sleep.

❖

Shay was so excited to get to stand up and take a shower by herself. The nurse hadn't put her on her schedule and said she was ready to solo. Chloe had been conveniently gone during her showers since she'd been able to take them, and she hadn't probed her as to why. She got out of bed and padded to the bathroom using her walker. When she didn't see the stool in the middle of the shower as it usually was, she realized that she'd underestimated the enormity of the task at hand. She turned around and looked at Chloe as she sat on the couch.

"I think I might need help." She glanced into the bathroom. "My stool is gone."

"Do you want me to call the nurse?"

"No. That'll take too long." She twisted the handles of the walker in her hands. "She's probably already helping someone else, and I need to shower before Jackson gets here."

"Oh. Okay." She bolted off the couch, crossed the room, and led her into the bathroom, which included an open, walk-in shower, and helped her undress.

Shay held the bar attached to the wall to steady herself, but washing was going to be difficult with one hand, and she didn't think she could manage standing the whole time without holding on.

She turned to Chloe with the bar of soap in her hand. "Can you help me?" The look on Chloe's face was one of pure terror, like she'd never seen her naked before.

"Uh...sure," Chloe said and quickly pulled off her sweater and rolled up her sleeves before she took the soap from her. She swiped a washcloth from the shelf, wet it, and lathered it. "How about I hold you up while you wash yourself?" She handed her the washcloth and then put her hands on her waist.

As Shay washed herself, she realized that Chloe was looking anywhere but at her. What was that about? She'd seen her naked a thousand times before and liked it. Why would she be uncomfortable?

She knew she'd lost weight and had multiple bruises, but was her body that off-putting? She leaned over to wash her legs but was having a tough time reaching her calves.

Chloe took the washcloth and soap and squatted down in front of her. The water spray didn't seem to even faze her as she gently took one leg in her hands and washed, no, caressed it and then reached for her injured one. The slow, methodical motions were perfect foreplay. With one hand on the railing and the other on Chloe's back, she balanced herself as the full effect of Chloe's touch resonated deep in her belly. If this were any other situation, she'd take full advantage of their proximity and insist Chloe take full advantage of *her*.

Chloe glanced up at her with her deep-blue eyes and lifted an eyebrow. "Don't even think about it." Apparently, Chloe had the same thing on her mind. She chuckled loudly as Chloe sprang up and moved around to wash her back.

Satisfied that her distance was due to the accident and not about her body, she tried to shake the thoughts from her mind. She couldn't wait to get out of this place and back home in her own bed, where she could take care of the needs burning within her.

CHAPTER THIRTEEN

Shay was coming home in a couple of days, and Chloe hadn't made any preparations other than washing and putting Shay's clothes back in the closet. She'd brought the list to the hospital with her to make sure she hadn't missed anything or that Shay didn't need something additional that she hadn't thought about. She took it from her purse and scanned it.

"Will they be giving you some bandages for your wounds?" They had almost healed, along with her bruises, but Shay had kept them covered to speed up healing and prevent her sweatpants from irritating them.

"Some, I think. But you should probably pick up more." She held up a package. "These are two by two." She rummaged through the container on the bedside table. Someone quietly knocked on the door and Shay said, "Come on in."

Rachel came through the door. "Are you ready for your session?"

"Yep." She plucked the almost-empty roll of tape from the container and held it up. "Can you get me some of this to take home?"

"Probably. We'll grab some on the way back up."

"I'll buy some," Chloe said. She didn't want Shay getting anything more than necessary from Rachel.

"Rachel's still going to be my therapist after we go home, because she does outpatient therapy as well." Shay climbed out of bed and reached for her walker. "She might even come out to the house once in a while."

"What? Why would she have to do that?" Her voice rose sharply, and Rachel raised an eyebrow. She'd failed miserably at hiding her annoyance.

Shay lifted her shoulders. "I kind of told her she could come see the beach. That's okay, isn't it?"

She glanced at Rachel and smiled. "Sure." The back of her neck burned like it was on fire. She didn't want Rachel anywhere near their home. It only gave her more opportunity to meddle in things that were none of her business. She stared at the next item on the list. Toiletries. She'd have to buy those as well. Erica had thrown them all in the trash. She put the list back in her bag and stood. "While you're in therapy, I need to pick a few things up and take them home, so I may not be here when you get back."

"Okay." Shay went to the door. "But you'll be here later, right?" she asked. She seemed to be walking incredibly well today. Maybe getting around at the beach house wouldn't be as hard as she'd anticipated.

"Of course." Chloe smiled. It wasn't such a bad feeling to be needed.

❖

Chloe put the oranges, bananas, and apples in the fruit bowl on the counter, the last of the four bags of groceries she'd bought to unpack. There hadn't been much in the refrigerator, and she'd thrown out what had been left because it was outdated. Now they had enough food to get them through the next week or two. Trying not to let her personal feelings get in the way, she'd even bought enough to have Rachel stay for dinner in case Shay wanted her to. Rachel was a great therapist. She had to give her that. Shay was up and walking fairly well at two weeks with the walker, much sooner than anyone had expected. She was truly thankful for that.

She'd already washed and put Shay's clothes back in the closet, but she needed to do her own laundry. She'd let everything slide since Shay had been hurt, and even though Erica had been at the beach house some of that time, she didn't do domestic chores for herself, let alone Chloe. She started the first load and then went into the bathroom and put a new toothbrush in the stand. All of Shay's things she'd boxed up were back in place. She checked a few items off her list, leaving everything else until Shay got home.

She plucked another journal from the pile in the closet, lay down on the bed, and began to read.

Is there such a thing as magnetism?

Some sort of gravitational pull draws me toward Chloe. I can't stop it. When she's here—I want her. When she's gone—I want her more. When things are bad—she makes them good again. When they're good—she makes them so much better. It's hard to explain the connection I feel with her, but it hasn't lessened over the time we've been together. It's only become stronger.

Dad always said, some people come into our lives who change us. We never know when, we never know how, and we never know why. The impact can be minimal, or it can change your whole life. Some will leave you crushed beyond measure, but it may be worth it. Chloe is definitely worth it.

Jesus. Tears flowed from her eyes, and she couldn't stop them. Sobs followed close behind, and she convulsed as she fought to take in air. The depth of her feelings for Shay tumbled back, throwing her into a painful uncertainty. Shay had been worth it too.

The doves cooed outside on the deck railing, and Chloe tossed the journal at the window. "Stop yearning for each other. That's not real! None of it! She'll leave you eventually, and then you'll have nothing!" She couldn't take their happiness. Not now, when her life was in such turmoil.

She needed to keep her mind off the battling emotions creating chaos in her mind. She bolted up, gathered the clothes from the floor, and took them to the laundry room. She felt like she was stuck in a bad romance novel, only it wasn't real because, any way she looked at it, she wouldn't have a happily ever after.

The journal lay open at the foot of the window. She picked it up, slapped it shut, and then stared at the stack of notebooks in the closet. The vault of information stared back at her like an evil blackmailer who knew all her secrets threatening to shatter her life at any moment. The guest bedroom would be a better place for them. Out of her sight, out of her mind. She picked up a stack and carried them to the doorway, then rethought her plan. Shay would notice them missing. She put them back in the closet, then pulled a few from the stack and hid them in the guest room at the other end of the house. She was far from finished reliving their romance through Shay's eyes.

❖

Chloe had been waiting at the door watching for them since her phone had chimed with the message from Shay that said they were almost home. She'd taken the last few days to arrange the furniture and remove the rugs from the hardwood floors so Shay would have a minimal chance of tripping and falling. Rachel had volunteered to bring Shay home, though Chloe couldn't remember why the hell she'd agreed to that. She didn't want that woman anywhere near her house. *Their house.*

She met Rachel's red Camaro convertible as it pulled up in the driveway. No big surprise. The car fit Rachel's arrogant personality perfectly. They both helped Shay inside to the couch, where Chloe had set up some pillows and a blanket, which she adjusted to make Shay more comfortable.

"What can I get you? Are you hungry?"

"No. We stopped on the way and ate lunch," Shay said as she shifted slightly to elevate her leg for Rachel to put a throw pillow under it.

Seriously? She took you to lunch?

"There's a new little Mexican restaurant in town. Have you been there?" Rachel asked as she seemed to take in the room.

"Yes. I have." *We both have. Many times.* She battled to keep her expression friendly.

Shay glanced at Rachel. "Did you bring in the chicken enchiladas?"

"I forgot. I'll get them."

"I brought you something. I thought you might be hungry."

Just that one sweet action wiped away Chloe's anger.

Rachel came through the door with the food. "Should I put these in the fridge?"

Chloe took the food. "Thanks. I got it."

"While you're in there, some water would be nice," Shay said.

Chloe went into the kitchen, slid the to-go box onto a refrigerator shelf, and grabbed a bottle of water from the door. In the short time she was gone, Rachel had wandered out onto the deck and was leaning against the railing looking out at the ocean. She set the water on the coffee table in front of Shay, then picked up the remote for the TV, clicked it on, and handed it to her. "Anything else?"

"No, but thanks. I'm kind of tired." She found a crime show on TV before she relaxed into the couch and closed her eyes. Mundane background TV had always put her to sleep quickly.

Chloe glanced at the deck. Rachel hadn't budged from the railing, so she followed her out. "You don't have to stay. I've got this now."

The deck creaked as Rachel turned around and crossed her arms. "So, this is the house she worked so hard to give you."

The hairs on the back of Chloe's neck stood on end. Shay had confided more in Rachel than she'd thought. "Just what exactly did Shay tell you?"

"That you'd always dreamed of having a place on the beach and she'd made it happen."

Chloe couldn't disagree. It was all true. "It was a wonderful surprise."

Rachel ran her hand back and forth across the railing before she focused back on Chloe, pulled her brows together, and tilted her head. "Yet, you still cheated on her."

The accusation stunned her. "I think you should go now." Why was this woman, this literal stranger, pushing so hard on this?

"I didn't see a single picture of you and Shay together in the living room and would assume there would be plenty, the way she talks about you. She's going to notice that detail."

Fuck. She'd forgotten the box of pictures she'd placed in the spare bedroom closet. After they'd split, creating new art had been her first priority. She'd needed to make the place different, and seeing pictures of her fractured life hadn't helped her creative process.

"What are you going to do when she remembers?" Rachel asked.

"When her memory comes back, I'll deal with the fallout."

Rachel raised an eyebrow and shook her head slowly. "I have no idea what made you look elsewhere. You must be an idiot. That woman in there is pure gold."

"Got it. I'm an idiot. Now leave." She followed Rachel to the door, opened it, and didn't say another word as she closed it behind her. *I am an idiot, but not for the reasons you think.*

She glanced at her watch. It was close to two o'clock, and Shay was awake again. "If you're good, I'm going to paint for a little while. We can have dinner at the usual time, okay?"

"We have a usual dinnertime?" Shay quirked up an eyebrow.

"They run a tight ship at the hospital. Seven, twelve, and five. No exceptions."

Shay laughed. "Maybe we can go out to dinner later?"

"Sure. If you feel up to it."

"I'd like to get out. Being confined to the hospital was driving me crazy. The only thing getting me through was knowing I was coming back here with you." The smile on Shay's face was beautiful.

"I'm glad you're home." And part of her was. Chloe had missed Shay more than she'd wanted to admit. She wouldn't be able to remove herself from Shay's life anytime soon, and oddly, she was okay with that.

❖

Shay had slept right through dinner, but Chloe had ordered in Thai and had a plate waiting for her when she woke up. After she'd eaten, Chloe had helped her move to the bedroom for more comfort. She scanned the room. The furniture had been rearranged. The bed was on a different wall, and the dresser was closer to the closet. Something else was different too, and she couldn't figure out exactly what it was. Things were definitely out of place.

"Why did we move the bed?"

"The sun was too hot in the morning on that side of the room," Chloe answered quickly.

That was plausible, but she also noticed that all the pictures of her and Chloe were gone. Had she taken them down for some reason? Were they back at the apartment? No. She clearly remembered setting some up here. "Where are all the pictures?"

Chloe hesitated. "They're in the guest bedroom. We moved them when we painted last month and just hadn't put them back in place." She left the room and came back with a box, then began setting the pictures on the dresser and nightstands. "There we go."

The color of the walls was different. Before, it had been off-white, and now it was a light sage-green. Maybe that's what was throwing her off. "Are my journals here somewhere?"

"I think they're in the closet." Chloe opened it, and she spotted them in a top corner on the shelf.

"Can you hand me a couple from the top?"

Chloe reached up, grabbed a few, and gave them to her. "I'm going to go paint some more while you rest, okay?"

"Sure. I'll read for a bit. These may help me fill in some of the blanks." She thumbed through the one on top, but it was dated close to six months ago. "What happened to the more recent ones?" she asked, but Chloe was already gone.

CHAPTER FOURTEEN

The week had been rough. Taking care of Shay while also working at the gallery hadn't been as easy as Chloe had thought. Her only time to paint was in the early morning, and Shay had changed her routine to match hers, getting up every morning at the same time and even fixing her breakfast to spend time with her. It was so sweet and endearing, but also frustrating since she wasn't getting any painting done.

The journals hadn't filled in all the blanks for Shay, and she'd continued to prod her with questions as well. This morning she'd slipped out early, packed up her canvas and paints, and taken them out on the beach. She'd captured a glorious sunrise, which had been difficult because Shay's face kept popping into her head. Finally, she'd abandoned the painting for another day and rummaged through her supplies until she'd found a piece of charcoal and sketched the beautiful face she couldn't seem to get out of her mind.

She'd been gazing at the ocean when she'd felt more than heard Shay's presence behind her. A cup of coffee appeared over her shoulder, and then Shay sat down beside her, pulled her knees to her chest, and buried her toes in the sand. Shay was still in her pajama pants and tank top, and Chloe could see the goose bumps on her shoulders, so she took the blanket she'd wrapped around her own shoulders and placed part of it over Shay's. Her hand landed around Shay's waist, and she couldn't seem to make it move from there.

"Thank you," Shay said softly and rested her head on her shoulder. "It's so beautiful and serene out here." She stared at the ocean.

In that moment, all seemed to be right in their world again. For a moment, anyway. Over the past few months, Chloe had felt as if she'd been tossed like a shell from the warmth of the sea and developed all these cracks for everyone to see. But Shay filled the crevices and ridges. *I'm just not me without her.* Even with its flaws, their connection was still strong. She wished the rest of the world would fade away, so they could fix the broken mess they'd created.

Rachel showed up for Shay's therapy session on time as usual. She was a huge pain in Chloe's ass, but she was a punctual one. At least she had time to prepare for the passive-aggressive battles Rachel solicited. After Shay's regular exercises on the all-in-one gym Chloe had purchased for her recovery, their session had moved to the beach. That was fine with Chloe. She needed a little quiet time to plan her next couple of paintings. In the past, she'd painted from inspiration, but that had become difficult in the past few months. Once she knew what she needed to accomplish, painting had become much easier. She wasn't sure if she liked this method, which made painting seem more like a chore than a passion, but it seemed to be working for the time being.

The sight she saw out her window alarmed her. Shay's arm was over Rachel's shoulder, and she was helping her walk across the sand. She bolted from her chair, through the house, and onto the beach. "Oh my God. What happened?" She took Shay's other arm and pulled it over her own shoulder.

"Her foot just went a little sideways in the sand."

"Do I need to take her to the hospital?"

"After I put some ice on it and give her a massage, she should be all right." Rachel didn't seem concerned as they walked her to the deck and settled her into a cushioned lounge chair.

Chloe's anger spilled out. "You shouldn't have taken her out there after a full session. You're pushing her too hard."

Rachel's hands went to her hips. "She was doing great. It's just an unplanned obstacle."

"Can you two stop fighting for a minute and listen to me?" Shay's voice was firm, and they both stopped talking immediately and gave her their attention. "It was my fault. I decided to race into the water. When the wave receded, the sand went too. End of story." She flopped back into the lounger. "Now fix me."

"I'll get some ice," Rachel said and headed into the house.

"I'll get a towel." She followed her in, took a towel from the hall cabinet, and met Rachel in the kitchen.

Rachel had pulled the bag of ice from the freezer and started filling a couple of quart-sized Ziploc bags. "You know you don't have to be here for these sessions. I'm sure there's someone else you'd rather be with."

This was all too much. Before Chloe knew what was happening, she felt the warmth of the tears streaming down her face. She didn't want this woman to feel sorry for her, but she didn't want her to hate her either.

When Rachel noticed the tears, she didn't show the slightest bit of pity, not that Chloe had wanted or expected any. She just stared over her shoulder as she continued with the ice, waiting for some kind of explanation.

Suddenly feeling stupid for crying, she swiped her hands across her face to dry her cheeks. "I didn't cheat on Shay."

The ice bag clanked as Rachel dropped it into the sink and turned around. "So, the woman at the hospital is just some crazy stalker?"

"No. We're involved, maybe, but probably not anymore. I don't know." She went to the table and sat in one of the chairs, motioning for Rachel to do the same. "It's a long story that I'm not sure you want to hear."

"Oh, I definitely want to hear it." Rachel relaxed in the chair.

"Shay and I have been separated for the past six months."

Rachel's eyebrows rose. "So, she was aware of the other woman?"

"Yes." She shook her head and chuckled. "You may not believe this, but Shay's the one who had the affair. After a while, I just moved on."

Rachel's face went blank, and she shifted in her chair. "I don't believe you. That woman out there is head over heels in love with you."

"I know, and I was head over heels in love with *her* a year ago."

"That's why you've been so sketchy."

Chloe closed her eyes and took in a deep breath. "This whole situation has been pretty fucked up."

"You've been having to act like it never happened." Rachel shook her head slowly and widened her eyes. "I can't imagine dealing with that. I'm so sorry. I've been judging you this whole time for something you didn't do." She glanced toward the deck where Shay was lying in the lounger with her eyes closed. "Wow."

Chloe still felt the need to protect Shay. "Please, don't hold it against her. She doesn't remember."

"And you're not going to tell her?"

"I want her to remember on her own. I don't want to put her through what I went through. It was such a shock, and with what she recalls now, it'll be for her as well."

"It would be devastating." Rachel spoke softly, as though she was still processing the information in her head.

"I don't want to set her recovery back in any way."

"So, you're just going to suck it up and take care of her?"

"We *are* still married and her mom's an ass. So yes." Chloe got up and went back to the sink to get the ice.

Rachel followed her. "I have to say my respect for you has increased considerably."

"Thank you, but that's not why I told you. And you can't treat Shay any differently than you have been." She wrapped the ice inside the towel, creating a cold compress.

"So, green light to continue flirting?" Rachel raised her eyebrows.

Chloe rolled her eyes. "If it makes her feel good about herself, then yes."

Rachel studied her for a moment. "What about you? Are you still seeing that woman?"

"Of course not. I'm not the heartless bitch you seem to think I am."

"That must be hard." Rachel seemed skeptical.

"Not as hard as you might think." Chloe brushed past her and took the ice pack outside. She'd already shared too much and refused to talk about her current situation with Erica. She would deal with it when the time came or, more accurately, when Erica pressed for more.

❖

Shay climbed into bed and watched as Chloe took off her jewelry and laid it on the dresser. She took a few pieces of clothing from the drawer and walked into the bathroom. The whole situation was weird.

Since when did Chloe feel the need to change her clothes in private? What was she missing? Chloe came out dressed in yoga pants and a baggy T-shirt, then gave her a smile and a slight glance as she padded to the doorway. They weren't going to have any physical contact again tonight. Chloe would end up sleeping in her studio or on the couch like she had for the past week.

"Can we talk for a minute?" Shay asked.

Chloe stopped in the doorway, turned around slowly, and leaned against the door frame like she was afraid to come any closer.

"You always seem to be in such a hurry these days." She patted an empty spot on the bed beside her.

Chloe hesitated a moment before she crossed the room and sat down. "Just trying to get some pieces ready for the gallery. I've sold a few, and it's starting to look a little empty."

"That's awesome. I'm so glad everyone has finally found you. I always knew once they did, you wouldn't be able to paint fast enough." Shay had always appreciated Chloe's art.

Chloe's lip pulled up on one side. "Well, thank you for that. It seems you were right."

They sat in silence for a moment, Chloe waiting patiently while Shay tried to find the words to ask what she wanted to know. Shay wanted to touch her so badly but rolled the blanket between her fingers to keep them busy instead.

She released the blanket and smoothed it across her lap. "We're good together, right?" She let her gaze skitter away from Chloe's. "I mean…sexually?"

Chloe nodded. "Yes, we've always been good together that way." She rolled her lips in and looked away for a moment. "It's just lately we haven't had a lot of time." Her voice sounded melancholy, sad even.

Disappointment settled deep in Shay's chest. They hadn't been having sex. That's why Chloe was so distant. "Seems I've got nothing but time now."

Chloe brushed her hand across Shay's thigh. "But I have a painting to finish." She didn't wait for a response. She was up and out of the room before Shay could counter.

Shay flopped into her pillow. *What am I gonna do about this?*

They'd always had a lot in common and never lacked conversation. But sex had been a large part of their life together, and the lack of it signified something bigger was happening in their relationship. No matter what differences they'd dealt with in the past, they'd always been able to come together and embrace their connection in bed.

CHAPTER FIFTEEN

Shay forced her eyes open. It wasn't early, but the sun was already blazing through the windows. She slid her hand over Chloe's side of the bed—empty. The sheet was cold, so she'd either not come to bed again last night or she'd gotten up early. The door to the bathroom clicked open, and Chloe quietly entered, already completely dressed.

"Where are you going?" Shay asked.

Chloe seemed startled. "Sorry. I didn't mean to wake you."

"I want you to wake me." Shay heard the neediness in her voice slip out.

"I've been up for a while." Chloe took a pair of earrings from her jewelry box on the dresser, flipped her hair over her shoulder, and put one in, and then with the same motion inserted the other.

A memory flashed in Shay's mind. Chloe's hair gathered in her hands, kissing her neck—Chloe giggling and telling her to stop, they needed to go. Not that she hadn't done that a thousand times before, but the look in her eye at that moment when she'd turned around in her arms had been so full of desire, there was no way they would've made it on time to wherever they'd been going.

"Since we've moved to the beach, I've become an early riser," Chloe said as she sat on the edge of the bed.

A different image of Chloe in a T-shirt coming across the room toward her and bouncing onto the bed flew through Shay's mind. "You have, haven't you? You used to sleep much later than me."

Chloe looked at her curiously. "You remember that?"

She nodded. "I saw you in the sunlight coming back to bed."

Chloe smiled as though remembering the same scene. "I like to be up with the sun, so I can catch beautiful sunrises on canvas."

Shay smiled and nodded. "Pieces of it, anyway." She saw the look on Chloe's face change. To what, she wasn't sure, but it looked more like concern than happiness. "Can you help me fill in some of the blanks? I'd like to remember, and I'd rather do it with you than alone."

"The doctor said not to push it. Let it come back naturally."

"What I just saw seemed like it would lead to the most natural thing in the world." She reached over, cupped Chloe's shoulder in her palm, and let her hand glide slowly down her arm.

Chloe watched the motion, and when their eyes met again, she saw the look in Chloe's eyes change. The kiss that came next was soft and seeking, like a kiss after a spectacular first date. It quickly morphed into something spawned out of pure need. They hadn't kissed with such urgency since...forever. Chloe was almost completely on top of her with her leg pressed to her center when a soft moan came from her mouth, fueling the desire bubbling inside her even more. She smelled of oranges and spice. God, she'd missed this contact. Every part of them touched—thighs, stomachs, breasts—and she wanted more. She reached up under Chloe's shirt, cupped her breast in her hand, and was rewarded with another moan, only louder this time. Receiving the signal loud and clear, she tugged at the waistband of her leggings, needing better access. Suddenly Chloe broke the kiss, cleared her throat, and stood up.

"I can't do this. I have to get to the gallery." Chloe's words were staggered as she fought for breath and straightened her clothes.

Shay watched her walk away, counting each step as she increased the distance between them, hoping she'd stop and come back. But Chloe was out of there before she could form a word, let alone a coherent sentence. She touched her swollen lips and let the feeling of being kissed so thoroughly wash over her again. What had just happened? She hadn't mistaken the want she'd seen in Chloe's eyes, the desire as Chloe had pressed her body to hers. Everything had rushed to her center, and she'd been ready for the woman she loved to take her. She didn't know what to feel—Anger, disappointment, fear. She'd been abandoned again.

❖

The surge of wetness had made it perfectly clear that Chloe's attraction to Shay hadn't diminished. She'd had to get out of there, escape the impending trap she'd set for herself. Walking to her car had been challenging, Chloe's legs were so shaky, she'd barely been able to move when she'd left the room. Thankfully, she'd already loaded the paintings into the back of the SUV.

Driving to the gallery had been a lame excuse. She'd have to apologize and, most likely, explain further when she got home tonight. What she would say and how she would say it was a mystery to her.

Suddenly she was at the gallery. Autopilot was getting to be a bad habit. She drove around to the back and parked. Whitney was already there waiting for her. She'd called her on the way and told her she needed to talk.

As soon as she was out of the car, Whitney pulled her into a hug. "What's going on? Are you okay?"

"I think so. I just don't know what to do." She searched for the key in her purse. "Can you help me unload these?" She didn't want to explain everything outside, where anyone could overhear.

"Sure. I brought coffee. Let me get it." Whitney rounded her car and took a coffee carrier along with a small bag from the front seat.

Once the door was unlocked and the alarm turned off, they unloaded the paintings from the back of her Chevy Tahoe and locked it.

Whitney didn't waste any time asking for information. "Okay, so now spill."

Coffee and a croissant miraculously appeared in front of her as she sat at the small table in the back of the gallery.

"I almost had sex with Shay this morning."

"Almost?" Whitney pulled a piece of croissant loose and put it into her mouth.

"She remembered something about me coming back to bed. The look on her face was just so sweet and innocent."

"And then she kissed you?"

"No. *I kissed her*, and my emotions were all over the place." She took a sip of coffee. "I felt like I was thrown back in time to when we'd first started living together. You know, the period when you have sex every day, sometimes twice because you can't get enough of each other."

Whitney raised an eyebrow. "Twice? Really?"

"The little voice in the back of my head brought me to my senses, and I got the hell out of there." *Thank God.*

"You *left?*" Whitney's brows drew together. "What did you tell her?"

"That I had to get here, to the gallery."

"She accepted that excuse?" Whitney stuffed another piece of croissant into her mouth.

"I didn't stay long enough to discuss it." She closed her eyes briefly. "You have no idea how hard it was to leave her like that."

"I can imagine." Whitney looked thoughtful as she sipped her coffee. "You started it. Why *did* you leave?"

"I don't know." She shook her head. "I want what we used to have. I just don't know if that's possible." She got up, took two smaller paintings from where they were hanging, and leaned them against the wall. "I'm so mixed up right now." She retrieved a painting she'd brought and held it up against the wall in the newly bare spot.

"Have you gotten past everything else?" Whitney asked as she stood behind her, checking the spacing.

"I think so. Maybe. I don't know. It's hard to forget. Especially when her physical therapist flirts with her all the time. Since she overheard me talking to Erica in the hall that day, I think she's trying to make me jealous."

"Have you told her what happened?"

"Some of it, though she probably still thinks I'm having an affair." She used the claw hammer to remove the two nails and pound one into the middle of the space she'd just created, then hung the larger painting.

"You should tell her the whole story, and then make her back the hell off."

"You think so?" She picked up the two smaller paintings and assessed where to put them, then carried them to another wall.

"Hell, yes. Shay is still your wife, and apparently, you're still in love with her."

The paintings thudded as she dropped them against the wall on the other side of the gallery. "I wish I'd never caught her or could erase the last six months of my life."

"Do it. Shay has. You should just move forward and let what happens, happen."

"Maybe I should. It's been so many days since I touched her, and she's still all I dream about. That certainly hasn't changed for me."

The bell on the door rang, and she looked up to see a customer enter the gallery. She let the conversation stop there. It was clear Whitney thought she should give Shay another chance.

Shay was thrilled when Rachel had told her during her therapy session the day before that she could ditch the cane and try walking on her own. She'd said to still be careful and not put too much stress on her leg, but she was progressing much better than Rachel had anticipated. When Chloe had called earlier and suggested they go out to dinner and celebrate her progress, that made her week even better. Maybe a change of scenery would do them both good. She'd dressed in khaki shorts and a light-blue V-neck shirt. Any worries she'd had about dressing too casual vanished when they'd arrived. Her choice seemed to be just a hint above the rest of the diners'. It was definitely a come-as-you-are place, which was fine as long as the food was good, and from what Shay could recall, it was.

"It's good to see you both here together tonight," James, the owner said, and his wife Kim walked over from the bar to welcome them as well.

The first time they'd been in for dinner, he'd come to the table and introduced himself. He had a place on the beach not far from theirs, and he and his wife Kim had quickly become good friends with them. They didn't have any children and spent most of their nights at the restaurant. She and Chloe had eaten at least one meal a week at the Marina Cantina ever since and had been invited to their home on numerous occasions as well.

"It's good to see you too." Shay hadn't missed the meaning in his words. Just who had they been frequenting the restaurant with, if not each other?

"We have your favorite table out on the deck ready for you."

Shay looked at Chloe and scrunched her eyebrows together.

"I called ahead," Chloe said as they followed Kim to the table by the railing. "I know how much you love the view."

And a beautiful view it was. The table looked right out onto the marina. While white lights hung in a zigzag pattern with torches filling the spaces between on the railing, the lights from several buildings on the other side glistened on the water. The weather was perfect, with just a slight breeze to keep the heat at bay. She remembered it being one of her favorite places to dine. At one time they'd even discussed getting a boat. Wait, had they? "We don't have a boat, do we? Did I miss that too?"

Chloe chuckled. "No. We decided to put that off another year until work slowed down."

"Your work or mine?"

"Both." Chloe smiled and then gave her attention to the menu.

Kim appeared again. "Can I get you ladies a drink or an appetizer?"

"Yes. We'd like a bottle of the Porer Pinot Grigio." Chloe glanced at Shay momentarily, seeking her approval. She nodded, and Chloe continued. "And I think we'll get the ceviche to start. It was so good last time. Shay loved it."

"I did?" She glanced at the menu. Fresh lime, ahi tuna, shrimp, scallops, vine-ripe tomato, avocado, and red onion. "You're sure I liked it?" She lifted an eyebrow.

"Trust me. You did." Chloe flashed her the beautiful smile that made her insides turn to goo.

"Okay." She set down her menu. "I have complete trust in you." And she did. She didn't trust anyone in the world more than Chloe.

"Then I'll go ahead and order." Chloe tilted her head, smiled, and rattled off both their dinner orders for the night.

James brought the wine to the table and filled both their glasses. Chloe immediately took a sip and closed her eyes. "Perfect." Then she took another drink and relaxed into her seat. "I'd forgotten how beautiful it is here."

"What's been keeping us from coming?"

"Just life." She took another drink of wine as she stared out onto the marina. "We need this break."

The lights danced in Chloe's ocean-blue eyes, and the beauty of her face overtook Shay. She reached for Chloe's hand, needing some sort of contact. "I agree." They sat in silence, holding hands and gazing out onto the water until the ceviche arrived.

Chloe dropped her hand and took control, as usual, dipping some of the cured fish onto a plate and sliding it in front of Shay, then doing the same for herself. "Go ahead. Taste it."

She pushed it around with her fork before scooping up a small bite and putting it in her mouth, holding it there a moment to take in the multilayered flavors before she chewed. It was the most delicious dish she'd ever eaten. She smiled widely and moaned as she chewed. "This is absolutely wonderful."

"Told you," Chloe said, her smile widening.

She raised her plate in both hands and held it out. "I need more, please."

Chloe spooned more onto her plate and took another spoonful for herself. "Are we going to need a second order?"

"Maybe." She scooped another bite into her mouth, closed her eyes, and moaned even louder this time.

"People are going to think we're doing something under the table." Chloe laughed. The low, sexy sound washed through Shay and made her want to make it happen a thousand times more.

"I don't care. Let them." Shay ate another bite. "How had I never tried this before last year?"

"You can be pretty stubborn sometimes when you want to be."

Shay wobbled her head. "You might be right." Another bite. "How did you get me to try it?"

"A little begging along with a little wine."

Shay quirked up an eyebrow. "Just a little?"

Chloe laughed. "Okay, maybe a lot."

Shay reached across the table and covered Chloe's hand with hers. "This is nice."

"It is." Chloe glanced around the place. "I love this restaurant."

"No. I mean this." She moved her hand between the two of them. "It's seems like forever since I've heard you laugh. I'd almost forgotten how much I love the sound."

Eye contact became sparse as Chloe twirled the stem of her wineglass between her fingers. "I was so scared, Shay. I thought I'd lost you."

"I know." She squeezed her hand. "But I'm better. I'm here, and everything is going to be okay."

"Is it?" Chloe stared into her eyes, and Shay saw a new uncertainty in them.

"Yes. It is. I promise." Shay picked up the bottle of wine, poured them each a glass, and held hers up. "To us moving forward."

After toasting, Chloe immediately drank down all her wine and poured herself more. By the time the main course arrived, she was on her third glass and ordering another bottle.

While Shay dug into her food and had eaten most of her carnitas, Chloe had only picked at her chicken quesadillas, eating only one and a half of the chicken and cheese-filled wedges, when she reached for the bottle of wine to fill her glass again.

"Maybe you should slow down a little." The words came out more like an order than a request, even though Shay hadn't meant it that way.

Chloe glanced up from the bottle mid-pour as she held it. "Why? We're celebrating, right?" She set the bottle on the table, picked up her glass, and took another swig of wine.

All her hopes for the night were slowly swirling down to the bottom of Chloe's wineglass. They wouldn't be intimate again tonight. "I was kind of hoping to celebrate a little differently when we got home."

The look Chloe gave her over her glass made her believe she was hoping to celebrate that way too, but the rate she was sucking down the wine totally contradicted that thought. It wasn't like they'd never indulged in alcohol. In fact, on more than one occasion they'd both had a little too much to drink and had explored each other's body thoroughly. But this wasn't tipsy Chloe sitting across from her. She was getting drunk at light speed. The only thing running through Shay's head now was why. Was she so upset by the whole accident that this was her way of coping with the stress, or was something else going on?

Dinner ended abruptly when Chloe got up to go to the bathroom and stumbled head-on into one of the waiters. After helping her to the bathroom, Shay fished out Chloe's credit card from her bag and gave it to Kim to settle the bill. She also used Chloe's phone to call an Uber. She hadn't expected to see a notification for a gazillion text messages from someone named Erica, all simply saying, *Call me.* She faintly remembered a customer of Chloe's by that name, but why would she be texting her nonstop like this? Had she commissioned a painting? Did she have a deadline? Chloe hadn't confided any information about her recent business at the gallery, which was something she would have to remedy.

She loaded Chloe into the Uber and told Kim that one of them would be back to get their car in the morning. Her mind was still clear, but she wasn't supposed to be released to drive for at least another week or two. Chloe had left the sober realm two glasses ago and was in no shape to drive. As it was, she was having trouble standing.

Chloe passed out in the car on the twenty-minute ride, and once they got home Shay took her straight to the bedroom, helped her undress, and only let her go to the bathroom alone because she insisted. She pulled the covers back on the bed and waited for her to come out and lie down. Being pulled into bed along with Chloe and the long, slow, erotic kiss that came next was a surprise. Chloe had barely touched her since they'd been home, and with one kiss all her nerve endings had been awakened. She finally broke away to gauge Chloe's awareness, remaining on top of her as Chloe stared up at her all glassy-eyed. One thing was certain tonight. She refused to make love to Chloe when she was this drunk.

When Chloe's hands went to her face and cupped it between them, she hadn't expected to see the tears that came next. "I still love you. You know. I shouldn't, but I do." She kissed her on the lips tenderly and then passed out.

"What?" She shook Chloe's shoulders. "Why shouldn't you?" She shook her again, but Chloe had passed out. "Why shouldn't you love me?" Her voice withered, and the question spun in her head as she laid her head on Chloe's chest and listened to the slow thump of her heartbeat—a heart that used to beat only for her. What had happened over the past year to change that fact?

Chloe's head was throbbing, and her mouth felt like someone had stuffed a bag of cotton in it. She opened one eye and then the other. Shay was snuggled in under her arm with her head on her chest asleep. Their legs were tangled together like they'd done more than just sleep last night, but they were both wearing T-shirts and panties. She reached under the blanket and checked. Yes, her panties were still intact. She had no idea how she was going to escape the awkwardness of this situation.

Shay shifted and snuggled closer, wrapping her arm around her waist. She pushed the usual thoughts from her mind and just let herself indulge in Shay's warmth and the strength in her arms as she held her. She couldn't remember the last time they'd been wrapped together like this with or without having sex. She'd missed the connection between them, and God help her, she wanted it back. She'd slept like she hadn't in a very long time.

She'd tried her hardest to resist her last night, and getting drunk had seemed to be the only way to avoid the intimacy she knew would follow when they got home. When the gorgeous smile came across Shay's face as she ate the ceviche, she'd felt it deep in her belly. More wine was her only option after that. It was the one thing that had kept her from taking Shay to bed last night.

When they'd arrived home from the restaurant, they'd gone into the bedroom and changed. Shay had asked her to stay with her, and she had. She'd been a little tipsy as well and had indicated more than once during the span of the evening that she'd like to continue the celebration after they got home. Chloe had made sure she was in no shape for anything like that, but she guessed Shay had fallen asleep in her arms.

What was she going to do about this? There was no in-between here. She could straddle the line for only so long. Shay would expect more soon, and Chloe wouldn't be able to make excuses forever. Was she going to be all in or out? She'd been the first to let go, to unravel everything in her life that had been so perfectly knitted together. The relationship had been meticulously, affectionately sewn together. It might literally destroy her to do it all again.

She carefully extracted herself from under Shay and went into the bathroom. The words written in bright-red lipstick in front of her on the mirror shocked her.

You love her, stupid! Forget about everything else.

Drunk Chloe had left advice for sober Chloe once again.

She spun a wad of toilet paper from the holder and tried to wipe the message away, but all it did was smear the lipstick. *Fuck!* She sprayed it with hairspray, but that made it worse. She looked under the sink for some alcohol, found a bottle, and doused a new wad of toilet paper with it, managing to clear most of the message. She didn't know what she'd have done if Shay had seen it.

"Come back to bed." Shay's voice echoed into the bathroom.

She rummaged through the medicine cabinet. "Trying to find some ibuprofen."

She heard the bottle rattle and peeked into the bedroom.

"I've been keeping it here, since I seem to live on it now." Shay sat up, opened the bottle, and held out a couple of capsules for her.

She brought a glass of water from the bathroom, scooped them out of Shay's hand, and dropped them into her mouth. "I guess I had a little too much wine last night."

"Little bit." Shay smiled and reached for her hand, tugging her onto the bed next to her. "Come back to bed and cuddle some more." Chloe didn't have the energy to do anything else, so she crawled back into bed. Shay immediately spooned her and kissed the back of her head. "I'll fix breakfast later." She wrapped her arm around her waist and pulled her closer.

The small voice in Chloe's head was screaming now, but she chose to ignore it. She was too tired to deal with herself right now. They had dinner plans with Jackson and Whitney before the gallery event tonight, and she was already dreading what new obstacles the night would present. She willed herself to sleep before reality could hit her again.

Chapter Sixteen

The restaurant was fancier than Shay had expected. Thankfully, she'd spent the better part of an hour choosing just the right outfit. After several botched attempts, she'd decided on a black slip dress and wedge heels. The dress fit her looser than she remembered, but when she looked in the mirror, she was happy with the way it hugged her curves. Chloe had dressed in half the time. She'd gone with her first choice of a light-gray shift dress with long puffed sleeves and a scoop neckline. She'd worn black-suede ankle-strap heels and had accessorized the dress with a black-beaded and fringed, drop-pendant necklace. With her long black hair pulled to one side and draped across her shoulder, she was stunning.

The dress might have been loose-fitting, but Shay knew exactly what was underneath. She remembered that for sure. When Chloe had walked out of the bathroom, Shay had been captivated by her beauty as usual, and she'd told her so. Chloe's cheeks had reddened immediately, and her eyes had become dark as Shay gazed at her. She would've liked to take more time exploring that look, but they'd been behind schedule because they'd had to call an Uber and pick Chloe's car up where they'd left it at the restaurant the night before.

As they were led to their table, Shay glanced around at the art on the walls. She tingled with excitement when she spotted one of Chloe's pieces hanging above the booth. "This is you?" She pointed to the painting.

"Yes." Chloe smiled softly. "They've been good to me here." She glanced around. "They've been letting me hang my art for a while. It's really helped get my name out there."

"So, we've been here before?" She glanced around but didn't recognize the place at all.

"You more than I." Chloe chuckled lightly. "If it hadn't been for your perseverance, my art wouldn't be hanging here at all."

"Me?"

"Yes. After Rob remodeled the place, you were relentless, calling him every day and even offering to pay him to hang it. I'm trying to think how he put it. Something like, you pushed him into taking the worst business risk that turned out to be the best marketing decision of his life." She smiled softly. "Apparently people come in just to see my paintings now."

"Wow. I always knew you'd be famous." And she did. Chloe put so much of her heart into her work. It just needed some exposure.

"Thanks to you, I am." Chloe's smile faded as she stared at her finger tracing the pattern of the tablecloth.

She reached over and took her hand. "That's a good thing, right?"

Chloe took a deep breath. "All our financial worries are gone now."

"That's a good thing, right?" she repeated, insisting on eye contact.

"Yes. Yes, it is." Chloe's smile returned, and she picked up the menu. "So, what are you in the mood for?"

The personal discussion had turned awkward and then faded quickly into the general topic of food and hunger, which had Shay wondering again what had changed in their relationship over the past year to make Chloe so distant.

The evening had been going well, the food was good, but Jackson and Whitney had been running late, so they'd missed dinner. Shay had been completely relaxed until they'd arrived at the gallery. Coming to the opening was a bad idea. The moment she stepped in the door, all eyes were immediately on her, but no one spoke. It was as though they were all afraid to talk to her, like she was too emotionally fragile to engage. The world around her had changed rapidly, and she didn't know why and couldn't do a thing to make it stop. Shay recognized a few people but also encountered many whom she apparently had met throughout the past year but didn't remember. Within an hour everyone seemed to relax, and she was overwhelmed by conversations about memories she didn't have. They were simple memories of events that should be easy to picture, but they still escaped her. It was frustrating to listen to people reminisce and laugh and not be able to join in the fun.

Shay moved to a quiet corner in the back of the gallery and pressed her fingers to her forehead as the pain in her head spiked. It invaded her thoughts, threatening to culminate in the usual splitting migraine. When she'd felt the signs, she'd taken her medication immediately, but it hadn't seemed to touch the incessant pounding in her head. She closed her eyes and leaned against the wall as she took in the various conversations in the room.

"You're hiding out in my spot." The voice in her ear was familiar, but she didn't recognize it right away.

She opened her eyes and sprang away from the wall. "Whitney." She instinctively pulled her into a hug.

"Hooray. Someone actually knows who I am." Whitney's animated smile warmed her heart.

"I understand. I always wonder how I can be surrounded by so many people and still feel so alone."

"Are you all right?" Whitney asked.

"My head's starting to hurt. I shouldn't have had that last glass of wine." She searched for Chloe in the crowd. "I need to go home, but it's Chloe's night, and I don't want to make her leave."

"I can take you."

"Could you? Really?"

"Of course. I haven't seen you in forever. It'll give us a chance to chat." Whitney seemed sincere. Her eyes were kind, not filled with the pity she'd been getting from others. "Just let me tell Jackson and grab Chloe, so she knows."

Shay watched her weave through the crowd as she crossed the room. Jackson fished his car keys out of his pocket and handed them to her. When she found Chloe, she peered over Whitney's shoulder at her as Whitney whispered in her ear. Chloe smiled at the person she'd been talking to and immediately came Shay's way. She really hadn't wanted to interrupt her.

"Are you okay?" Chloe asked, her eyes wide and soft.

God, she loved those beautiful ocean-blue eyes. She wanted so badly to ask her to take her home, but she refused to ruin her night. "I'm okay. Just had a little too much wine."

"I'll take you home." She set her glass on a tray propped up in the corner.

"No. Definitely not. These people are here for you. You need to stay."

"I've got this," Whitney said. "I just wanted to let you know that we're leaving."

Chloe's gaze went from Shay to Whitney and back again. "Are you sure?"

Shay nodded. "Yes. Please stay and enjoy all this." She took Chloe into her arms and hugged her. The warmth was so soothing that she held her for a few moments longer before she reluctantly let go. "I want you to stay." She kissed her lightly on the cheek.

"Don't worry. She'll be safe with me." Whitney put her arm around Shay and ushered her toward the door.

Shay glanced over her shoulder to see Chloe still watching them. She waved and said, "I'm fine."

Chloe smiled softly. "Okay. I won't be late."

She left the party with Chloe's perfume on her clothes and in her head. The bouquet of orange and spice was almost suffocating. She never should've hugged her. The mere scent of Chloe could turn her on completely.

The lights on the black Audi A5 in front of her blinked on and off, and a memory of her and Chloe snuggled closely in the back seat together flashed through her mind.

"Here we are," Whitney said.

"We've been out in this car before. The four of us. You, me, Chloe, and Jackson."

Whitney smiled. "Yes, we have. Many times." She opened the door for her.

Shay hesitated before getting in. "When was the last time?"

"Sometime last year." Whitney twisted her lips slightly.

"Another event like this?" Shay slid into the seat.

"I think it was dinner," Whitney said before closing the door.

Shay waited for Whitney to buckle in and start the car before asking more questions. "Were Chloe and I happy?"

"Very." Whitney's voice was soft, contented even.

"Things are different now."

"Different how?" Whitney asked, acting like she had no idea.

"I feel I can be candid with you, that we trust one another. Is that right?" Shay shifted sideways in her seat.

"We always have in the past." Whitney glanced over and then back at the road.

"She doesn't kiss me, touch me, nothing at all like she used to." She took a deep breath. "That's not entirely true. She has a few times, but after it happens, she immediately backs off like she's done something wrong."

Whitney shrugged. "Well, you've been in an accident and need to recover." She said it like it was the most obvious statement in the world.

"How can I fully recover if the woman I love refuses to have sex with me?"

"She's just being careful." Whitney glanced at her and then focused on the road again. "I'm sure that will come."

"I don't want careful—I want passionate and reckless." She hadn't intended the growl she let out to be so loud, but the sound filled the car.

Whitney grinned. "Don't we all? Maybe she's worried about moving too fast. What does the doctor say?"

"To go on with life normally. The memories may or may not come back."

"But you want to remember." Whitney was making a statement.

"Of course I do. Wouldn't you?"

Whitney took a minute, then nodded and smiled. "Yes, I believe I would."

"Can you fill in the blanks for me?" She was grasping at straws now because no one had been forthcoming with any information. Shay wondered who she'd confided in before. Where that person went— where they were now. Why weren't they here now?

"Only the blanks I know." Whitney didn't look at her but kept her eyes focused on the road in front of them. They were almost home. After they pulled up in front of the beach house, Whitney put the car into park but didn't turn off the engine.

"Will you stay with me until Chloe gets home?" She wanted the blanks filled in now.

Whitney hit the ignition button and the car died. "Of course."

❖

It was a little past eleven when Chloe arrived home, and she was surprised to see Jackson's car in the driveway. Whitney had taken his car, and he'd stayed to help with cleanup. She'd dropped him off at their apartment on her way home, thinking Whitney would be there already. She opened the door, took her shoes off in the entryway, and padded quietly into the living room, where Whitney and Shay were asleep. Shay lay on the couch and Whitney in the club chair with her feet up on the coffee table, a habit she'd had since before Chloe met her. Although tempted to push her feet to the floor, she didn't want to wake Shay. She circled the coffee table and stood next to her. Her eyes opened immediately.

"You're awake."

Whitney nodded. "I wasn't really sleeping." She checked the time on her phone. "You got done a little earlier than usual."

"Yeah. I wanted to get home as soon as possible. Jackson was a big help."

"That's my man." She looked over her shoulder. "You took him home?"

She nodded. "I didn't think you'd still be here."

"She wanted me to stay." Whitney sat up, stretched, and slid on her shoes.

"I was worried. Is she okay?"

"She's fine." Whitney looked over her shoulder at Shay on the couch and motioned with her hand to move to the kitchen. "Curious, but fine."

"What did she ask you?"

"Everything."

"And you told her?"

"Of course not. I filled in a few blanks about your career, but I left the hard stuff for you." Whitney opened the refrigerator, took out a couple of bottles of water, and handed one to her. "She misses the old you."

"The old me is gone."

"Is she?" Whitney raised an eyebrow. "I think I saw quite a bit of her tonight." She twisted the cap off the water bottle and tossed it onto the counter. "You still love her."

"I never said I didn't *love* her, Whit. But our lives have just changed so much in the past year. I don't know if I can get back to the way we were."

"Well, she's already back there, and you have to do *something*."

"Do what, Whitney?"

"Remember. Forget. Start all over." Whitney shrugged. "If you don't, you're both going to get hurt again."

"That's probably going to happen anyway."

"She wants sex—primal, mind-blowing, take-me-now sex. She sees the line you've drawn and wants to blow right past it." Whitney pressed her finger to the counter and trailed it between them.

"Jesus, Whit. There's nothing more I'd rather do than forget everything that happened over the past six months, but I was totally blindsided. Wrecked for months, and still not totally recovered. What if she does that to me again? I don't know if I can handle it."

"That's possible." Whitney tilted her head. "Isn't what you had worth the risk?"

"I don't want to talk about it anymore." She took in a deep breath. "Thanks for bringing her home."

"The kind of love you and Shay had is rare. We don't come across it more than once in a lifetime. If you let her go, you'll just end up searching for something to measure up to what you had. Fate has brought the Shay you fell in love with back to you. You have a second chance, so save yourself some grief and just let her in."

She took a gulp of water. Everything Whitney said made perfect sense. "When did you become so wise?"

"I married your brother." She chuckled. "But seriously. I know you moved on, but you haven't really been happy without her." Whitney squeezed her shoulder. "Think about it."

"Believe me. That's all I think about now." She walked her to the door and gave Whitney a hug before she opened it and clicked it closed silently after she left. She leaned against the door for a few moments before she went back into the living room, sat in the chair adjacent to the couch, and watched Shay sleep. So beautiful and innocent. This was the woman she fell in love with. She reached out to touch her, hovered momentarily, then balled her hand into a fist and pulled back.

Her instincts told her to slide in next to her and take her into her arms like she would've a year ago, but she couldn't move. Even though

Shay had blocked the memory of her indiscretion, Chloe hadn't and didn't know if she was ready to fully forgive her. And if Shay ever remembered, would she be able to forgive Chloe for moving on so quickly with Erica? She shook her head. The biggest fucking mistake of her life.

❖

Ruby-red lips, green eyes, and auburn hair seeped into Shay's dream. The scent of cherries and vanilla permeated her senses. The memory was so vivid she shuddered. It was as though the event had happened only yesterday. She was working late with someone she knew, but it wasn't Amber. This girl was much younger. *Lila.*

They'd been concentrating on the new product specifications when she'd looked up, and the girl was just watching her. Staring, in fact. Then she smiled and moved in for a kiss.

"Whoa. What's that about?" Shay backed up and stared. Why was this happening? Had she given her any signals? She hadn't, had she?

"I just thought…" The girl shrugged. She seemed just as confused as Shay was. "You seemed to like it the last time."

What the fuck? The last time? She was semiconscious now, trying to pull the rest of the memory in clearer. She had to know how and why this had happened.

The girl looked away, seemed a little guilty, and then caught eye contact again. "When you told me about the issues you're having with Chloe, your suspicions about her and that customer she's been spending so much time with."

Shay's mind spun as the memory surged into her head. She bolted up on the couch. They *had* gone out a few times. She *had* kissed those lips before, and she'd enjoyed the attention she'd given her. What else had she done? She wasn't getting a good feeling about it now.

Something was stirring in her heart—guilt, fear, anxiety. She couldn't pinpoint it, but something wasn't right. Chloe was clearly protecting her from herself. At least now, she had a starting point. She would gather more information and then move into deeper waters.

❖

Shay had been awake most of the night after her awkward dream. She hadn't been able to shake the vision from her head and felt extremely guilty for having it. Overhearing Chloe and Whitney talking in the kitchen had added to her insomnia. Their words were faint, but she got the gist of the conversation. Between the vivid dream and what she'd overheard, now she knew there were reasons for Chloe's distance. Something major had happened between them. Later, as she lay on the couch pretending to be asleep, she'd felt Chloe's hand hover above her cheek, but she hadn't touched her, another indication that something wasn't right. What it was, she didn't know, but she intended to find out.

She wasn't supposed to drive yet, but Chloe had already arranged a rental car for her, and it was sitting in the driveway. It was an automatic, so her left leg didn't come into play at all. She pulled up in front of the office building and sat in the car for a moment, staring up at the huge mirrored high-rise in front of her. It looked familiar, and she hadn't forgotten the way here or the way people darted in and out of traffic on the highway. Not even the shortcuts she'd always taken to avoid the morning commute traffic had escaped her memory.

She'd accepted the job three years ago. No, that would be four years now, leaving the small insurance firm she'd worked at before for bigger, bolder opportunities. Chloe's art hadn't been selling, and they'd been struggling to pay their monthly bills. Even though this job was a little farther away and required her to work more hours, it had alleviated a lot of the pressure.

It was now or never. She got out of her car and headed inside. She checked the directory—same floor as she remembered. She waited and caught the next elevator and punched the button next to the number four. When the doors opened, she stepped out and stopped, rethinking her decision. Her breathing shallowed and the room became smaller. She turned and punched the down button. Glancing toward the stair door, she took in a few deep breaths, trying to calm herself, and headed that way.

She heard voices in the stairwell and retreated into the hall. Where could she go? There was no place but inside the office. She pulled open the door and took a sharp left away from the cubicles located in the main room, one of which used to be hers. She had no idea if she even still had a place here. She came upon an office with her name on the door and stopped. *Shay Buchanan, Chief Actuary.* She'd actually gotten the promotion she'd been working so hard for.

She turned the knob and went inside. All the things from her cubicle were here, and someone seemed to have arranged them carefully. Probably her. She picked up the picture of herself and Chloe. They seemed happy. The sun was shining, and the ocean was foaming behind them on the beach. She smiled. That had been a good day.

A voice sounded behind her, and she whirled around to find a young man with short, dark, spiked hair that seemed to point whichever way it wanted. Dressed in a navy-blue suit that seemed tighter than necessary, he didn't look much older than eighteen.

"How did you get in here?" he asked.

"The door was open." She turned back to the desk, searching for any sign that she'd actually used this office before the accident. A vision of being pushed up against the wall and being kissed flew through her mind, and she shuddered. Apparently, she'd used it in more ways than one.

"It was unlocked, but not open," he said, moving toward her. "Ms. Buchanan isn't in. Can I direct you to someone else?"

The young man had absolutely no idea who she was. Did she look that different? Maybe he was new. She turned and rested a hand on the desk. "Amber. I'd like to see Amber if she's available."

He narrowed his eyes and assessed her for a moment, possibly contemplating whether it was safe to leave her alone in the office. "Stay here. I'll be right back."

After a few minutes, she heard the young man talking to someone with a familiar voice.

When Amber came through the doorway, her eyes widened. "Oh my God. I can't believe you're here," she said with a squeal as she pulled her into a hug. "I've missed you so much." She turned to the young man and held out her hands as if presenting her prized pig. "This is Ms. Buchanan."

"Oh. I had no idea. She just appeared in here." He didn't smile, just shook his head and left the room.

"Sorry, he's new." Amber rolled her eyes. "Interns."

That made her feel a little better. She hadn't forgotten everyone.

Amber continued to smile and stare. "What?" Shay put her fingers to her mouth. "Do I have something in my teeth?"

"No." Amber shook her head. "You just look really great."

The heat of a blush took over her face. "Thanks." She'd never been good at receiving compliments.

"You want to go say hi to everyone?"

"No." That wasn't in her plan for today at all. "If you don't mind, I'd just like to talk to you. Get some things straight in my head."

"Right." Amber's eyebrows pulled together. "Jackson told me you have some blank spots."

That was an understatement. She'd lost a whole fucking year, or close to it—at least eight or nine months. "Yes, that's true. Can you help me?"

"You bet. I'm happy to fill in wherever I can." Amber moved quickly out the door. "Let's go talk in my office."

She stopped and stared at her name on the door, touched it with her fingers, felt the ridges in her name. This had been one of her life goals, so why couldn't she remember it?

Amber seemed to notice her confusion. "The plaque finally came in. Looks good, huh?" She rolled her lips together. "You don't remember the promotion?"

"No. One of the blank spots." Shay shook her head. She seemed to be doing a lot of that lately. She had no recollection of the promotion at all.

"Lila can probably help refresh you on that, but she's out until the end of the week." Amber pulled the office door closed and led her farther down the hall.

Lila. A face flashed in her memory. Green eyes, wavy auburn hair, and a magnetic smile. Her stomach knotted, an unexpected reaction. "I don't remember much about her."

"Really?" Amber stopped and arched an eyebrow.

"Green eyes and auburn hair, right?"

Amber nodded and lowered her voice. "And drop-dead gorgeous legs. The kind most twenty-five-year-olds have." She took her hand and pulled her into her office. "I'm kind of surprised you don't remember her. You two were working together quite a lot before your accident." She slid into place behind her desk.

"I remember the name and the face, but that's it." She sank into the chair across from Amber. "Was something else going on with Lila?"

"Well, there were rumors, but you squashed them right away." Amber avoided eye contact. "Lila never denied them."

"Rumors? What rumors?"

"Never mind. I shouldn't have said anything. They were exactly that. Unsubstantiated office gossip. I don't know if any of it was true."

"Jesus, Amber. *I don't remember anything about her.* You have to tell me."

Amber rubbed her forehead before she got up and closed the office door. "Listen. All I know is that before we rolled out that new policy, you and Lila were spending a lot of time together working on it."

"That's not unusual. That's what it takes when you're defining statistics for new products."

"No, I mean *a lot*. Like after hours here and away from the office too."

"Away from here?" *Oh, shit.* She'd never done that before. She'd worked from home when necessary, but never outside of the office with anyone else.

Amber nodded. "I don't know anything more than that, except that people noticed how familiarly she talked about you. She acted like she knew things about you. Personal things. Who knows if they were true."

Shay shot out of her chair and paced the floor. The room suddenly became suffocating, and the back of her neck tingled. How could people think that of her? "Well, rumors are created by lonely people who don't have lives of their own." Her voice sounded low and angry even to her.

Amber leaned back and held up her hands. "Hey. Don't get mad at me. You wanted to know."

"I'm sorry. It just bothers me that people think I would do anything to jeopardize my marriage to Chloe."

"I get that." Amber shrugged. "I think we're pretty good friends, and you never said anything to me about it. Well, only about how Chloe's art career had exploded and that she was spending a huge amount of time at the gallery and events."

"That was this past year?" Shay had missed it all—the good and the bad.

Amber's eyes widened, and she nodded. "Yes. She's amazing." She pointed to the wall behind her. "You brought me that, remember?"

She turned, moved to the wall, and studied the abstract oil painting hanging there. She didn't remember. Not even a glimmer of recollection. "Did I mention anyone else in Chloe's life?" she said, hovering her fingers above the lines of the painting and tracing them in the air.

She shook her head. "No. Nothing about anyone else."

Her stomach churned. She'd done something wrong. Crossed a boundary. Created friction between them. Maybe they both had. She'd worked hard and gotten the promotion, but at what cost? Now what did she have? "When will Lila be back?"

"She's been splitting her time between the two offices. I think she's coming here this week, but let me make sure." Amber made a few clicks on her computer keyboard. "Yep. In town on Wednesday night. She'll be in the office Thursday." She stood up and joined her in front of the painting. "You're lucky to catch her on her weekly visit."

"She doesn't work in this office?"

"Nope. She's in the Atlanta branch now. She transferred there a couple of weeks before your accident. She's been traveling back and forth since you've been out."

"I knew about the transfer?"

Amber nodded. "After you got the promotion, you made it happen. I hear you gave her an awesome recommendation."

"So, she's in charge in Atlanta?" Something was terribly wrong with this picture.

"Technically, no. You're in charge everywhere, at least you will be when you come back, but she's higher up than she was here. Some people in the office grumbled about that."

She took out her phone, scrolled through the list of names in her contacts, and didn't see Lila's. "Do you have her cell number?" She clicked on the button to create a new contact.

"I do." Amber picked up her phone from the desk and opened her contacts. "You ready?" She nodded, and Amber rattled off the number.

When she started to save it, the number came up under the contact of Work main. *What the fuck?* She closed her eyes and realized she hadn't put it in under Lila's name for some reason. Why would she do that? "Don't tell her about this conversation, okay?" She turned and looked into Amber's eyes, knowing tears were ready to spill out of her own.

Amber seemed to get it and pulled her into a hug. "I won't say a word. Promise."

"Thanks." She turned quickly and sped out the door, managing to make it to the parking lot before the first tear ran down her cheek. She stopped, took a breath, and swiped it from her face before she slid into her car.

All of Whitney's vague answers from last night made sense now. She and Chloe had more than drifted apart, and one of them had moved on. She didn't know which one and why, but her gut told her she wasn't innocent in whatever had happened. She had to find her newer journals.

CHAPTER SEVENTEEN

Chloe was completely surprised when she saw Shay pull into a parking space in front of the gallery. She'd picked up the rental car her insurance provided when Shay came home but hadn't realized she'd been released for driving yet. The vision she saw get out of the car made something stir deep in her belly. Shay was dressed in a flower-patterned, sleeveless sundress and sandals. Her hair was swept up into a short ponytail that exposed the beauty of her long, luscious neck and the space where it met her jaw. The perfect place, one that Chloe used to love to kiss.

Stop! She shook the thought from her mind before she met Shay at the door and opened it for her. "Hey, this is a nice surprise."

Shay tilted her head and raised her eyebrows. "Is it?"

"Of course it is. I just didn't know Rachel had cleared you to drive yet."

"Some decisions I can make on my own." Shay seemed irritated by the comment, but then she smiled. "I wanted to come help you clean up since I had to leave early last night."

"Oh, okay—" All she heard was the door clang shut before Shay swept her into her arms and kissed her with intent, but also with tenderness. Chloe didn't fight. She let herself fall into it, feel every moment of it, from the soft sweetness of Shay's lips to the magic of her tongue as it slipped across her own lips and into her mouth. *Sweet Lord*, she'd forgotten how good it felt to be kissed so thoroughly and with such care and glorious passion. She'd been kissed by many women in her life, but never, ever like she'd been by Shay. She silenced the voices in her head telling her to stop, let her arms snake around Shay's waist, and kissed her back with all she had. And she enjoyed it.

When they parted, Shay touched her lips gently again with hers and stared into her eyes. "Sorry. I've been wanting to do that since last night," she whispered. "But there were too many distractions, too many people around."

She fell back against the doorway, rested for a few minutes trying to find her balance and cool the heat consuming her body.

Shay left her there, moved across the gallery, and said, "Now, what can I do to help?"

Chloe cleared her throat, found her footing. "Well, there's not a whole lot to do. I've just been cleaning up the remnants from last night." She scooped up a cup that had been left on the window-display platform. "You know how people find the oddest places to leave their trash."

"Even though there's a garbage can in every corner." Shay picked up a feather duster from the counter and started swiping it across the framed and glassed watercolors.

Chloe chuckled. "Exactly." She couldn't help but smile at Shay as she wandered around the gallery from painting to painting, dusting them and making sure they were all perfectly straight. She was so much more like the woman Chloe fell in love with and yet still so different.

"The gallery is a success. You've done wonders with it."

"That's the most depressing thing I've heard in weeks."

"What?" Shay's sundress flew up as she spun around. "I meant it as a compliment."

The garbage can rattled as she dropped the trash she'd collected into it. "I don't want to run the gallery. I don't want to deal with the books. I don't want to handle advertising. I don't want any of that. I just want to paint." She pushed the curtain aside and stepped into the back room.

Shay followed her. "Okay. Then I'll run it."

"You can't do that. You already have a job." She picked up a stack of invoices and dropped them onto the desk again.

"Not right now." Shay took some papers from the desk and fingered through them.

"But you'll be going back to it soon."

Three stacks of papers turned into two as Shay sorted them. "When I go back, it'll probably be part-time to begin with."

"I can't ask you to do that. It would be too much."

"Tell you what. I'll take over the books for now, make sure they're in good shape, and then we can find an accountant. We can also hire someone to work the gallery during the days it's open and help out during events. That'll give you more time to paint."

"You'd do all that?"

"Of course. I'd do anything for you." Shay stared into her eyes, and Chloe could see she was sincere.

Her eyes began to well with the impact of the statement. She looked away and cleared her throat. "That would really help." This new Shay was so different from the old one. It wasn't that Shay hadn't lent a hand before, but she'd never understood Chloe's passion for painting the way she seemed to now. Previously, everything had always been black and white with Shay. Chloe's creativity had remained a mystery to her. Now she seemed to get what it took for Chloe to find the frame of mind she needed to be in to paint, to figure out what came next.

"I'll get an ad ready for the paper this week, okay?" Shay said, like it was the easiest thing in the world.

Relief overwhelmed Chloe. "Okay." Suddenly all the weight from her shoulders had disappeared. Well, the gallery piece of it anyway. Her personal life was a different story. A couple of months ago she was so ready to move on with Erica, but now she wasn't so sure. How long would this new Shay last? Would everything fall apart again when her memory returned? Could she take that chance?

They'd been having a wonderful day getting organized, and then the bell on the door chimed. Shay said she'd get it, so Chloe hadn't gone out front, but she immediately recognized the voice as Shay greeted the customer. Coffee spilled out of her cup onto the papers in front of her as she launched out of her chair behind the desk. She ran to the bathroom, spun a few paper towels from the roll, and dropped them on top of the spill before she raced to the front of the gallery.

"Hi, Erica." She held out her hand. "It's good to see you."

Shay looked uncertain as she spoke. "Oh, you know each other?"

"Yes." The back of her neck burned as she tried to calm herself. "Erica has become one of my best customers."

"You might say I'm her biggest fan," Erica added. A moment passed before she spoke again. "I was just hoping to get a status on that painting I commissioned. The one of the beach?"

"Right. Yes. I've started it but haven't seen just the right sunset I need to complete it."

"Maybe we could have dinner later and discuss that and another project I'd like you to consider." Erica's code for "I need to see you immediately."

She glanced at Shay, who seemed to be listening intently, taking in the whole conversation. "Do we have anything planned tonight?"

"No. Not at all." Shay shook her head. "Go ahead. I'll just take some of the paperwork we've been working on home and catch up on the books."

Erica smiled widely. "That's very generous of you…"

"Oh, I'm sorry." She motioned between them. "This is Shay… my wife." The words tumbled out in the weirdest of ways, and she hated herself for that. She was irritated with Erica for showing up unannounced. She'd specifically told her to call or text before she came to the gallery to prevent a situation like this.

Erica held out her hand "I'm Erica. Pleased to meet you."

When she turned back to Chloe, Shay clasped her hand tighter. "Is that like Cher, or do you have a last name?"

Erica glanced at her hand then back at Shay. "Freeman," she said slowly, without expression.

Shay released her hand. "Nice to meet you, Erica Freeman."

Erica smiled briefly before she turned her attention to Chloe. "The usual place at sevenish?"

Damn it, she was being way too familiar, and she was doing it on purpose. "Which place was that again?"

"That Italian place you like so much," Erica said.

"Grattzzi's?" Shay asked.

Erica scrunched her eyebrows. "La Terrazza."

The grimace that appeared on Shay's face almost made Chloe burst out laughing. "The place with the server who averaged our drinks? We swore to never go back there."

The memory flashed in Chloe's mind, and she chuckled. "I believe that server has moved on." The last time they'd eaten there with Jackson and Whitney, the server had neglected to keep count of the beverages they'd ordered and had decided to settle on one an hour for each of them on the bill. "The food is good, and Erica likes it." She glanced at Erica. "Right?"

"I do, but I'm fine with Grattzzi's."

"No. La Terrazza is good." She walked to the door. "I'll see you there at seven."

Shay had remembered that incident correctly. Chloe didn't particularly like going to La Terrazza, not because of the food, but because of its location. The restaurant was in Ybor City, which was farther away than Grattzzi's. She'd purposely gone there with Erica because she knew they wouldn't run into Shay.

"What was that about?" Shay asked.

"Grattzzi's is our place to eat and relax. I don't want to take customers there." She smiled. It was true. The restaurant had been special to her since the first time they'd eaten there together, and she hadn't wanted to share it with anyone else. "Are you sure you'll be all right tonight without me for a little while?"

"Yeah. I'll be fine." Shay glanced at her phone. "Rachel's supposed to come by for a therapy session this afternoon. I'll text her and see if she wants to have dinner." She worked the keypad with her fingers.

The knot in Chloe's stomach resurfaced. Nothing like giving Rachel a perfect opportunity to get even more cozy with Shay. "You've become pretty good friends with her, huh?"

Shay shrugged. "I guess you could say that. She's smart, funny, and a good listener." The phone chimed, and she read the message. "She's in." She dropped her phone into her bag.

Amid this whole disaster, Shay had managed to make a friend. She wasn't quite sure how to feel about that being Rachel. She should be happy that Shay had found someone other than her to confide in, even a possible love interest for her in the future, but she hated it all in the same thought. Deep in Chloe's heart, she still ached to be the smart, funny girl Shay wanted to talk to and was suddenly very aware that she might lose her again. Why did it matter? She'd moved past that point, hadn't she?

"Your therapy sessions are almost done. Do you think you'll remain friends with Rachel after they're finished?" She tried to stop the questions from spilling out of her mouth, but something inside her needed to know. "Do you like spending time with her?"

"Well, yeah. She's nice and we get along well. She kinda gets me. I think we need to find her a girlfriend, though. Then we can all go out together." She went to the desk, gathered the laptop and the receipts, and slid them into Chloe's computer bag.

Relief washed over Chloe. Rachel's attempts at flirting hadn't seemed to faze Shay in the slightest, or if they had, she wasn't letting on.

"I didn't realize how late it was. I need to leave if I'm going to beat her to the house."

Chloe raised an eyebrow and smiled. "You mean, so she doesn't get there first and catch you driving."

"Exactly." Shay moved with lightning speed toward her, took her into her arms, and kissed her before she turned and headed for the door. "See you later."

It wasn't a peck on the lips or a long, slow kiss like before. This was something in between that set each of her senses on fire, a kiss that held the promise of what was to come. Who was this new Shay who seemed to be taking charge as she never had before? Chloe didn't know, but she liked the change.

Chloe had purposely arrived at the quaint, upscale restaurant, La Terrazza, early. The hostess had seated her at their usual table in the corner by the large oak cabinet where wine bottles lined the top and an old tapestry hung. With deep-rust-colored walls, the place had a dark, clandestine feel, which she'd enjoyed in the past, but tonight it felt a little too romantic for the conversation she had planned.

She'd debated whether to get a table in the middle of the restaurant instead, to make sure the conversation stayed on a level tempo, but she didn't want to become the main attraction if the conversation took a bad turn. The waiter had brought their usual bottle of cabernet, and her first glass of wine was almost gone. The situation Erica had put her in earlier at the gallery had made her extremely uncomfortable and angry, and Erica hadn't seemed to care.

Erica's voice echoed through the restaurant when she arrived. She never did anything quietly. Her straight, blond hair bounced on her shoulders as she swept through the restaurant without assistance to the table.

"You're early," Erica said with a smile as she kissed her on the lips softly before taking the seat adjacent to her.

"The gallery wasn't busy, so I closed up. Figured I'd avoid some of the evening traffic."

"Good idea." Erica squeezed her arm and then let her hand drift down it and land on Chloe's leg. "I've missed you."

"I know. I'm sorry. The hospital, the house…" She broke eye contact and stared at the black tablecloth between them. "Everything has just been so hectic."

"Can't Shay's family help her with that? Or whatsername?"

"I told you Shay's family will not be involved in her recovery, and whatsername is out of the picture." At least she thought she was. Lila hadn't been back since she'd told her to stay away that day at the hospital. Either she really wasn't concerned about Shay's well-being or she wasn't invested enough in whatever they'd had between them to deal with the fallout from the accident. Either way, she was glad she hadn't had to contend with her again.

"Okay. Then get her a nurse."

"I'm not going to do that. She's a big part of my life, and I won't abandon her." She finished the wine left in her glass.

"*Is* a big part of your life? Don't you mean *was*?"

Just then the waiter appeared. Perfect timing. "Are you ready to order?"

"Yes." She didn't give Erica an opportunity to respond before she rattled off her order. "I'll have the capellini primavera." She needed something light to keep her stomach settled and to absorb the wine.

The waiter looked at Erica, who seemed a little flustered at being put on the spot. "I'll have the filet mignon, medium rare. Bring us a caprese salad as well." She handed her menu to the waiter, and he picked up the bottle of wine and filled both their glasses. She waited for him to leave before she said, "What's going on with you?"

"Nothing. I just don't like to be pushed." She picked up her napkin, put it on her lap, and smoothed it across her legs. "This is something I have to do, and you're going to have to accept it." Erica's hurt expression was unexpected and had her rethinking her words. "I know it's a horrible situation, Erica, but I can't do anything else about it."

The wounded look disappeared, and Erica scowled. "Actually, there's a lot you can do about it."

"I'm doing the best I can. What do you want from me?" Chloe fiddled with the silverware next to her plate, aligning each piece with the other.

"I want you to tell her how she broke your heart and that I was there to pick up the pieces." Erica tossed her napkin onto the table. "It's not fair to anyone to keep it all a secret."

"I can't do that right now. The doctor says it could set her back." He hadn't, but she wasn't ready to deal with the repercussions if it did. Her life would be impacted as much as Shay's would be.

"Then at least stay with me tonight. I miss you. It's been lonely without you."

That was the second time Erica had said that tonight, but strangely Chloe didn't feel the same way. "Okay."

Erica smiled, the answer seeming to appease her for now. The waiter dropped off the caprese salad, and Erica added a few slices of mozzarella and tomatoes to each of their plates before she dug in like she hadn't eaten in days.

She didn't doubt that Erica missed her, but she was fairly certain that she wasn't lonely. Erica always seemed to find someone to occupy her time when Chloe wasn't around. She saw multiple women and didn't commit to any one of them. She'd made Chloe well aware of that fact when they'd first started dating. When the break happened with Shay, Chloe hadn't been ready for any type of commitment, so it wasn't a big deal to her then. That situation hadn't changed.

When their meals came, she used eating as an excuse not to talk, but Erica continued to lead the conversation, as usual. Instead of trying to keep up, she let her mind wander. Today had been the best day she'd had in a long time. No worries were clouding her head, and no tension existed between her and Shay. It was just the two of them being *them*, like they used to be, and she couldn't wait to get home to see her again. Her feelings completely baffled her.

"Hey, are you with me?"

The fork clinked as she set it on her plate. "Sorry. Just got an idea for a new painting and was fleshing it out in my head." Her second glass of wine now gone, she took a drink of water. She needed her mind clear by the time she left the restaurant.

"You want to tell me about it?"

"It's not fully formed yet." Erica seemed to notice her reluctance to share her thoughts. A glimpse of Shay at dinner looking out onto the marina flashed in her mind. "A watercolor of the marina at sunset. Lots of different lighting shadows to consider." It would make a beautiful painting.

"Sounds nice. Should I commission it or wait until it's done?"

"You don't have to buy everything I paint, Erica."

"I know I don't have to, but I love your work." The sweet talk again.

Would that still be true when she stopped sleeping with her? She'd soon find out. She took one last bite of her pasta and pushed her plate away. "I'm stuffed."

"Cannoli?" Erica asked.

"I couldn't possibly eat anything more."

Erica glanced at her watch. "It's still early. Why don't we go to my place? We can open another bottle of wine and talk more there."

"Okay. That sounds nice." She agreed but knew there would be no talking once they got there, and she wasn't feeling any of that with Erica tonight. During dinner, she hadn't been able to keep her mind off Shay. The kisses they'd shared earlier had set something within her in motion that she absolutely wanted to explore further.

Erica insisted on getting the bill and walked with her to her car. She'd followed Erica out of the parking lot but had purposely hung back to catch a red light after Erica had already gone through the green one. Her phone rang a few minutes later, and she ignored it. She knew it was Erica. Her phone chimed again as she pulled into the driveway at home. She took it out of her purse and typed in a quick message.

Not feeling so good. Went home.

She held down the power button and turned her phone off before another text message could come through. She'd made her decision to go home as soon as she left the restaurant. She wouldn't have sex with Erica again until she figured out her feelings for Shay.

She didn't see Rachel's car and the house was dark. Shay must have already gone to bed, she unlocked the door and moved silently through the hallway to check the bedroom, only to find that Shay wasn't there. That wasn't strange. She knew Shay was having dinner with Rachel but had thought she'd be home by now. After changing into her yoga pants and T-shirt, she headed into the kitchen and opened the refrigerator to get a bottle of water.

Numerous Chinese-food containers were stacked on the shelf. Rachel must have brought dinner. As she screwed the top off the water and took a drink, she wondered where they'd gone afterward. She looked at the time on her phone. It was close to ten. Thinking she might have missed a text from Shay, she turned her phone on and checked her messages. None from her and several from Erica, which she didn't read. Her jealousy flared, and she tamped it down. Even if she didn't trust Rachel's motives, at least she knew Shay was physically safe.

She took another drink of water, went into the bedroom, and got into bed. The day had been filled with exhaustingly chaotic feelings. Being asleep when Shay arrived home would be the best way to avoid more of the same.

CHAPTER EIGHTEEN

S hay had brought the laptop Chloe used at the gallery as well as all the current paperwork home with her. Rachel wasn't due for another hour, so she'd had time to sort through the invoices and receipts. She hadn't been able to get them all entered into the computer, but once they were in date order, she noticed how many pieces Erica had purchased recently. She did a search through the bookkeeping software on the laptop and found that it wasn't a recent trend. Erica had started buying Chloe's art during the fall of the previous year, and the quantity had risen quite a bit since then. Chloe had several other regular customers as well, but none had purchased as many pieces as Erica.

After texting back and forth with Rachel, they'd decided to stay in and eat Chinese food for dinner. She'd ordered and paid for the food, and Rachel was planning to stop and pick it up on her way to the beach house. When the doorbell rang, she was engrossed in researching the gallery customers. She glanced at the clock, surprised to find it had been close to an hour since she'd texted Rachel.

Rachel stood in the doorway dressed in white capris and a hot-pink V-neck shirt, holding two brown paper bags of Chinese food.

"Thanks for saving me from a boring night alone."

"Same," Rachel said as she entered. "I was glad to hear from you, and I'm starving."

Shay took one of the bags from Rachel and led her into the kitchen. "Same." They both chuckled and went to work unloading the bags and setting the food cartons on the table.

"Where's Chloe tonight?" She pulled open a couple of drawers. "Silverware?"

She pointed to the next one down the line. "Dinner with a client."

After opening each container, Rachel dropped a spoon into each one before taking the chopsticks from the bag to the table along with a couple of forks. "Oh. Does she do that often?"

"I don't recall that she ever did before. I've been putting the receipts into the computer, and this one seems to buy a lot of her art." She took a couple of beers from the refrigerator and held them up. Rachel nodded, and she handed them to her.

"So, she has a fan."

"It appears so." She hadn't meant to sound petty, but something about the way Erica had acted today bothered her. Like she had some familiarity with Chloe she wasn't aware of.

"You don't sound happy about that," Rachel said as she twisted the tops off the beers. She must have caught the tone of her voice.

"It's sort of an excessive amount." She took a couple of plates from the cabinet and set them on the table. "Makes me wonder what exactly she's trying to buy."

"Is she buying for herself or for another business? Maybe she's an art dealer." Rachel used her chopsticks to pluck some noodles from the container and drop them onto her plate.

"I don't think so. There's no tax ID on any of the receipts." She spooned some chow mien onto her plate and then traded containers with Rachel.

"Did you order orange chicken?" Rachel asked.

Shay pushed one of the cartons to her before she twirled her fork in the noodles and stuffed them into her mouth. Rachel offered her the orange chicken, and she waved her off. She had plenty on her plate right now.

"Do you think it's odd that Chloe never kisses me?"

Rachel's eyes widened. "Hell yes, it's odd. If you were my wife, I'd be kissing you all the time."

Heat rose in her cheeks, but she ignored the comment. "We're not having sex either. Not since that time in the hospital I told you about."

Rachel talked into her plate. "The woman must be crazy."

"I kind of get a weird vibe whenever I kiss her. You know, like she's not all in. And if she does let herself go and kisses me back, it gets really awkward when we get anywhere close to going further. She always finds some reason to stop."

"Wow." Rachel dropped her chopsticks onto her plate and wiped her mouth with a napkin. "Not the kind of conversation I was expecting tonight." She raked her fingers through her hair and let out a breath.

"I'm sorry." Shay reached over, touched her leg. "I know we have this flirty thing going between us, but I'm hopelessly in love with my wife." She'd been letting the banter between them persist because it made her feel good about herself, not realizing the impact it was having on Rachel.

"No. I'm sorry." She took her hand in hers and squeezed it. "I'm your physical therapist. You don't owe me anything. It's inappropriate of me to expect anything more."

"You're more than just my therapist. You're my friend." The only friend she had. The only one she could discuss any of this with besides Jackson and Whitney, and they wouldn't tell her anything Chloe didn't want her to know.

Rachel smiled and returned to her dinner. "She seems to be patient and caring. Maybe she's just worried about your memory issues."

"I'm so tired of patient and caring, I'm ready to scream." They ate in silence for a bit, and Shay found herself lost in thought. She'd cleared most of the food from her plate when she glanced up to see Rachel watching her. "Sorry. I was hungry. I went to the gallery today to help Chloe but didn't eat much."

"I can see that." Rachel chuckled. "Didn't you tell me you kept a journal?"

She nodded as she chewed and swallowed the last bit of chow mein on her plate. "I found them, but there's nothing recent in the ones here at the beach house." She relaxed into her chair and took a pull of her beer. "It's bizarre. I've kept journals all my life, and suddenly I stopped six months ago?"

"Can they be somewhere else?" Rachel pushed her plate away and relaxed in her chair as well.

"Maybe at the apartment. I would've thought we'd have sold the place by now."

"Where's it located?"

"Downtown Tampa." She shot up from the table, grabbed her bag, and searched for her keys. She fished them out and held them up by one key. "I still have this." She looked at each key individually, and they were all the same as she remembered. "I'm gonna go look. You wanna come?"

"You're not supposed to be driving yet."

"I won't tell if you won't."

"It's my rule. Remember?" Rachel plucked the keys from her hand and tossed them back into her bag. "I'll drive you."

"Whoops. I forgot."

When they arrived at West Park Village, Shay directed Rachel through the area to their multilevel apartment and instructed her to park in front of the single-car garage.

"Wow. This is a nice area. It seems kind of far from the beach. Are you going to keep it?"

"That wasn't the plan. The last I remember, we were trying to sell the furniture because we'd bought new for the beach house, except for certain things. Something must have happened to change that." She slid the key into the door, hoping it would work, and it did. She pushed open the door, stopped, and glanced around. The furniture was what she remembered. "Anyone home?" She glanced over her shoulder at Rachel. "Don't want to surprise anyone in case we decided to sublet or just forgot to turn in the key."

"Looks clear," Rachel said as she moved past her to the stairs.

"Hang on." She opened the door directly in front of them, which led to Chloe's studio. For the most part it was empty, but a few items were left—an easel, a stool, some old paints, and a few paintings of Shay on the wall that Chloe had done years ago. Including one of Shay in bed naked only half covered by a sheet. *Why are these still here?*

"Is this where Chloe painted?" She moved to the depictions of Shay on the wall. "These are beautiful." She assessed the nude and seemed to take in the entirety of it. "You look gloriously happy here."

"I was." Chloe had sketched it one morning right after they'd made love. Shay had woken up more than once and found Chloe sketching her.

She went out the door and up the stairs to the main floor. The living room and kitchen looked the same, so she continued up to the bedrooms on the third floor. Nothing was the same in the master suite. She pulled open the closet, which was half empty. Only her clothes remained, but none of Chloe's. Suddenly she was dizzy, and she sank onto the bed. *What happened?* The loss hit her square in the chest, and she couldn't stop the tears from streaming down her face. They had split up.

"Did you find the journals?" Rachel said as she entered the room. "This is a really nice place. Do you think maybe you decided to keep it?"

Shay swiped at her face. "I don't think so."

"Wait. Are you okay?"

"No. I'm not." She launched off the bed and reached for the journals on the shelf at the top of the closet where she'd kept them. The stack was small, probably only a few months' worth. So, whatever occurred between them had happened about the time these would start. She took the oldest one from the stack and read the first entry.

Chloe hates me, and I don't blame her. I hate myself.

She shook as she continued to read and found out all she needed to know about her own betrayal. This was the journal entry where she had done the act, the deed that had shattered two lives. She immediately noticed the tearstains on the pages and ran her fingers across them, knowing they were her own. She *had* regretted what she'd done. Tears poured from her eyes. Chloe must have been shattered, hurt beyond repair. She wanted to curl up in a ball on the bed. She had absolutely no reason to be jealous of Erica then or now.

She heaved out a sob. Chloe was a beautiful woman. She had the right to move on after the love of her life betrayed her—tore her heart out and stomped on it until all the love she had for her drained out. The pain in her heart caused by knowing what *she* had done to Chloe was unbearable. How could she lose everything in an instant and expect Chloe to be there for her, take care of her without question? Yet she had.

Rachel came across the room, sat on the bed next to her, and wrapped her arm around her shoulder. "I'm so sorry."

She wiped the tears from her face with the back of her hand before she closed the journal and held it tightly in to her chest, leaning into Rachel for support. "This is why Chloe's so different."

Rachel hesitated. "It's bad, huh?"

She nodded, scrubbed her face with her hands, and then cradled the book. "I fucked it all up. I just don't know why." She glanced at Rachel, who didn't seem surprised. "You knew this already."

Rachel rolled her lips in and tilted her head. "I don't know the details, but yes."

"Who told you? Chloe?"

"She didn't want to, but I pressed her."

"My God. I've been pushing her to be intimate with me. I can't imagine how difficult this has been for her."

"She's still here, so she must still have some feelings for you." Rachel tried to console her.

"What an absolute asshole I am."

"It's not like you remembered and pushed her."

"But still." She shook her head. "Fuck. What am I gonna do?"

"Do you remember any of this?" Rachel held up the journal.

The bed shook as she flopped back onto it. "Absolutely none."

"Do you still love her? Chloe, I mean."

"More than anything in the world." She closed her eyes. "She crashed into my life, and it's never been the same since."

"In a good way, right?"

"The best way. It was a fucking miracle. You have to understand the kind of family I came from. I never thought love existed, was even real, until I met her. She swept in and captured my heart—shifted my whole reality. Now I feel like I can't even hug her."

"Why can't you just start again?" Rachel thumbed through the journal and paused to read an entry. "Would you do it all again?"

"In a heartbeat."

"Then what are you waiting for? Make it work this time. Make her love you again." She dropped the journal onto the bed and got up.

"You don't understand. I didn't do anything to make it happen before. She did it all. She chased me." She closed her eyes and took in a deep breath. "My life was perfect until I fucked it up."

"I didn't say it would be easy." She picked up the journal. "It's going to be even harder to read these." She held it up. "Figure out what went wrong and fix it."

"What if I can't?"

"You can. She still loves you." Rachel tossed the journal onto the bed and took the rest of the stack from the closet. "Don't be so hard on yourself. You're not the only one at fault here."

"What do you mean? Did she do something too?"

"That's not what I said. Relationships don't fall apart in an instant. Clearly you two had issues leading up to this. A relationship like you're describing doesn't break on its own."

"I wonder if we were even trying to make it work." She opened the latest journal and read the last entry. The morning of the accident. The pain in her heart magnified as she read more about what she'd done and how Chloe had found out. What she didn't understand was why.

I have to talk to her one more time, get down on my knees and beg her to forgive me if I have to. All I can do is hope she will.

Rachel hovered over her shoulder. "Looks like you wanted a second chance, and now you have one."

"I'm trying to do the right thing here." Was this really a second chance or just more humiliation for Chloe?

"Fuck the right thing. You need to do what's right for you."

"I can't just insert myself into her life if she's found someone else. What if she's fallen out of love with me and in love with someone else?"

"Um, you're already inserted into her life—and, from my perspective, falling in love with you would be easy, make her remember who you really are."

Thoughts flooded her mind and went to the worst possible place. "I can't even imagine how she felt. What if one day you woke up and found yourself sleeping next to someone you'd fallen out of love with? Someone who'd trusted you with their very soul? Someone who'd never expected you to feel this way? Someone who believed you when you said you'd love them for the rest of your days, even if it had nothing to do with another person? What if it's just you? You've changed, they've changed, life has changed? Do you tell them, or do you go on living a lie for their sake? What if the opposite happened? What if they fall out of love with you? Would you want another chance? Would you expect it? Would you want them to go on living the lie when deep down in their soul they want to be with someone else?"

"Wow. That's a lot of what-ifs. You need to stop thinking so much." Rachel held her by the shoulders. "You don't know any of that to be true, right?"

She shook her head. "No."

"So, take what you do know and use it to win her back. Live for the little victories, remember. Anything to get you back to where you were."

"What about the woman I had the affair with?" She rubbed her face with her hands. "Jesus. Where the hell is she now?" She knew where she was because she'd sent her away. It seemed she'd regretted everything she'd done.

"It must not have been very serious. It looks like whatever happened between you is over for both of you."

"Maybe." She certainly hoped so. She knew it was probably Lila, but she didn't intend to tell anyone.

"If it doesn't work out, you always have me." Rachel pulled her lip up to one side and winked, then ducked as the pillow Shay threw at her sailed by her head.

"There's that." She picked up the pile of journals and placed them back on the closet shelf. Taking them to the beach house would be a mistake, a distraction she couldn't deal with right now. She had to focus on getting her life back.

❖

When Shay's phone rang on the ride back to the house, the last voice she expected to hear when she answered was her mother's. She hadn't talked to her since she'd been released from the hospital, and before that, contact had been minimal. It wasn't a secret that their relationship was strained. Shay would never be the daughter her mother wanted, and Mary would never be the mother Shay needed.

"Hello."

"Hello, Shay. This is your mother."

"I know who it is. What do you need?"

"I wanted to make sure you're all right. I hadn't heard from you."

"I'm just awesome, Mom. I've got a big metal rod in my leg and just found out I was screwing around on my wife before the accident."

"I see." Her mother was silent, which was rare.

"Did you hear what I said, Mom? I cheated on Chloe." She spoke resolutely as another piece of the puzzle snapped together in her mind. Her mother was aware of what had happened. Ironically, she would've been the first to tell her if Chloe had been the one cheating. She would've used anything to break up her marriage and steer her back to the opposite sex.

"You had every reason to. Chloe was off doing her art. She wasn't giving you the attention you deserve."

She cringed. Had she confided in her mother, or had she just found out somehow? "That's no excuse, Mother." Yet those were the exact reasons she'd used to justify her own behavior in the journal. When had she become so much like her?

"I'm just trying to make you feel better. You're more like your father than you know," her mother said. Not the subtlest way of telling her about her father's indiscretions.

"Nothing can make me feel better about this whole fucking mess." The throb in her head began to pulse, and she rubbed the back of her neck. "If there was one thing in my whole life you could've done for me, you should've told me this."

"I didn't want to hurt you," her mother said.

"We both know that's not true. You didn't want me to be with Chloe. You hoped I'd forget everything we had together." All the arguments they'd had about her sexuality filled her mind, and her head hurt more. "I have to go." She didn't give her mother a chance to respond again before she pulled the phone from her ear and ended the call.

"Are you okay?"

She chuckled. "Yeah. I'm fine." She glanced at Rachel while she drove. "How are you liking the glimpse you're getting into my fucked-up life? I bet you're glad I'm married now."

Rachel reached across the console and took her hand, the gesture soothing her. "We all have our demons. Some of us have valid reasons for them."

Rachel seemed to understand even if Shay didn't understand it all herself.

After Rachel dropped Shay off at home, she was surprised and somewhat relieved that Chloe had beat her there. Not wanting to wake her, she didn't bother to change clothes, just went to the couch and again read the words in the journal she'd written. The hurt deepened within her each time. Even after Shay read them repeatedly, she couldn't believe they were true.

An auburn-haired woman with green eyes flashed in her mind, and her stomach clenched. It wasn't enough that she'd been careless about phone calls and texts, but for her to actually leave Chloe waiting in the car while she was fucking her upstairs in her office was unconscionable. Was she seeking a rush? Had Lila manipulated her? Or was she just plain cruel? Outrageously, fucking cruel. She couldn't imagine how Chloe felt when she'd walked into her office and discovered them, found out her wife was betraying her. Yes, she could. She would've been devastated. If the situation had been reversed, she would've been crushed beyond measure. She had no idea if she'd ever be able to forgive herself for the pain she'd put Chloe through.

Shay was the one who had broken the relationship between the two of them. Whatever reasons she'd had, they weren't valid enough to justify hurting Chloe the way she had. There would never be anything that could justify that. How could she *not* forgive Chloe for anything that happened after that? She now knew the reasons for Chloe's distance and what they'd been through together. It was only natural that Chloe needed space. She was amazed that Chloe hadn't already told her, left her alone to heal after the accident. She was still trying to protect her even after her betrayal.

CHAPTER NINETEEN

Chloe had no idea why Shay's usual navy-blue pants and button-down shirt wouldn't do tonight for the gallery event. Shay had tried on more dresses than Chloe ever had before when preparing for one. She wasn't even sure why Shay was going. She'd had her regularly scheduled physical-therapy session today and had seemed pretty worn out after it. She'd told Shay it was fine if she wanted to stay home and rest, but she'd insisted.

"So that's the dress you've settled on?" She watched Shay from the doorway as she assessed herself in the mirror.

"I think so. Do I look okay?" When Shay spun around, and Chloe caught the full picture of her in the black fringe dress, her stomach took an unexpected dip. She was stunning. Shay wasn't full figured like herself, but the dress fit her snugly and accentuated her subtle curves in all the right places. The fringe started right where Chloe should be keeping her mind away from, and the neckline dipped just low enough to let her cleavage peek out. The silver, strappy heels set off the outfit perfectly.

"I'll take that as a yes." Apparently, Shay had caught her reaction. She smiled and went to the dresser. "Can I borrow your pearls?" She opened the jewelry box and plucked something out. "Why is this in here and not on your finger?" She held up Chloe's wedding ring.

Chloe stumbled for an answer that would make sense. "It was loose, and I don't want to lose it."

Shay took her hand and slid the ring onto her finger. "Fits just fine now."

Chloe fiddled with the band. "Seems to, doesn't it?" She took in a breath and smiled.

"Is mine in here too?" Shay rummaged through the rest of the jewelry.

"Um...yes. They took it off when you were in the hospital." She lied. She'd put it in the jewelry box after she'd found it on the entryway table the day Shay had come to the beach house. The day of the accident. Something inside her hadn't been ready to let go of it then.

Shay fished hers out, handed it to Chloe, and wiggled her finger, clearly expecting her to place it on her ring finger just as she had hers. "Just like our wedding day." The smile on Shay's face was beautiful. "Back to normal."

"Back to normal." She smiled at her, but they were still far from back to normal. She took the pearls from the jewelry box, unhooked the clasp, and put them around Shay's neck. "Perfect."

Shay moved closer, wrapped her arms around her waist, and kissed her. The gesture wasn't unexpected. She'd felt the electricity between them the moment she'd brushed her fingers across the smooth spot between Shay's shoulder and neck, the spot she loved to taste. She didn't back away. She took Shay's face in her hands and fell into it, let it happen just as she had before. It was a soft, searching kiss, one that reached in, touched her soul, and left her wanting more, something deeper. Her stomach tightened, and her heart actually felt as though it was struggling to beat. She felt Shay's hands on her back, then on her breasts, and she dragged her lips away, tried to catch her breath.

A soft whimper came out of Shay's mouth, and she whispered, "You're so beautiful." Shay looked at her with such love and desire, she immediately kissed her again and found herself being pushed onto the bed, Shay pinning her to it, her hands moving down her body, across her waist, up her thighs, between her legs. She gasped at the touch, and the little voice in her head screamed. She shoved Shay to the side, got up, and tried to clear her mental fog. She could see Shay was confused, and rightly so. Desire bubbled inside her, but she couldn't do anything to relieve it. She wouldn't, not until she'd straightened out her emotions.

"I need to be there on time." *You can do this, Chloe.* Without looking back, she stepped through the doorway, closed her eyes, took a deep breath, and plastered on a smile. Life would go on.

❖

The evening had started awkwardly and remained that way since they'd arrived. Chloe couldn't bring herself to look at Shay for more than a moment, afraid she might feel confused again. They hadn't spoken in the car on the way nor since they'd arrived. In fact, a bystander would think they didn't even know each other.

She stopped mid-sentence when she heard the door chime and glanced over to see Erica enter, a tall blonde trailing closely behind her. *Fuck!* She'd known Erica would resort to some sort of retaliation. She'd just hoped Shay wouldn't be present when it happened. It was the first event of the month, and the gallery was full of customers. Avoiding eye contact, she focused her attention across the room on Shay, who seemed to have noticed Erica's entrance as well, with a flash of irritation. Had the encounter with Erica a few days before at the gallery sparked any of her memories? When she'd arrived home that night, Shay hadn't come to bed. She'd slept on the couch. She'd also been somewhat antisocial the next day, quiet to the point of almost ignoring her, which had been unusual for her since she'd come home. She'd said she'd gotten in late and hadn't wanted to wake her, and Chloe hadn't pressed her. If some memories had floated to the surface, Shay was keeping them to herself.

"Chloe, darling." Erica's voice echoed loudly. She wouldn't be able to avoid her tonight. Erica swept her into her arms, hugged her more tightly than usual, and said, "I've missed you."

The motion had come so quickly, Chloe hadn't had a chance to dodge her. She glanced at Shay again, who was now heading her way with determination in her step. The irritation in her eyes seemed to have vanished, but she wasn't smiling.

"It's good to see you again," she said and smiled at Erica and the tall blonde with dazzling blue eyes and a knockout body. Erica's weapon of choice didn't faze Chloe in the slightest. She had never completely formed an emotional attachment to Erica, so jealousy would never be a factor in their relationship—or whatever it was they had.

"Forgive me. Where are my manners?" Erica turned to the blonde. "This is Barbara."

"Most people call me Barb." She reached out to shake Chloe's hand.

Of course they do. "It's nice to meet you, Barb." The stereotypical name fit her features well. She felt Shay's arm slip around her waist and immediately did the same after she shook Barb's hand. "You remember my wife, Shay," Chloe said.

Erica's attention zoomed to Shay. The closeness between them didn't seem to have escaped her. "Hello again. You seem to be doing well," Erica said.

"I am, thanks," Shay said as she pulled Chloe closer while simultaneously offering Erica her hand.

Erica took her hand, held it for a moment. "Well, I have a feeling we're going to be good friends."

Chloe narrowed her eyes when Erica glanced her way. She was straddling a thin line, and if she dared to cross it, the fragile existence Chloe was living would come crashing down around her.

"Come on, love. Let's get some champagne." Erica moved Barb in front of her and sauntered to the makeshift bar in the corner of the gallery.

Relieved that she'd escaped the encounter with no visible injuries, Chloe released the breath she'd been holding. Ditching her the other night had been immature, and she hadn't returned any of her calls or texts since. Arriving with a knockout blonde on her arm tonight was a clear sign that Erica was angry about the situation, but that was out of her control. She had to focus on Shay's recovery whether she wanted to or not. She had an obligation to fulfill no matter what the circumstances had been between them before the accident and hoped Shay would do the same if the situation had been reversed.

The warmth of Shay's arm was still around her waist as she turned toward her. "I'm sorry."

A tingle shot through her when Shay reached up, moved a stray strand of hair behind her ear, and let her fingers drift down to the hollow of her neck. The feeling had been something she'd grown to love but had lost over the past year. "I know," she whispered and kissed her gently. Something in her eyes told Chloe she understood the turmoil in her heart. Had she remembered something?

Shay took her by the hand. "I could use a glass of wine. How about you?"

Relief washed through her. All seemed to be normal again, for a moment. "Wine would be good."

❖

The evening was progressing nicely. Chloe had sold several pieces of art, and Shay seemed to be having a good time mingling with people as well. Close to an hour had passed when Chloe caught Erica in her peripheral vision. Barb was being entertained by another artist, and Erica was leaning against the bar staring at something. She followed her gaze and spotted Shay, who seemed to be having an in-depth conversation with yet another artist. She focused on Erica again and wasn't sure what she saw in her expression, but it certainly wasn't pleasant. Erica narrowed her eyes, took the last swallow of her drink, set it on the bar, and pushed away. She was heading across the room to Shay.

No, no, no. Chloe's vision tunneled, and all she heard was the rapid beat of her heart in her ears as she bolted across the room, took Erica by the arm, and led her to the back door and then outside, letting the metal door clang shut behind them.

Erica yanked her arm free. "What the hell are you doing?"

"Bigger question. What the hell are *you* doing?" She glanced over at the door to make sure it was still closed.

"I was just going to have a friendly chat with Shay," Erica said.

"I didn't see anything friendly about the way you were looking at her." She'd seen that expression before, more than once. It was pure jealousy.

"This isn't working for me," Erica said matter-of-factly as she smoothed her hands down the front of her blouse and then clasped them in front of her. "You're going to have to tell her about us."

"She's not ready for that."

"She's not ready? Or you're not ready?"

"I told you the doctor said she needs to remember on her own, or her memory may be permanently damaged and never come back."

"Her memory is already damaged. Why would it hurt to speed it up?" Her finger stung as Erica took it between her fingers and tugged at her wedding ring. "Why are you wearing this?"

"Shay found it in my jewelry box. I couldn't very well refuse to put it on." She could've, but the look in Shay's eyes at that moment had made her not want to refuse her anything.

"I think it's time she and I have a talk." Erica spun around and headed for the door.

Did she think this was some sort of game? This was Shay's

memory they were talking about—and Chloe's life. Did she even care? "Erica, stop. Please. For me?"

Erica was almost to the door when she stopped and turned around. She came at Chloe so quickly, she thought she was going to strike her. Instead, she took her face into her hands and kissed her with a force she'd never felt from Erica before. Chloe swayed into her. All the right areas came to life in an instant. She couldn't deny that Erica could make her body react, but there were places in her heart Erica would never be able to touch. Shay had already claimed them long ago.

She heard the door open and close through the fog clouding her head. *Shay.* Panic shot through her. She broke the kiss, glanced at the door, and was relieved to see Jackson leaning against it. He'd been the one she was in mid-sentence with when she'd bolted across the room to intercept Erica.

He gazed at the stars for a moment and then at them, with no judgment in his eyes. "It's a beautiful night. Erica, I think your date is looking for you." He'd come to rescue her. The man was a godsend.

"I doubt that. She's very capable of mingling on her own."

"Well, if she isn't, she should be by now. She's on her fourth glass of wine and ready for you to take her home." He arched an eyebrow. "Isn't that the way you like your women, plied with alcohol and uninhibited?"

Jackson knew how Erica had seduced Chloe the first time. Chloe's anger and too much alcohol had pushed her into bed with Erica. The guilt had overwhelmed her, and she'd gone to his house the next day and told him and Whitney everything, crying through the whole sordid story. Everything she'd discovered about Shay and Lila had made her incredibly vulnerable, and all it had taken was a few margaritas to send her crashing over the edge. And crash she had, right into Erica's bed. She'd sworn she would never go there again, but she was weak and had ended up there again the following week. Erica had taken full advantage of the situation, and soon there'd been no coming back from it.

Erica's eyes narrowed. "Fuck you."

"Au contraire." Jackson's eyebrows rose. "Fuck *her*."

Erica took in a breath and focused on Chloe. "You know I'm not going to fuck her, right?"

"You brought her here for me to see. I don't know what you're going to do with her." Nor did she care.

The muscle in Erica's cheek quivered as her face tightened, and she flattened her lips. "We'll talk about this later."

Chloe shook her head. "No. I don't think we should talk. Clearly, you need attention that I can't give you right now, and I don't want to upset Shay."

"*Clearly*, Shay is more important to you than me." Erica looked shaken.

"I'm not having this argument again. Not here. Not now. Just go home, Erica."

Erica opened her mouth as though she intended to say something and then snapped it shut. She went to the door, yanked it open, and headed inside.

"Don't forget your date," Jackson sang after Erica as the door closed behind her.

Chloe slapped him on the shoulder. "Stop. She'll never leave if you keep that up."

"She may never leave you alone anyway."

Chloe wasn't even sure she wanted Erica to stay away. "I don't know what's wrong with me. I'm in this state of indecision all the time now. I saw Erica tonight with Barb, and it bothered me. I hate to admit it, but I was jealous." She spoke to the wind as she paced, unable to look at Jackson. "Then I think of Shay with Lila doing the intimate things we used to do, and it makes me sick to my stomach. Visions of Shay holding her hand and whispering in her ear pummel my mind, and I feel like I've been gut-punched. Then my mind wanders to Shay, and I think about doing those same things to her—Shay doing them to me as well, and my body reacts in ways it never has with anyone else." She didn't tell him about what had happened at home before they got to the gallery tonight. "How did I lose that? Why did I even think of looking elsewhere? What the fuck is wrong with me, Jackson?"

"Nothing." He stepped in front of her, touched her chin with his fingers, and forced eye contact. "Absolutely nothing. You're human and want to be desired. Erica is hot. Even I have to admit that. But Shay." He shook his head. "Shay is hot, smart, and ridiculously unpretentious. I always thought Shay was your perfect match."

"She *is* my perfect match." She held her hands out in front of her. "I just let something unimportant get in the way and forgot that fact."

"I wouldn't call it unimportant. Another woman was involved. You should've communicated with Shay about it, not Erica. She purposely caught you at a weak moment, stole you away before you had a chance to deal with the situation you'd been put in."

"Before I even realized what was happening. I fell right into it."

"You've learned that lesson the hard way."

She nodded. "The hardest lesson *ever*."

"She's not going away, you know. It may get worse because her plan to make you jealous backfired, and she knows it." He put his arm around her shoulder and squeezed. "Erica's the kind of woman who likes to be the one who walks away, not vice versa."

"I can handle her as long as she stays away from Shay."

The frown on Jackson's face made it clear he didn't think she could. "I'll run interference whenever I can."

It was entirely possible that Erica had already told Shay everything in the few minutes she'd been inside without her. All Chloe could do was hope she had a sliver of compassion in her heart for them both. Dreading what she might encounter when she got back inside, she moved toward the door.

Jackson took her hand and pulled her in the opposite direction. "Let's walk around front. You don't want to go in after Erica, do you?"

She shook her head. "No. You're so smart, Jackson. How did I ever get so lucky to have you as my brother?"

"You were in the top three when I chose. I took a chance." He flashed his perfectly white teeth and laughed.

He wasn't only her brother, but also her mentor, confidant, and best friend. She would be forever in his debt for all the times he'd saved her from herself—before and after she'd met Shay.

When Shay had slid Chloe's wedding ring onto her finger, their wedding day had flashed in her mind and her heart had felt heavy instead of warm and contented, like she usually felt with Chloe. She would have to overcome the guilt she had no memory of. She'd taken a deep breath, ignored it, and when Chloe kissed her the second time, she'd made it clear that she wasn't done with her, not completely. Everything had faded away at that point. She'd wanted so much more and had intended to take it, but Chloe had put on the brakes, and she hadn't pressed for more. Chloe had to choose when the intimacy progressed between them. It had to be that way.

She'd watched her from across the gallery as Chloe laughed and mingled with the guests. The chunky, multicolored, handmade necklace Chloe had chosen to wear with the mint-green, sleeveless, flowing dress set off the outfit perfectly. Her tanned legs and arms were glorious against the color. Chloe was still the most gorgeous creature she'd ever seen. It was a miracle she'd even married her in the first place.

She wasn't particularly fond of the gallery events, and after Chloe had left her on the bed earlier, she hadn't wanted to go at all. Staying home and wallowing in self-pity seemed so much more appealing than dealing with a bunch of strangers. But, irritated or not, she had to remain close to Chloe if she wanted to have any chance of winning her back. She intended to do everything in her power to make her fall in love with her again.

The night had dragged on longer than Shay had thought it would. Chloe had actively avoided eye contact with her for most of the night until Erica arrived with her date. The look she'd seen in her eyes wasn't clear. Panic, fear, maybe. She didn't know, but whatever it was, something told her Chloe needed her. So she'd sucked up her pride, gone to her, and slipped her arm around her waist. Shay was pleasantly surprised when Chloe had done the same. She was still hers, at least for the time being.

Once Erica and Barb had left them alone, they'd exchanged a few words. She seemed to enjoy herself for a while after that, and then she'd seen her go out the back door with Erica. She didn't follow. They would have to work out whatever they needed to without her, whether it was business or personal.

Chloe's mood had changed again when she'd returned with Jackson. She was guarded, almost defensive. What had happened to prompt the change? She was afraid to ask. When Chloe had introduced her to Erica and Barb, she felt friction between them. Not with Barb, but definitely with Erica. She recalled seeing her at these events before the accident. Then she felt a headache start, and she'd tossed back a couple of glasses of wine to hold it at bay. She didn't dare go home early. Something was very familiar about Erica, and it had made her uncomfortable. She wasn't about to leave Chloe alone at the gallery while Erica was still there.

Conversation had been sparse on the way home. It wasn't until they'd gone into the house that she decided to ask, "What happened to you tonight?"

"What do you mean?" Chloe seemed distracted. "Nothing happened."

"You were gone for quite a while."

"Sorry. I was getting claustrophobic with all the people in the gallery. I went out back with Jackson for some air."

A half-truth. She'd seen her head out the back door with Erica, and then Jackson had followed soon after. Why hadn't she mentioned Erica?

"Your friend Erica seems nice." She tossed her sweater onto the couch. "I didn't get to talk to her much, but Barb and I visited quite a bit."

Chloe stopped in the bedroom doorway momentarily. "That's nice. What did you talk about?"

"Lots of things. Her, me, you, Erica. She was very engaging. Not sure why Erica left her all alone most of the night." Shay sat on the edge of the bed and slipped off her shoes. "She said Erica seems to be a huge fan of yours. She has several of your works in her house." She'd also noticed that from the receipts but hadn't asked Chloe about it yet.

"She's been to her house?"

"They're dating, so I would say yes."

"Right." Chloe's voice weakened. "That makes sense." She took in a breath. "Well, I'm glad someone likes my art."

"Have you known her long? She seems to be a good customer." She pulled her dress over her head and put on a T-shirt. "While I was getting the books organized, I noticed that she's purchased quite a few of your paintings."

Chloe looked away quickly and rushed into the bathroom. "She's a very good customer. Sometimes keeping her happy is more work than the sale's worth." When she came out, she was dressed for bed. "I'm kind of tired. Can we talk about this another time?" She slid under the sheets, rolled onto her side, and faced the wall.

"Yeah, sure." Shay stared at the ceiling. Sleep wouldn't come right away. Something wasn't right about tonight. She didn't like Erica's involvement with Chloe, and something in her head told her she knew why. Yet it was lost somewhere in her foggy brain. She wanted to be held, needed to be held, but she wouldn't ask. Not while another woman was on Chloe's mind.

CHAPTER TWENTY

Chloe had left the beach house before sunup this morning. She'd left a note for Shay on the counter telling her she'd gone to paint the sunrise from one of the rooftops in Tampa. Avoiding sex had become her first priority now. The fact that Shay *wanted* to make love with her was weighing heavily on her mind. It was becoming much easier for her to go back to a place before they'd split up. But Shay hadn't even come close to her in bed last night, and she had an idea why. She wasn't sure if Shay had noticed the tension between her and Erica, but it was obvious to anyone who knew them. Jackson had seen it right away.

When she walked into their apartment in downtown Tampa, it was like walking into a past life. Shay hadn't removed any of her paintings from the walls, and she hadn't put the pictures of them into a box as Chloe had done. Everything in the apartment had remained undisturbed, exactly the same as when she'd first moved to the beach house alone.

She went into the bedroom, searched the closet, and found the remaining months of Shay's journals on the upper shelf. There weren't nearly as many here as at the beach house, which contained her thoughts from years past. Was she prepared to read any of them? She took the first one from the stack. This would be the last before Shay's accident, and she already knew Shay had come to the beach house to ask her to reconsider the separation. She dropped it back on top and slid the bottom journal from the stack. She knew how it ended. Now she wanted to know what went wrong between them.

A miserable discovery.

I got off work early tonight and went by the gallery to see Chloe. The door was locked, and the sign that hung in the window said

Closed. I knocked, but no one was inside. Chloe's Tahoe was there, but she wasn't answering her phone, so I walked down the block to the restaurant across the street where we'd become regulars while we were getting the gallery ready to open. I saw her through the window from across the street, laughing and smiling with the beautiful blonde who'd been at all the gallery events since it opened. I didn't go in. I couldn't. I didn't want to believe Lila when she'd told me she'd seen them together. But she was right. While I was working all the extra hours to save enough money to buy the beach house, Chloe had been seeing another woman. How blind could I be?

The more she read, the more she realized how it had all happened. She let the journal fall to her chest. "Fuck me." When had the universe started working against her so relentlessly? She'd made so many mistakes in her younger days—drugs, alcohol, too many women. She'd dealt with her struggles in life, hadn't she? That was all before Shay. She hadn't even thought of another woman since she'd come into her life.

Everything had spiraled out of control so quickly. If Shay had only talked to her, they wouldn't be in this mess. She'd been so jealous of the attention Chloe had been getting from Erica, innocent attention that an admirer gives an artist. But she hadn't been able to convince Shay it was all purely business on Chloe's part. When Chloe had found the text messages to Lila on Shay's laptop, she'd been so hurt. When she'd found the two of them together, the hurt had morphed into an anger she couldn't control.

Erica had been there for her, and she'd taken advantage of the situation. She'd woken up the next morning in Erica's bed and knew there was no going back. Her life had been forever changed at that point. Looking back, Erica had never been innocent, and she'd made sure Shay knew that. The messages, the looks, every one of her actions made it seem as though they were having an affair. God, she was so naive.

"Damn her for not trusting me." She shot up in bed and threw the journal across the room. "Damn me for not paying attention."

She took out her phone from her bag and hit Jackson's number. It was early, but she knew he'd be awake. He answered right away. "I need to show you something. Can we meet?"

"Do you mean, good morning, Jackson. Can I buy you breakfast at that new little restaurant by your apartment?"

She smiled. "Yes. That's exactly what I mean." Jackson always had a way of lightening her mood.

"Oh, good. The reviews have been awesome, and I've heard the food is divine."

"Where is this new place where the food is so spectacular?" she asked.

"Just a couple blocks down on the corner, between our complexes. Are you coming from the beach?"

"No. I'm at the apartment. I'll see you in ten." Chloe knew exactly where the restaurant was. She'd noticed the diner-style place on the corner several times before she'd moved to the beach. When it first opened, she'd thought she and Shay would be spending a lot of time there. Chloe wasn't a bad cook, but neither of them had much spare time to spend in the kitchen. As it worked out, they hadn't had the opportunity to try it before Chloe had moved permanently to the beach.

People were waiting in front of the restaurant when she arrived, but she didn't see Jackson. She went inside to put her name on the list, and the hostess directed her to where he was already seated. "You must have just beaten the crowd," she said as she slid into the chair across from him.

"No. We have connections. We eat here a lot." He looked across the restaurant and waved. Whitney was coming in the front door. "I hope you don't mind. She's hungry."

"No. Of course not." She stood and gave Whitney a hug. "Why are you wearing a hoodie? Aren't you hot?"

Whitney slid into the chair next to Jackson. "You dragged me out of bed. I'm still in my pajamas."

The table rattled as Jackson slapped his hands to it. "Before you show me whatever it is you need to show me, we have some news."

"Oh?" He was smiling, so it looked like good news.

He pointed to Whitney, who unzipped her hoodie and gave her a flash of the T-shirt underneath, then smiled widely.

Chloe caught only a glimpse but thought the shirt said *Tacos for two, please.* "Wait. What?" Does that say what I think it does?" She sprang from her chair, reached across the table, and pulled Whitney's hoodie open. She read the shirt again and saw two baby feet on the bottom. "Oh my God. You're pregnant?"

Whitney nodded eagerly.

She squealed, rounded the table, and hugged Whitney again. "I'm so excited for you two." After rubbing Whitney's belly a few times, she went back to her chair and sat, but she couldn't stop grinning. This was the best news she'd heard all year.

"Where's my favorite-aunt shirt?"

"Don't feel bad. I didn't get one either." Jackson pointed to his plain blue T-shirt.

"When are you due?"

"January fifth. I'm already in my second trimester. We didn't want to say anything just in case."

Chloe understood their reasons. Whitney had been pregnant twice before and had miscarried early each time. "Wow, you've been hiding it well. I can't believe I didn't notice."

"Morning sickness was a bitch." Jackson twisted his face into a grimace, and he hooked his thumb toward Whitney. "She actually lost weight." He picked up the menu and perused it. "But now she's eating like a horse."

Whitney slapped him on the shoulder. "I am going to get so fat, and you're gonna love it."

"You bet I am." He put his arm around her and kissed her.

They were both beaming like they'd just won the lottery, and it seemed as though they had. They'd been ready to start a family for some time now, and it was finally happening. What she wouldn't give to be that happy again. She decided to leave the journal in her bag. Today was not the day to talk about her problems. It was a day to celebrate new life and having the opportunity to be the best aunt ever.

CHAPTER TWENTY-ONE

After having a long, leisurely breakfast with Jackson and Whitney, Chloe had gone to the gallery and done everything and anything she could to avoid going home. After several missed calls from Shay, she called her back and apologized for being out of touch. They discussed dinner plans and decided Chloe would pick up tacos and enchiladas from a nearby restaurant on her way home.

During dinner she told Shay the good news about Jackson and Whitney's baby. Shay had known their struggles and was excited they had finally succeeded. She also posed the question of whether Chloe would be content to only be the cool aunt rather than a mom herself. She'd reassured her that she would be happy to be the best cool aunt ever. Shay's upbringing had instilled many doubts about raising children in her mind, and Chloe was unsure about her own parenting skills as well.

Once they'd finished dinner, Chloe had gone into her studio to paint, stayed there well into the night, and gone to bed late to avoid sex as usual. She'd woken up with Shay tangled in her arms again this morning, Shay's head on her chest and their legs intertwined. How or when it had happened, she didn't know. They'd had a huge gap between them when she'd finally drifted off to sleep. Holding and being held by Shay was the safest place she'd ever been, then and now.

So many thoughts were running through her mind. The gallery event the other night had been a huge pile of awkward that almost erupted into an explosion of Shay's memories that wouldn't have been easy to explain. The moment Erica had strolled into the gallery with Barb on her arm, Chloe knew she would never go back to that kind of relationship. When she'd gotten involved with Erica, she'd known that she dated more than just one woman at a time and had chosen to ignore the subtle looks and interest she gave other women in her presence. But Erica had never actually brought another woman around before and flaunted her in her face as she had the other night. Erica might have thought that would push Chloe into a decision, and it had. Only it wasn't the decision Erica was expecting.

After receiving Jackson and Whitney's news about the baby yesterday, she'd decided that from today on, she wanted to recapture the happiness she had with Shay. She planned to commit to making her marriage work. The whole thing might end up in disaster, but it would be her number-one priority no matter what the little voice in her head told her.

She untangled herself from Shay and slipped out of bed. Stopping in the doorway, she checked to make sure Shay was still asleep and then pulled the door almost completely shut, leaving it only a small crack open. She stopped in the guest room and picked up one of Shay's journals that she'd hidden before she went into the living room and sat in the club chair by the window. It was a dreary day at the beach, forecast to rain all day. Coffee would have to wait because that would wake Shay immediately. She wanted to get some reading done before that happened. She opened the journal and read the first line.

We moved to the new gallery today!
The weather was beautiful this morning when we started moving Chloe's art from the old gallery to the new, but mid-morning the clouds became thick and dark. We both knew the sky was going to open up any minute and soak us with rain. We had to move fast to get the paintings from the Tahoe into the gallery. We ran back and forth so quickly, I was surprised I hadn't fallen on my face. Chloe held the huge golf umbrella as I carried the art. By the time we were done I was soaking wet. The umbrella had done me no good at all, but the paintings were safe. We did it without damaging a single one, and Chloe was happy. The best reward of all was after we were inside, Chloe closed the umbrella, dropped it to the ground, and threw her arms around me. I felt like her hero again.

She was my hero. Chloe remembered it well. She was excited and nervous all at once. Shay had done so much to help make her successful—the beach house and the new gallery—but it had made life more stressful for them both. Yes, her paintings were selling, but the pressure to sell more to pay the bills was ridiculous. Her creativity had been horribly hampered. The only time she'd been able to envision anything was as she was drifting off to sleep, and then her vision had disappeared when she'd woken up in the morning. In their quest for Chloe to become more successful, her creative process had been somehow broken. *She'd* been broken. It had been the beginning of the end for them.

At that moment, she wanted to run into the bedroom and tell Shay everything about their life together—the good, the bad, and the ugly. She wanted to share all the things that had changed in recent months, and why. But she couldn't crush her reality so easily, so thoughtlessly. Shay needed to find her own way back to her memories. If she forced the process, Shay might resent her and possibly not even believe her. Her own new reality, the one she was actually beginning to enjoy, would be decimated. Maybe she was being selfish, but she didn't want to give up her own choices for the future.

Chloe heard the floor creak as Shay padded down the hallway. The house was exceptionally quiet this morning, except for the soft patter of rain on the roof. She quickly hid the journal under the cushion of the chair and waited for her to emerge into the living room. When Shay came up behind her, she attempted to get up from the chair, but Shay fell to her knees next to the chair, wrapped her arm around her neck, and pressed her face into her shoulder.

"I feel so alone right now. Please tell me you love me and still want me."

She felt the warmth of a tear hit her shoulder, and her heart ached. "I'll always love you, Shay," she said as she moved Shay around to her lap, gathered her in her arms, tucked her in under her neck, and held her. They both cried together until she drifted off to sleep again. It seemed like an eternity but was probably only minutes. She breathed in the scent of Shay's hair, felt the softness of her face against her shoulder. Her body reacted. She *did* still love her, and she wanted her so much more than she cared to admit.

Chapter Twenty-Two

When Shay had woken up on Chloe's lap in the chair, she'd been reminded why she'd fallen in love with her. Chloe had always been so selfless, taking care to make sure Shay was happy, especially after she'd told Chloe about her childhood and her strained relationship with her mother. Even though she hoped they could rekindle their romantic connection, even if she and Chloe could never be intimate again, she was still going to become Chloe's best friend and never let go of that part of their relationship. Trying to make her fall in love with her all over was a risky plan that might very well blow up in her face, but she had to do something. To live with her and know what she'd done, how much she'd hurt Chloe, devastated her. She had to make it up to her, to make it right.

After Chloe had gone into her gallery to paint, Shay had called Rachel and set up an appointment to see her at the hospital rather than have her come to the beach. She'd told Chloe she had a doctor's appointment, and since she would be at the hospital, she'd scheduled her regular therapy session with Rachel there as well. The apartment was on her way, so she'd stopped by to pick up a couple more of her journals. She needed to talk to someone about them, and Rachel had become her only confidante.

She followed Rachel into her office and flopped down in the chair across from the desk. The therapy session had been longer than usual because Rachel had pushed her on the equipment. It wasn't nearly as painful as it had been the last time, so that was a plus.

Without asking, Rachel took a bottle of water from the mini-fridge and handed it to her. "You're doing really well."

"Thanks." She wiped her face with a towel. "Trying to make

sure I can use this leg well into my nineties. Lofty goal, isn't it?" She chuckled.

"You tell me, Chief Actuary. You know the statistics."

"Thirty percent chance of making it that long."

"That's a grim forecast."

"That's for average people. Fifty percent for me. I'm well above average." Shay gave her a huge grin.

"Jesus. You've developed quite an ego."

"That's your fault." She pointed at Rachel. "You fixed me and gave me the confidence to succeed."

"I've created a monster." The grin on Rachel's face was adorable.

She laughed as she reached into her bag and took out the journals. "Don't worry. These will take me down a notch." And they would. Every time she read them, she hated herself more.

Rachel's smile morphed into a frown. "I thought we talked about this. You're going to stop punishing yourself for something you don't remember, right?"

"Right." She slid the journals across the desk, making sure the one that revealed her biggest regret was on top.

"And you're going to make Chloe love you again, right?" Rachel asked.

"I'm going to try." She pushed the journal close to Rachel. "Go ahead. Read it."

"Good, because if you're not, I'm going to throw my hat back into the ring. No sense in helping you woo another woman unless you're all in." Rachel picked up the journal and held it in the air as she spoke.

Shay raised her eyebrows and grinned. "Did you just say woo?"

"I like romance." Rachel quirked up an eyebrow. "You have a problem with that?"

Shay bit her lip. "Nope. No problem. Not here." The fact that Rachel was a hopeless romantic was endearing. If circumstances were different, she would definitely be first on Shay's playlist.

Rachel thumbed through the pages. Shay had bookmarked the exact spot for her and could see her expression change as she read. Shock, horror, disbelief, disappointment, disgust—there were plenty more reactions where those came from. She saw every one of the emotions on Rachel's face that she'd felt as she turned the pages.

Rachel's face was blank when she closed the journal and dropped it to the desk. "You're gonna have to do some major, industrial-strength wooing to get past this."

"I know. Now that you see what an absolute asshole I am, will you still help me?"

Rachel nodded. "You have to promise not to read this again." She tapped the journal with her finger. "You have to focus on the positive."

"I promise." She reached for the journal, and Rachel snatched it away.

"I'll keep it here just to make sure." Rachel slipped it into her top drawer along with the other one Shay had brought.

They spent the next several hours figuring out ways to make Chloe forget the pain. Shay told Rachel everything about their life together and all of Chloe's favorite things. She was a little surprised at how the whole process made her feel so much closer to Chloe. If she could make the same feelings happen for Chloe by reminding her of their life before, she might actually have a shot.

When she finally left and headed for home, Shay felt like she might possibly be able to make Chloe fall in love with her again. She could never erase what she'd done or the pain she'd put Chloe through, but hopefully she could make up for it by loving her even more.

❖

Since Shay had gone to the hospital, Chloe had called Whitney and invited her out to the house for lunch. She'd asked her to pick it up on the way, but Whitney was okay with that. Whitney had brought a couple sandwiches and a salad for them to split from Panera Bread. And it was such a beautiful day they decided to eat outside on the deck.

Whitney unpacked the food and set a turkey-and-avocado sandwich on each of the plates Chloe had brought from the kitchen. She opened the box with the salad and pushed a couple of forkfuls onto each plate as well.

"So, how's it going with Shay?" Whitney asked as she took a huge bite of her sandwich.

"She asked me if I still love her this morning. She fucking cried in my arms."

Whitney stopped mid-chew, swallowed, and wiped her mouth. "Oh my God. What did you say?"

"I told her I love her, of course. I just can't stand to touch her." The look of shock on Whitney's face made her rethink her answer. "I'm only kidding."

"When did you become so passive-aggressive? That's not going to help her recover any faster," Whitney said as she forked a pile of salad until she couldn't get another leaf of lettuce attached.

"I know that, but it helps me keep my distance. I can't fall back in love with her, Whit. She fucking tore my heart out." She'd been rethinking her decision to go all in on her marriage and was hoping for reassurance from Whitney.

"No. *She* didn't." Whitney talked through her food. "This Shay still loves you with her whole heart. Can't you see that?"

Chloe closed her eyes and shook her head. Whitney was right. She was punishing her for something she didn't even know she did. "So how do *I* get past it?" She took the bread off the top of her sandwich and rearranged the avocado into the middle of it.

"Keep reading her journals. Remember how good it was. It *was* good, wasn't it?"

"Phenomenal. I never thought it would end. Certainly not like it did."

"Apparently, the universe doesn't think so either, because here you are right back in the thick of it again." Whitney picked up half of her sandwich and dug in.

"Maybe so." Was Whitney right? Were she and Shay destined to be together? Could she go back to that place in time when they were gloriously happy? Let go of the heartache, the betrayal? Build from today forward and possibly repave their fate? "I think I'm already falling in love with her all over again. She has that 'wow' factor that makes me want her. I should be picturing Erica naked, not her. Technically, I'm with someone else. *She's* with someone else." She nibbled at her sandwich, not really hungry.

"Has Lila been around at all?" Whitney asked as she scooped more salad onto her plate.

"No. I don't believe so."

"Okay, so what if the circumstances were different, with Lila out of the picture and Erica not involved?"

She blew out a heavy breath. "If circumstances were different, I'd pursue her to the ends of the earth, but they're not and aren't likely to change if she finds out about Erica."

"Jesus, Chloe. Tell her about Erica *and* Lila. Tell her the whole story. More important, tell her how much you love her. Tell her you love her more now than you ever thought you could."

"I can't let her know about Lila or Erica. It would crush her. She had an affair with a woman because she thought I was having an affair. That was totally irrational thinking and ridiculously immature. It's really both our faults. If I'd just paid more attention, talked to her more, none of this would've ever happened."

"What are you gonna do?"

"I don't know. I have to wait out her recovery period and then tell her. I'm not sure I can do that. Not when I still love her so much. It's so hard to be just friends."

"Well, there's your answer." Whitney pushed out of her chair and headed back inside. "Talk to her."

"You don't understand."

Whitney emerged from the house again and dropped a cookie onto her plate. "Then explain it to me. Make me understand."

"Have you ever been stung by a jellyfish?"

Whitney stopped eating the cookie just long enough to respond. "Yeah. It hurts like hell."

"Well, finding Shay with Lila together was a thousand times worse." She was a huge, messy jumble of emotions. She felt like Armageddon had happened in her heart. Then, now, and everything in between was swimming in her brain like a hurricane. "I love her so much more now than I did before—if that's even possible. I'm just not me without her. The whole situation is so fucked up. What if I go back to her and it happens again? What if neither one of us has truly changed?"

"Did you fall out of love with Shay?"

"No. She fell out of love with me."

"Why would you think that?"

She raked her fingers through her hair. Although she suspected Whitney and Jackson had discussed them many times, she hadn't told them the complete story. "We weren't having sex anymore."

Whitney's eyebrows rose. "At all?"

"Nope. We were both too busy, too tired, too whatever."

The crumbs flew off Whitney's hands as she rubbed them together. "I guess that means you have something to look forward to then, right?"

Chloe chuckled. "You always know how to find the bright side in any situation, don't you?"

"Yep. My glass is always half full." Whitney held up another cookie and waved it in front of her. "More?"

"No thanks. You and the baby need it more than me."

She hadn't gone into detail about everything that had happened between them. She couldn't place all the blame on Shay. They hadn't shared many moments of affection during the past year. They'd both been doing their own thing without considering how it made the other feel. She'd been so wrapped up in the new gallery she'd ignored Shay's needs just as much as Shay had ignored hers.

CHAPTER TWENTY-THREE

The evening was going along smoothly at the gallery, and Shay was a little bored. Chloe was busy with customers and other artists, so these events were rather uneventful for her. But watching Chloe mingle was a pleasure she would never deny herself. They'd been stealing glances at each other all night long that seemed to convey hidden messages, and each one made her stomach fly into a huge somersault. Chloe glanced her way again and smiled that beautiful smile of hers. Shay had to take a deep breath to calm herself. She wanted to sprint across the room, pull her into her arms, and kiss her like nobody's business. She wasn't very patient.

The bell on the door chimed, and she saw Erica enter the gallery and search the crowd. When she seemed to have found what she was looking for, she headed straight for Chloe. The woman was gorgeous with her blond hair, blue eyes, and perfect smile. Shay hadn't expected the jealousy that raged through her and had to calm down or she'd give herself away. Chloe seemed reluctant when Erica pulled her into a hug. If nothing else, Shay knew Chloe's facial expressions. It relieved her to see that Chloe was smiling, but it wasn't her usual happy smile. The body language between them seemed barely cordial. One little victory for the night.

Shay hadn't objected when Erica wanted to meet her for dinner to discuss a commission the week before. But if she'd have known Erica was her competition, she would've never let it happen. She took out her phone and sent a text to Rachel.

Where are you?

After a minute or two a message came through from Rachel: *Trying to find a place to park.*

She hadn't thought of that. She typed back, *Ugh. Parking is miserable here.*

Found one. I'll be there in a minute.

Hurry!

The door chime caught her attention again, and she was excited to see Rachel enter the gallery. She looked absolutely gorgeous tonight, dressed in a flower-patterned sundress with her dark hair loosely scattered around her face. She looked so much different than the Rachel she saw during her therapy sessions. If she didn't know better, she'd think it was all for her. Maybe it was. She rushed through the mingling crowd to greet her and hugged her tightly.

"Wow. That's quite a greeting." Rachel chuckled and held on for a little longer than necessary.

"Wow. You look stunning." She watched the blush take over Rachel's face.

"I don't get out much and thought I might find one or two single lesbians hanging out. They come to these events, right?"

She couldn't help the grin that took over her face. "They do, usually in packs."

Rachel took in a breath. "Okay, then. I'm ready for them. I think."

She wasn't quite sure how to feel about letting Rachel into the wilds of art lesbians. She was a treasure, and she kind of liked keeping her to herself for now. "Yeah, you are."

"That's her, huh?" She glanced over at Erica.

"Uh-huh." She nodded and took a deep breath. "How do I compete with that?"

Rachel turned to face her. "From what I see in front of me, there's no competition."

"Listen, that's very sweet, and like I said before, if I wasn't completely in love with my wife, I'd totally let you romance me."

Rachel let out a soft chuckle that held a tinge of sadness. "Well, there's that." She held her gaze for a moment and smiled. "Okay, then, let's see what you're up against."

❖

Chloe had finally managed to get away from a customer who had talked her ear off for the better part of an hour. She needed a glass of wine and wanted to check in with Shay. She'd seen Rachel come in about the same time Erica had shanghaied her. She hadn't paid a bit of attention to the first few sentences that came out of Erica's mouth because of it. Rachel looked beautiful tonight, dressed in a sleeveless summer dress with her hair falling loosely around her face.

Chloe's jealousy burned deep in her belly and made it hard to breathe. Rachel was just waiting in the wings to pounce as soon as Shay learned of their relationship status before the accident. Leaving the two of them alone together for too long was a mistake. It was ridiculously obvious that Rachel had more interest in Shay than physical therapy.

She was on her way across the room to the bar to see them when Shay headed her off halfway with a fresh glass of wine.

"You're a lifesaver, Shay."

"That's my job. Keep you happy and ply you with liquor." Shay gave her a sexy smile and winked.

"Keep it up, and you just may get to take me home tonight."

Shay's voice was low and sultry as she leaned in and whispered, "Ooh, my wildest dreams are about to come true."

Chloe's heart thumped. She'd missed the banter and laughter between them.

Rachel joined them and pulled her brows together. "What's so funny?"

"Nothing," Shay said. She seemed to be content to keep the banter just between the two of them. Chloe liked that. They had something new to them alone, unsullied by the outside world.

Rachel finished her glass of wine and excused herself to go to the bathroom, so she and Shay moved to a quiet corner in the back of the gallery for a few moments of privacy. Erica suddenly appeared when she was in mid-sentence, so wrapped up in the feelings Shay was stirring in her that she hadn't seen her coming.

"There you are. I've been looking for you," Erica said as she slipped in between them.

Shay threw up her hands. "Fuck! Do you mind? I'm trying to have a private conversation with my wife." This was totally out of character for Shay. Erica dropped her mouth open and blinked. Shay wasn't the least bit affected by her stunned reaction.

"What are you doing? I'm working," Chloe said, and Shay

clenched her teeth and stared into her eyes. Her arm stung when Shay took her by the hand and pulled her outside behind the gallery.

The door clanged shut, and she found herself pushed up against the brick building being kissed so completely and expertly that she had to grab hold of Shay to keep from melting to the ground into a puddle. A jolt of electricity hit her when she felt the softness of Shay's breasts against her own as the length of their bodies touched. Every nerve ending snapped to attention when she pressed into her as the kiss deepened. *Holy fuck.* She wanted her now more than she'd ever wanted her before. And when Shay broke the connection, Chloe felt cold and hollow.

"That's what I'm doing. If you want to finish that, let me know." Shay pulled open the door and left Chloe plastered against the wall, stunned and searching for balance. She didn't know what that was about, but she'd never been so turned on in her life.

❖

Shay had rushed through the gallery, grabbing Rachel on her way to the front door. Conversation between them had been slim on the way to the car, and it hadn't gotten much better once they'd hit the road.

"You wanna tell me what happened? I mean, I came back from the bathroom just in time to catch you pulling Chloe out back."

"Just who the hell does that woman think she is? She's not that special."

"Erica?"

"Yes. Erica." Shay blew out the words, letting her exasperation ring through.

"Nope. Nothing special there."

"She had no right to butt into our conversation like that."

Rachel nodded as she drove. "You're absolutely right."

"Chloe is married to *me*."

"Right again."

"She has a lot of nerve acting like she's more important than me."

"Let's take the bitch out." Rachel's voice lowered to a growl.

Shay broke into laughter. "I'm being totally irrational, aren't I?"

"Little bit." Rachel smiled. "But I'm loving every minute of it."

She held her head with her hand. "Oh, God. Did I make a scene?"

"Not too bad. You sure left Erica with her mouth open. What happened outside with Chloe?"

"I kissed her." She closed her eyes. "Long and hard." A tremor ran through her as she remembered the feel of her lips, her tongue, her body against hers.

"That little green-eyed monster came at you hard."

"I couldn't stand seeing Erica with her, knowing she'd fucked her." She shook her head. "I have no idea where this is coming from. I've never been jealous before." But then again, she'd never had reason to be. When Erica had interrupted them, that had been the last straw. This woman clearly had no boundaries, and she was tired of it.

"Okay. So now Chloe knows you're serious."

"She sure does. She's probably afraid to come home, and I'm kind of afraid of her coming home too." She raked her fingers through her hair. "We'll fight, or she'll just reject me again."

"Do you want to stay with me?"

"I don't know. Should I?"

Rachel shrugged. "I think it'll remove the awkward. Give you both time to cool off."

"Let's do it. I need to get some clothes."

"I'm sure I have something you can borrow." Rachel took a U-turn at the next stoplight and headed back into the city. "It'll be fun. We'll pop some popcorn and watch a movie."

She sent Chloe a text letting her know she was going home with Rachel. Chloe didn't carry her phone with her at gallery events, so she wouldn't see it until later, after everyone was gone. She wasn't sure how Chloe would feel about her not coming home tonight, but she wasn't up for being rejected again. They both needed a short break.

Shay woke up the next morning on Rachel's couch snuggled up against her. It was a little weird and definitely uncomfortable when she'd realized where she was and who she was clinging to. Rachel might have felt differently, though.

They'd stayed up late eating popcorn and watching old horror movies. They'd started at either end of the couch and had soon both decided they needed to be in the middle, sitting thigh to thigh, so they could hang on to each other during the scary parts. Rachel was quickly becoming her closest friend, and she seemed to be respecting the boundaries Shay had set.

The text she'd received from Chloe last night had been a simple question mark. She'd replied with, *I think we need a break from each other tonight.* Although the bubbles had appeared on her screen indicating a return message, Chloe hadn't responded again, which she took as agreement. It left a huge knot in the pit of her stomach, but it was the right thing to do. Forcing intimacy would just push them further apart.

Chapter Twenty-Four

It was close to six p.m., and Shay wasn't home yet. Chloe had spent the day in her studio painting. It was funny how her creativity had been sparked again. The banter and flirty smiles she'd shared with Shay last night had opened that door again so easily. When Shay had pulled her outside, she'd thought they were going to fight, so the gloriously intense kiss had been unexpected. Every one of her senses had come to life. They'd been awakened, and all the layers of hurt and anger had begun to fall away like a mummy that had been wrapped in thousands of rolls of cotton and buried for a thousand years. It was clear now that she was still in love with Shay, or perhaps she was falling in love with her all over again.

Waking up alone had been more disappointing than she'd realized. When Shay had sent the text letting her know she wasn't coming home, that she was staying with Rachel, she'd been ridiculously jealous. She'd even written and erased multiple texts before deciding not to respond at all. Though she hadn't been sure how their night would end, she'd wanted the opportunity to choose. Shay had made the choice for her, which irritated her, a control issue she needed to contain. Shay had always been the level-headed one. Emotions always got in the way of Chloe's choices. Shay had made the best decision for both of them. If Shay had come home last night, she very well might have ended up making love to her, which she would have regretted.

Even though she'd had to admit it felt good to be flirted with— wanted somehow—she wasn't at a point with her emotions to deal with the confusion that intimacy with Shay would create. Clearly, with all that was going on in their lives, they'd lost something long before Shay had strayed. Had the money and success been worth it? No, she didn't think so. Life had been so much simpler before, and she'd always felt loved.

One of Shay's journals lay on Chloe's lap as she sat on the deck and stared out onto waves while they crashed against the beach. She'd pulled it from the stack in the bedroom closet after she'd cleaned up in the studio. She ran her fingers across the cover, wondering how Shay would feel about her reading her innermost thoughts. Then she opened it.

Pizza, sunset, and stars…

We ate pizza in the car tonight. The restaurant was too busy, the wait for a table over an hour. I hadn't eaten since breakfast and was so hungry, I thought I was going to pass out. Chloe was so sweet. She ordered a pizza and a couple of sodas to go, and we drove to the beach. She put on some jazz music, opened the liftgate of her SUV, and we sat in the back and ate as we watched the sunset. She even picked off all the onions because they'd gotten the order wrong, and one of the sodas turned out to be diet, so we shared. The whole night should've been a colossal fail, but she made it work. That was the moment I knew I loved her. The sunset was gorgeous, and the night was so clear when the stars blanketed the sky everything else besides her heartbeat and mine fell away. The whole night turned out so impossibly romantic. She kissed me, and I truly felt it to my toes. Tonight made it crystal clear. I will be with Chloe forever if she'll have me.

Chloe shook her head. If life could only be so simple again. As she remembered it, the night *had* been a colossal fail. She'd planned for a nice romantic dinner, then a visit on the roof of her apartment building where they could watch the stars, and after that who knew what. But the reservation mix-up had scrambled her plans. They'd given her table to someone else, and even though she'd planned well in advance, she wasn't the kind of person to insist they eject someone else to make it right.

Shay had been so gracious about the whole thing, it hadn't even entered her mind that the subpar substitute venue of the back of her SUV would impact her the way it had. The sunset had been dreamy, and when the stars came out, Shay had told her stories about each one as though she'd created them all herself. The kiss they'd shared had only made the night more magical.

The sound of the door rolling across the rail as it opened pulled her out of her thoughts. Shay was home. Her stomach vaulted, and she quickly slid the journal into her sketch bag.

"Listen, I'm sorry about last night." Shay touched her on the shoulder. "I don't know why I acted that way. I know it's not your fault that I don't remember. It won't happen again."

Still a little dreamy from the memories brought back by the journal, she smiled and asked, "You want to walk down to the beach and watch the sunset?"

"I would love that." The excitement in Shay's eyes was vivid. "Can we get a pizza?"

Chloe chuckled. "Wouldn't think of doing it any other way." Something had changed in Shay since the accident. She seemed so carefree now, a shining light amid all the darkness in recent months.

The night went almost exactly as the date had gone before. Only they'd picked up the pizza and a bottle of wine, come back home, and found a nice spot on the beach behind the house to watch the sunset. It was romantic as hell, and Chloe knew it was a bad idea.

She couldn't help but notice Shay smile as she watched Chloe meticulously pick the onions from her slice before she ate it. They hadn't been a mistake on their first pizza date, and most people would think it was odd that she liked her pizza cooked with onions yet didn't like to eat them, but Shay had always called it an endearing quality. Shay finished her piece and tossed the crust into the box. That hadn't changed. She never ate the crust, but Chloe loved it, and she saved it for her. Part of the reason they blended so well—the perfect balance. Shay moved the pizza box and the wine from between them and scooted over closer to her. "Can I kiss you?"

Chloe wiped the remnants of pizza from her mouth. "You don't have to ask to kiss me."

"Lately, it kinda feels like I do."

A sigh whooshed out of Chloe's mouth as she pulled her knees up to her chest and rested her chin on them. "I'm sorry. There's just been so much going on lately. I haven't been myself."

"Join the club. I don't know who I am anymore." Shay stared up at the sky. "I feel like the clouds in the mist above the ocean. One creeping up on the other just to have another gust of wind push it farther away until it becomes too far out of reach."

She didn't know how to fix that for Shay. As it was, she was holding on by a thread to what they had. She couldn't feel sorry for her right now. "How was your night with Rachel?" It was none of her business, but she needed to know.

"Fun. We made popcorn and watched horror movies." The smile on Shay's face was beautiful as she spoke, and Chloe grew curious about what else might have happened.

"You're wearing her clothes." The Largo Medical Center T-shirt hadn't escaped her notice when Shay had shown up on the deck tonight, and it hadn't left her thoughts much during the night since. She couldn't help but wonder if Shay had slept with Rachel.

Shay plucked at the front of the shirt and looked down to read it. "I was cold, and the dress would've been uncomfortable to sleep in."

"So, you changed last night?"

"Are you asking me if I slept with Rachel?" Shay looked sideways at her and tilted her head. "'Cause it kinda sounds like you are."

She rolled her lips in and shook her head. "You can't tell me she doesn't want that. She's been flirting with you since day one."

"Oh, she definitely wants that." Shay had her full attention now. "But *I* don't want that. The only one I want to touch is you, and you won't let me." She blew out a heavy breath. "I'm doing anything and everything to get some sort of reaction from you."

Chloe raised her eyebrows. "So you're trying to make me jealous?"

"You've been ridiculously passive. Forgive me if I need some sort of emotion from you. Good *or* bad." She threw her hands up. "Say it! Say I'm fucking driving you crazy! Say something! Then at least I'd know you care. It's better than nothing at all."

The pained look in Shay's eyes was too much to bear. She grabbed the empty bottle of wine and glasses and stood up. "Of course I care. In fact, I care too fucking much." She slogged through the sand to the deck and then went inside the house.

"Wait," Shay said, and Chloe could tell she wasn't far behind.

The trash can clanged as the wine bottle crashed to the bottom. "I'm doing everything in my power to help you recuperate, and all you do is make it harder for me."

"I'm not going to break, you know." Shay took her by the arm and swung her around. "I give up. Can we just forget about my recovery and be what we were tonight? Do a little less fighting and a little more of this?" Shay pulled her into a scorching kiss, and every part of her was ready to do exactly what Shay wanted.

She broke away and took in a deep breath. Shay had no idea what she was asking. "I can't." She held her palm to her forehead and paced the kitchen. "Because you—"

"What? What did I do?" Shay held up her hands, and Chloe could see by her pained expression that she was truly confused.

Out of pure need, Chloe rushed to Shay and took her face in her hands. "You made me forget everything else and fall in love with you." *Again.* She kissed her—long, deep, and slow—and every particle of her zipped with pure pleasure. Kissing Shay was the most arousing thing she'd experienced, *ever.* Shay's hands roamed down her back, cupped her ass, and every bit of her resistance was gone. She kissed her as every ounce of raw emotion that had built up within her over the past month and a half spilled out. The dam had broken, and the desire that had been rising inside her since she'd brought Shay home from the hospital spilled out. Shirts came over heads and dropped to the floor. Bras were unhooked, pulled from arms, and tossed, landing only God knows where. *Slow down.* Chloe dragged her mouth away and stared into Shay's beautiful chocolate eyes before she took Shay's hand to lead her into the bedroom.

The phone chimed in her bag and then rang immediately afterward. She tried to pull her hand free from Shay, turned, and saw the confused look in her eyes. She backtracked, kissed her, then went to her purse and grabbed the phone. It wouldn't power down fast enough as she held the button firmly and moved the slider to Off. The phone slid from her hands back into her purse and she returned to Shay, took her into her arms, and kissed her like she'd never done it before. They were skin-to-skin at this point, at least from the waist up, and it felt so much better than she remembered, if that was even possible. They were fusing together so perfectly, but she had to pull herself away or they were going to end up right there on the kitchen floor, which would be hell on both of them, especially Shay's leg.

She led Shay into the bedroom and stood by the bed gazing at her for the slightest of moments. God, she was beautiful. She squatted in front of her, slid the sweatpants and plain white underpants from her hips. Stopping only to briefly kiss the spot she'd missed so much, she then moved slowly down her leg to the wounds on the inside of her thigh, now almost completely healed. Who knew that wounds so deep could heal so much of her soul. She glanced up, saw the desire in Shay's eyes, and wrapped her arms around her legs, pressed her cheek to Shay's belly, and gorged herself on the warmth of it.

Shay touched her shoulders, coaxing her upward. She complied, and then Shay pushed her to the bed and took complete control as she'd never done before. Chloe let her, and take her she did.

Looking up at Shay, seeing her hair down, wild and thick around her face, made her arousal surge to heights it had never reached before. She wanted her now, but Shay wasn't yielding as she trailed her tongue from her jaw to her collarbone, then across to the hollow of her neck. She arched her back and squirmed beneath her.

Shay laughed as she sucked on her neck. "Uh-uh. You're mine tonight." The low, sultry voice rumbled through her.

The warmth that engulfed her when Shay's lips surrounded her nipple was amplified a thousand degrees by the jolt that shot through her when she sucked it hard into her mouth. She lifted her hips and pressed into her, wanting more, now, but Shay wasn't giving in. Shay's teeth raked across her nipple, and she shifted again.

"I know what you're after," she whispered, and Shay's mouth closed over the neglected nipple. This one was so much more sensitive than the other, liquid gushed between her legs. The time Shay spent licking and sucking had her pleasure topping out. She was almost ready to come, and then Shay let the nipple slip from her mouth, replacing it momentarily with her fingers as she moved down her body.

Chloe was usually so in control of everything, but letting Shay take her this way was astonishingly gratifying. So many new sensations were zipping through her as Shay's mouth made its way across her stomach and her fingers glided across her hips. The whimper that escaped her lips when the heat of Shay's mouth found her center was uncontrollable. Shay's tongue moved slowly and expertly between her folds. She raised up into her, and Shay's mouth pressed against her firmly, her tongue moving faster and harder as she clasped her hands around her ass, holding her there. The orgasm came in strong, plunging her headfirst into mind-shattering euphoria. Shay's name tumbled from her lips as she fought for air and lifted her hips, wanting to be so much closer.

Shay slowly made her way back up Chloe's body and kissed her gently before resting her head on her shoulder.

"Sweet Lord," Chloe blew out with a breath.

"I'm right there with you on that." Shay's arm snaked across her stomach and tightened around her.

She'd just moved into a lazy haze when she felt Shay raise her head and blow a breath across her nipple. It zipped through her, and all her senses came to life again. It was amazing how she knew exactly what to do.

"Definitely not," she said as she lifted Shay's chin with her finger, intercepting her mouth with her own and kissing her. But Shay wasn't giving up control. She crawled on top again, hovered her breast just above Chloe's face, then lowered herself enough for Chloe to take a nipple into her mouth. This was new and had Chloe wet all over again.

She felt the smooth skin of Shay's sides as she skittered her fingers across them, felt Shay quiver as she slipped her fingers between her folds and inside. She rocked back and forth above her, setting the pace. Shay's breaths became quick and shallow, and as Chloe watched Shay's beautiful body begin to react above her, she couldn't stand it anymore. She sat up, wrapped her free arm around Shay, and drew her in, breasts to breasts, enjoying the friction between them. Shay's eyes remained glued to hers as they moved together in perfect rhythm. In a matter of minutes, Shay clenched her arms around her, buried her face in Chloe's neck, and cried out as the orgasm ripped through her hard and fast.

Still quivering, Shay collapsed against her and held her tight as the words came in a whisper out of her mouth. "I love you."

Chloe pressed her face into Shay's neck, breathed in the natural musky scent she adored, and in that moment, she let everything go. "I love you too."

Shay moved next to her, and Chloe snuggled against her. She'd never been this comfortable with any other woman. She'd forgotten how Shay knew everything about her body, every pulse point, every sweet spot, when it reacted, how it reacted, how to bring her to orgasm quickly, slowly, completely, whichever was warranted at the time. But Shay had never taken her with such power before, and letting it happen felt incredible.

Earlier, when Shay had stood there looking at her that way, the choice had been totally out of her hands. She couldn't refuse her again. She didn't want to anymore. She wanted everything back to the way it used to be, and it seemed all she'd had to do was let it happen. In an instant the void in her soul had been filled.

It was so much better than Chloe remembered. Had she really forgotten, or had Shay just become more experienced? She purged the thought from her mind. She refused to let anyone ruin this moment, including herself.

CHAPTER TWENTY-FIVE

Shay had been afraid to go to sleep last night, worrying that Chloe might not be there next to her when she woke up. Her fears had come true. When she opened her eyes, she found herself alone in the bed. She hadn't dreamed it, had she? As she slid out of bed and put on her robe, her muscles told her just how much they'd enjoyed each other last night. No, it wasn't a dream. The aroma of fresh coffee hit her as she padded down the hallway. A full pot was in the coffeemaker and two cups on the counter. She poured coffee into each of them and added just a dash of creamer to Chloe's.

Then she stood in the doorway to Chloe's studio watching as Chloe sketched the beginnings of a new painting. From where she stood, she couldn't tell what it was, but Chloe's hand was flying madly across the canvas as she created something with charcoal.

Chloe stopped and looked over her shoulder. "I had an inspiration and didn't want to wake you." The smile on Chloe's face was sweet as she dropped the charcoal onto the table, wiped her hands, and swiveled around on her stool. "How long have you been up?" she asked as she intercepted her halfway across the room.

"Just long enough to bring you this." She handed Chloe a cup of coffee, and she took a sip.

"Mmm. Just the way I like it." Chloe wrapped her free arm around her waist and kissed her softly. "Thank you."

The warmth in Chloe's eyes took her, and she didn't want to let her go. "You're welcome." She took in a breath and released her. "May I see what you're working on?" Chloe moved aside and let her view the canvas. It was a sketch of her lying blissfully naked, covered by the tiniest swatch of sheet tangled around her legs.

"I hope you don't mind. You were so beautiful this morning, I couldn't help myself."

She set her cup on the small table by the door and moved closer to better see the sketch. "I don't mind at all." Her face looked relaxed and calm. The happiness had shown through, and Chloe had captured it perfectly. "You made that happen." She took Chloe's face in her hands and brushed her thumbs lightly across her cheeks. "You make my heart happy."

Tears began to well in Chloe's eyes. "I didn't know if I'd ever hear you say that again."

She pulled her into her arms and squeezed. "I'll never stop saying it." Tears streamed from her eyes as well, and soon they were standing there clutching each other as they cried.

How had she ever lost interest in this woman? Shay loved her more today than she ever had before, and she wanted to make her happy every day going forward. She wanted to prove her love to her, but only making love to her wouldn't be enough to erase everything they'd been through.

❖

The view from Shay's office was stellar—at least one perk to becoming chief actuary. Going back to work was the last thing on Shay's list of things to do, but she couldn't keep living in a fantasy world. She had work to do, people to take care of—to deal with.

Shay had spent most of the morning catching up on email and reviewing documents she'd been working on before the accident. She heard Lila before she saw her, and the voice sent chills down her spine. She wasn't scheduled to be in the Tampa office until Wednesday. Shay had purposely started back on Monday to get a handle on everything before she had to see her, wanting to be prepared both professionally and personally. Now she wouldn't have time to do either.

When her office door pushed open, she wasn't at all prepared for what she saw in the doorway. Lila was dressed in a powder-blue skirt and jacket, a crisp white shirt tucked in underneath. She was stunning. The temptation was clear now, though the reason was still blurry.

"Hi, Boss. I'm glad to see you're here and back at it." Lila didn't wait to be invited in. She crossed the room and took a seat in one of the chairs in front of Shay's desk.

"Thanks. It feels good to be back."

"Yeah?" She lifted an eyebrow. "I bet you were going stir-crazy at home."

"Not really. Chloe and I have plenty of things to do there, but I needed to catch up here." The mention of Chloe prompted the smile to leave Lila's face. "Thanks for taking care of everything while I was out."

Lila took in a breath and smiled again. "Glad to do it." Her smile faded again, and she looked at her hands in her lap. "I was worried about you." She looked up and flipped her hair out of her eyes with a quick movement. "When I went to the hospital, they told me you'd lost some of your memory. Is that true?"

She nodded. "Almost all of the past year." Chloe hadn't told her Lila had come to see her in the hospital, and there was no doubt in her mind why she hadn't. The fact that Lila *had* come led her to believe there was more than sex between them. She hoped that wasn't the case.

The muted sound of Lila's hands dropping to her legs filled the room. She seemed relieved, as though she'd thought someone had lied to her. "That means you don't remember…all the hard work we put in on the new product." She stood up. "Let me get settled in, and I'll go over it with you."

"Sounds good."

Lila turned and crossed the room but hesitated before she left the office. "I'm really glad you're okay."

That had gone better than she'd thought it would. She relaxed into her chair. Hopefully, the next hour or two would go just as well.

Lila returned with a few manila file folders under her arm and a cup of coffee in each hand. She set them both on table in the corner of the office, along with the file folders. "You want to work over here? I think it'll be easier."

"Sure." She picked up a pad and pen and then took a seat at the table.

Lila picked up one of the cups of coffee and set it in front of Shay. "Black, right?"

Shay nodded, and Lila moved a chair closer to where Shay was sitting, sat down, and opened one of the folders. The close proximity made her a little uncomfortable at first, but that soon faded as Lila got right down to business.

After Lila had caught her up to speed on everything, she sat back in her chair and seemed to be assessing her. "You look great."

"Thank you, but you haven't seen me naked." The comment was out of her mouth before she remembered who she was talking to. Her cheeks warmed, and she hoped Lila hadn't seen her reaction. Lila continued to stare. "Or have you?" Lila seemed to balk at the question. She had to know what, if anything, Lila was going to share with her about their affair. "This question may be out of line." She rolled her lips in momentarily. "Were we doing anything together besides working?"

Lila hesitated for a moment before she smiled and shook her head. "No. During the time we were working together, you were absolutely head over heels in love with your wife."

Not the answer she'd expected. Maybe Lila wasn't so bad after all. Or maybe she had just been fucking her to get the job like everyone else in the office thought. Either way, although Lila was plenty beautiful, Shay couldn't imagine anyone else making her feel the way she did when she was with Chloe.

When eleven thirty rolled around, Shay was ready for a break. Once she'd settled on when her first day back to work would be, she'd immediately made plans to have lunch with Rachel. She hadn't seen Rachel's car when she pulled into the parking lot of the diner near the hospital, but that didn't mean she wasn't there. The coffee shop was within walking distance, so she figured Rachel had most likely walked—a habit she'd urged Shay toward now that her leg was healing. She spotted Rachel waving at her from a booth at the back of the diner and sped her way. She had so much to tell her.

"So, how's the first day back?" Rachel asked as she got up and pulled her into a hug. "I went ahead and ordered the club sandwich for you." They'd been there a few times before.

"Exhausting."

"I figured you'd have lots to catch up on. I can't go away for a day without my email filling up."

"I was caught up on email. I had to meet with Lila this morning and wasn't as prepared as I should've been."

The surprise on Rachel's face was clear. "I thought she wasn't coming in until Wednesday."

"Me too." She adjusted the silverware in front of her. "I thought I had more time to get up to speed."

"How'd it go with her? Did she say anything?" Rachel asked in a whisper as though everyone in the diner would know who she was talking about.

"Really well, actually." She took a drink of water. "I asked her point-blank if we'd done anything together other than work, and she said no."

"Seriously?"

As they ate, Rachel listened intently as she told her about what she'd said about her love for Chloe as well as what Amber had told her about the rumors.

"What's her angle? Do you really think she was fucking you to get the job?"

"It's possible." She chewed a bite of her sandwich. "I mean, she's a gorgeous twenty-something, and I'm just…well, I'm just boring old me."

"Stop that." Rachel immediately dropped her fork and reached for her hand. "There's nothing boring about you."

"If you say so."

"I do. Remember our deal?" Rachel seemed dead serious.

She rolled her eyes and moved her head from side to side. "If things don't work out with Chloe, you're next in line."

Rachel lifted her eyebrows. "I mean that."

"Got it." She chewed on her lower lip.

"I know things are going well between you and Chloe, but don't you think you should tell her that you know?" She took a drink of water. "I mean rather than let her find out for herself?"

"I'm hoping that will never happen."

"Those are dangerous waters you're treading in, love." Rachel let go of her hand and returned to her salad.

"Tell me about it. They're getting deeper every day. I'm just not ready to risk it without the lifeboat yet."

"I'll talk to her if you want me to," Rachel said quietly.

She stopped mid-bite. "You'd actually do that for me, wouldn't you?"

Rachel nodded. "I'd do anything for you." She looked away, but Shay saw everything in her eyes. "You're my best friend."

Knowing Rachel had revealed more of her feelings than she'd planned, Shay reached over and took her chin in her fingers, forcing her to look at her. "And you're mine."

Rachel's advice was sound, but even if she still didn't remember, telling Chloe now about what she knew could kill any love she had left in her heart. She wasn't ready to take that chance yet. Not until she was cemented securely into Chloe's heart again.

❖

With minimal interaction with Lila, the rest of Shay's day had gone well. Working a full eight-hour day was exhausting and had taken more out of her than she'd expected. She didn't know how she'd managed to pull off the twelve-hour stints she'd worked in the past. The thought of going home to Chloe was all that had gotten her through the final hour.

When she opened the door to the beach house, the magnificent aroma of her favorite mushroom risotto hit her square in the nose. She dropped her bag just inside the door and headed into the kitchen. Chloe stood at the stove stirring the risotto as she gazed out the window at the beach. She was dressed in a pair of white leggings and a flowy quarter-sleeved, royal-blue top that left her shoulders bare—shoulders that begged to be kissed as her midnight hair draped lazily across them. She couldn't imagine a more beautiful sight than that of her wife standing in front of her right now.

Chloe leaned into her as she moved in behind her and wrapped her arms around her waist. "How was your day?"

"Tiring. Who knew I did so much?"

"I did." She chuckled. "You're super smart."

"You think so?"

"I know so." She turned in her arms and gave her a wonderful "hello" kiss. "I missed you today."

Shay had never thought she'd hear that again, and her heart pounded. "I missed you more." She kissed her again.

Chloe spun around to the stove and returned to stirring the risotto.

"Now go change." She bumped her with her butt. "This will be done soon, and I don't want it to get lumpy."

"On it." She brushed Chloe's hair to the side and kissed her neck. "I can think of so many things to do besides eat dinner." Chloe squirmed against her, which only prompted her to move closer.

"Not going to happen. I want to hear all about your day," Chloe said, but Shay couldn't leave the sweetness of her neck, not yet. "I said go." Chloe rested her head back on Shay's shoulder and blew the words out slowly.

She growled against Chloe's neck as she backed up and took the hallway to the bedroom. Chloe seemed to have forgiven her for her transgression, and that made her happy. Even though she hadn't remembered the affair, it had been apparent that the impact on Chloe had been significant. Seeing Lila at the office today had brought it front and center in her mind again. She still wondered why Lila hadn't mentioned anything about it. Would she in the future? She had the job she wanted, the one most of the other people in the office didn't think she deserved. Perhaps Lila had only thought of her as a means to an end. Now that she couldn't remember, she was content to let it stay buried in her own lost memories.

By the time she made it back to the kitchen, Chloe had already plated the mushroom risotto and set the small, round oak table they rarely used for eating. They ate most of their meals either out on the deck or on the coffee table in front of the TV.

"Is there anything I can help you with?"

Chloe pointed to the bottle of pinot gris on the counter. "You can open that."

"Finally, something I can do." She smiled widely at Chloe as she opened the drawer, took out the wine opener, and pulled the cork. The glasses were already on the table.

"Tell me about your day."

"It was a struggle at first, but Amber helped me get logged into my computer and get organized." She took a bite of risotto and moaned. "This is delicious."

The smile on Chloe's face was radiant. "It's not my best. There are a few lumps because someone interrupted my process."

"The lumps were made with love, which just makes it better."

Chloe covered her mouth as she laughed, trying to hold in the bite she'd just taken. "I'll remember that the next time you complain about them."

Shay batted her eyes and let her mouth fall open. "Me? Complain about something so delightfully delicious?" She shook her head. "Never."

The tip of Chloe's fork glistened as she pointed it toward her. "I'll be sure to remind you of that remark in the future."

The future. Chloe was talking about their future. Maybe life would go on after all. Shay couldn't contain her smile as she ate. She couldn't imagine any other place she'd rather be than right here with Chloe, and it seemed she felt the same way too.

After dinner, they cuddled up on the couch to watch a movie, a romantic comedy, Chloe's choice. The mushroom risotto had tasted just as wonderful as she'd remembered. The wine that had accompanied it had made her sleepy. Preventing her eyes from fluttering shut was impossible.

❖

"Baby." Chloe's voice resonated in her head. "You're going to be late if you don't get up now."

Light blinded her as she tried to open her eyes. "I don't want to go to class."

Chloe chuckled. "Not class, silly. Work."

"Can't I stay home today?" She found Chloe's hand lying on her stomach and laced their fingers together.

"You can, if you want, but I have to go to the gallery today," Chloe said softly.

"Well, that's no fun." She snuggled in tighter and breathed in the citrusy scent of orange and spice she'd come to adore. "I'm sorry. I fell asleep last night." She should've never moved to the couch. She'd been so tired, she'd fallen asleep after the first scene.

"It's okay. We have plenty of nights ahead of us." Chloe kissed her on the head.

Did she really mean that? She twisted to look into her eyes and saw her eyes twinkle. Yes, she did.

Shay hadn't told Chloe about knowing what she'd done with Lila as Rachel had suggested. It was the wrong thing to do, but she wanted to remain in this new bubble of euphoria as long as she could. It was only wishful thinking to hope her indiscretion would be lost in her memory forever.

CHAPTER TWENTY-SIX

For some reason, Chloe was nervous as she waited for Whitney. She'd asked her to come to the gallery for lunch and to pick something up on the way, as usual. She didn't know how she was going to tell her the news. Whitney had urged her to reconcile her feelings for Shay and move forward. At the time, she wasn't quite sure she could manage it, but she'd done just that. She'd forgiven her completely and let her back into her heart. She looked up when she heard the chime on the door, her heart racing when Whitney entered, hands full of food.

"Wow. Did you buy everything on the menu?"

"Possibly," she said with a slight lilt. "The baby is hungry." She set the bags of food on the table in the back of the gallery.

"How's the little bambino doing?" she asked as she touched Whitney's stomach.

"The little bambino is eating like the Hulk."

"Well, hopefully he or she won't come out with that nasty green hue to their skin."

After the food was all unpacked and they'd each sat on a stool at the high-top table in the corner, Whitney took the first bite of her pasta and stared at Chloe. "What's the emergency?"

"No emergency. Is it a crime to want to have lunch with my best friend?"

Whitney gave her a sideways smile as she swirled another forkful of spaghetti. "Not that I mind an impromptu lunch, but you're fairly predictable." She put the pasta into her mouth and chewed. "A lunch invitation the morning of usually indicates you need to talk something out."

She rolled her eyes. "I guess I'll have to plan better next time."

"No need. I'm here whenever you need me." She touched her belly. "You may have to start coming to me, though."

"I can do that."

"What's up?"

"I slept with Shay."

Whitney choked on her pasta and reached for her drink. "Jesus. Warn me when you're going to tell me something like that." She wiped her lips with a napkin. "Was it good?" She took another drink. "I mean, how do you feel about that? How does she feel about it? I need all the details."

Chloe chuckled. "I love that you don't hold back." She took a breath and thought about the other night. "It was absolutely wonderful." Her face filled with heat, and suddenly she was smitten all over again. "God, I must have been blind. I think I've fallen harder for her than the first time."

Whitney held her fork in front of her mouth and smiled. "You have. I can see it in your face every time you talk about her." She took another sip of her drink. "You were reluctant when we talked last. What changed your mind?"

"Shay's different now. Better somehow."

"Paying more attention to you?"

She nodded. "Like she used to, and she's so much more relaxed."

"Makes sense since she doesn't remember all the stress of buying the beach house and opening the gallery." Whitney raised her drink in the air. "It's like fate has given you a do-over."

"Seems so." She lifted her own drink and touched it to Whitney's.

Whitney sucked a gulp through the straw. "By the way, don't plan on taking your cat back anytime soon. Jackson has gotten pretty attached to her. This father thing is really kicking in, and Ginger's loving it. Besides, it's good practice for him."

"That's fine. Shay doesn't remember her. We got her during the blank period. Thanks for taking her in. I've just been so busy lately, I wouldn't have been able to take care of her."

"Busy exploring your wife's body, I hope."

"That's new, but yes. I've also been prepping for a show in St. Augustine this coming weekend."

"Is Shay going with you?"

Chloe shook her head. "I haven't told her about it yet."

"Why not?" Whitney spun another wad of pasta on her fork and ate it.

"Before things evolved between us, I was planning to go alone."

"I think it would be good for the two of you to get away for a weekend together. You can stay at your mom and dad's getaway place in town."

"I guess I should." A weekend away from everyone with just the two of them sounded incredible.

"Damn right you should." Whitney took a bite of bread. "I'd kill for a romantic weekend away right now."

"What's stopping you?" Chloe asked.

"We're trying to get the nursery ready." Whitney widened her eyes. "Who knew there were so many shades of yellow and green."

"You're sticking with not finding out the sex?"

"Absolutely." She tilted her head. "Well, maybe. I want to know, but Jackson's staying firm."

"Does he go to every appointment with you?"

"Pretty much."

"You can always make a phone call."

"Believe me, I've thought about it more than once since I had the ultrasound."

"Lavender's a good color. You can accent with violet."

Whitney raised her eyebrows as though she hadn't considered that choice. "I do like purple."

"I'll be happy to help you paint."

"Nope." She picked up their plates and took them to the trash can. "You'll be too busy doing other things with your wife this weekend."

The thought made her warm. Being that close to Shay again had been wonderful. From that moment forward, Chloe knew she would want her every day. Whether her heart was ready for that, she didn't know. Shay's intentions seemed to be pure, and considering she didn't remember that they had separated, Chloe had to believe they were.

As soon as Whitney left the gallery, Chloe flipped the sign to Closed and got in the car. She couldn't wait to share her idea of a romantic weekend with Shay.

"Hey…" Shay drew the word out slowly when she answered the

phone. "I was just thinking about you." The smile in Shay's voice rang through the line.

"I bet you say that to all the girls." She hadn't thought about what she'd said until the words were out of her mouth.

Shay rebounded quickly. "Nope. Just the love of my life."

"I'm in the parking lot. Can you come down?"

"Be right there." The excitement in Shay's voice was unmistakable, and it made her smile.

She'd gotten out of her Tahoe and was leaning against the hood when Shay came out the door and rushed to her. The huge smile on her face was beautiful, and Chloe couldn't contain the thrill that filled her. Suddenly she'd been swept into Shay's arms and was being fully kissed. There was no warning, no preamble, just a full-on take-me-now kiss, and it felt wonderful.

When they parted, she caught movement in her peripheral vision. She glanced over to see Lila standing between the parking lot and the door staring. Shay seemed to notice her too but didn't pay her any attention. She refocused on Chloe, touched her bottom lip with her thumb. "Sorry. I've been thinking about doing that since I left this morning."

"It felt *exactly* like that."

They both laughed before Shay kissed her again, longer, deeper this time. When she came out of the blissful haze Shay had so easily taken her to, Lila was hurrying into the building.

"I know you just went back to work, but do you think you can take Friday off?"

"Let me check." Shay took her phone from her pocket and checked her calendar. "I think I can arrange that."

"Great. Then let's do it. Better yet, why don't we take the weekend away from everything? I have a show in St. Augustine this coming weekend. We can go early and have some alone time." She raised her eyebrows, waiting for Shay to respond.

Shay blinked a couple of times and then smiled. "Just the two of us? Really?" She nodded. "I'd love that."

"Sounds like a plan." She welcomed the blissful peace she felt. It was wonderful to be in love again.

❖

They'd gotten on the road later than planned. Chloe had woken up early to pack the Tahoe with all the paintings she had at the house, but they'd had to stop by the gallery to pick up a few more. The gallery owner had been very specific about the pieces she'd wanted Chloe to display, which included a few already on display at the gallery in town.

The three-plus hour drive to St. Augustine had been filled with laughter and carpool karaoke. Chloe had to admit that Shay took home the prize for that one. You'd never know it, but she was always into the newest music, whereas Chloe could barely remember every other word in the chorus. She already owed Shay another home-cooked meal, a back scratch, and whatever that led to, which she was actually excited about.

By the time they'd delivered the paintings to the gallery in St. Augustine and had made it to the house, she was worn out. Shay had let her off the hook for cooking, and they'd ordered Chinese to eat in. She'd make good on the bet when they got back home to the beach house. She didn't have any excuses. She'd lost fair and square and would deliver on her promise.

She was so full of noodles she could barely move when Shay started the music on her phone and pulled her to the middle of the room. The Bluetooth speaker they'd brought along was small, but mighty. "Let's dance like we used to." Shay must have sensed her reluctance because she did some weird, crazy moves.

Chloe shook her head and laughed. "God, that's horrible. No self-respecting woman would set foot on the dance floor with you."

Shay raised her eyebrows and danced around her in a slow, fluid motion. "Is this better?"

Chloe tilted her head and squinted. "A little bit."

Shay's mouth dropped open, and her hands went to her hips. "You're tough." She toed off her sandals and moved across the room with a sensuous grace that lit each of Chloe's senses. Her black, skinny jeans wrapped her legs perfectly, and the yellow tank top she wore clung to her like a woman with desire. Each movement was filled with purposeful clarity, a sort of seductive certainty she'd never seen in Shay before.

Shay danced closer, near enough for Chloe to feel her breath on her cheek as she whispered, "How about this?"

She nodded as Shay danced in place in front of her. "Much better."

"Then what are you waiting for?" Shay held her hands up in front of her and wiggled her fingers, silently begging her to join in.

God, Shay was sexy, she thought as she slid into place across from her, matching her rhythm. She'd never forgotten just how attractive she was, but it had been so long since they'd danced together like this. The only thing stopping her from taking her into the bedroom right now was her fear of discovery, the terror of opening the vault to her emotions and letting them spill out into the unprotected jungle between them. The gashes had healed, and she wanted to let go so much, but the fear was still there, tamping down her emotions. She had to let go, or this would never work between them.

A slow tune came through the speakers, and Chloe picked up her phone to change it. Shay took the phone from her hand and set it back on the counter. "Just leave it. We can dance to this. Right?" Shay took her into her arms.

She nodded. "We can." She could feel Shay's heart beating against her chest. It made her own heart race. This was a dangerous position to be in—right here in Shay's arms with every part of their bodies touching. All her erogenous zones came alive.

The evening crackled with possibility as Chloe's feelings came back full force. Thoughts of being pressed up against the door into a passion-filled kiss that blossomed into so much more shot through her head. She didn't push them away. This was the Shay she'd been captivated by so many years ago, only different. The old Shay seemed to mingle with the new, and she'd somehow fallen in love with both of them, yet so much deeper this time.

Soon Shay's lips were on hers, her tongue doing magical things in Chloe's mouth that were creating incredibly erotic sensations in the rest of her. They somehow made it to the couch. Air whooshed out of Chloe's lungs as she fell backward onto it. Shay followed immediately, straddling her—hands in her hair, mouth on her neck. Where had this strong, bold Shay come from? Chloe had no idea, but she wanted more of her. She reached around, grabbed her ass, and tugged her closer as she reveled in the sensation of Shay's tongue bathing her neck, her fingers curling under her shirt collar, drawing it back, and starting on her shoulder. She let her hands glide up Shay's back under her tank top, felt the warm, soft skin beneath it and moaned. This wouldn't do. The shirt had to come off. Cool air chilled Chloe's neck when Shay's mouth abandoned her to raise her arms in the air, letting her slide the shirt over her head. The motion quickly reversed when Shay grasped the edges of Chloe's shirt and slid it off as well.

Chloe took in the glorious body in front of her, dressed only in black skinny jeans and a black bra with the soft, white flesh of her breasts brimming over the top. Her hands went to the clasp, and in a split second, Shay's breasts were spilling out into her hands and then into her mouth. Shay pressed against her and tugged on her hair as Chloe flicked the nipple with her tongue. The taste of Shay's skin was exquisite, a sweetness she'd missed. Suddenly Shay was off her lap, standing in front of her and shoving her jeans to the floor. Chloe leaned forward and stopped her when she started on her panties, gazing up into her eyes as she drew them down her legs. The desire was clear, and Chloe was sure her eyes conveyed the same. It was all she could do to stay in place as Shay's nakedness blanketed her again.

Shay moaned as Chloe slid a finger between her folds, felt the glorious hot wetness, twirled her finger in it. Soon Chloe's fingers were deep inside as Shay moved up and down, her breasts pressed into Chloe's face. Within minutes, she began to quiver, let out a cry, and Chloe embraced her as the orgasm ripped through her. Her rhythm slowed, and Shay collapsed against her. She sat, fingers still inside with Shay draped across her as her walls clenched around them, tiny spasms gripping them sporadically. She would've stayed holding her like that for hours if she could, but when Shay stood up and held out her hand, she let her lead her to the bedroom.

After they reached the bed, Shay turned her around and unfastened the clasp of her bra. A jolt of electricity shot through her when Shay's lips pressed ever so slightly against her back, and she felt the heat of her breath trail downward as she slid the skirt from Chloe's waist. Light touches from Shay's fingertips taunted her, willing her to press into her. When she did, the pure erotic feel of Shay's breasts against her back toppled all her willpower, and she moaned. She felt Shay's breath hitch, and then she spun her around and said, "You are so beautiful." Chloe took her face in her hands and kissed her, fought for control as their tongues danced together perfectly. Soon her arms were wrapped around her, tugging her closer, making each part of their lengths touch.

The whole thing was surreal. A month ago, Chloe hadn't thought she'd ever be this close to her again, and at this moment it was all she wanted. When they fell onto the bed, Shay took control again, and Chloe let her. Every inch of her needed to be touched, sucked, taken. Shay didn't waste any time doing just that. She moved between Chloe's legs, spread them, and let out another moan as she pressed her mouth against the heat waiting for her. She knew exactly what to do, where to touch her, and suddenly without warning the orgasm took her, and a rush of pleasure shot through her.

Shay's name flew from her lips, and she whimpered. With that, Shay grabbed her ass tighter, crushed her mouth against her as she hit the top and came back down again. She lay there still feeling the beats of her body as each aftershock went through her. Every muscle felt like jelly. Shay crawled up beside her, kissed her lightly, and laid her head on her chest. Any awkwardness left between them was completely gone.

Chloe was greedy, wanted so much more of the treasure she'd rediscovered in Shay, but she was spent. The warmth of Shay against her soothed her, and soon she couldn't keep her eyes from closing.

❖

The show had gone well, and Chloe had sold several pieces. Shay had left for the restaurant a couple of doors down to order food to take home. Chloe was shocked to see Erica walk through the door. The gallery was almost empty, but the owner and a few of her friends were still milling about in the back.

She rushed to the door to intercept her, glancing out the front window to see if Shay was anywhere in sight. She wasn't. "Erica, I didn't expect to see you here." She said it politely, as though she were only a customer.

Erica dropped her purse on the table by the sign-in book. "It would've been nice if you'd told me personally, rather than just sending me a postcard."

Fuck. She'd forgotten to remove her from the mailing list. She glanced out the window again.

"Shay's here with you, isn't she?" Erica's voice seethed with jealousy.

She nodded. "She's gone to get dinner. You need to leave."

Erica raised her eyebrows. "So, you don't have any love left in your heart for me?" The mix of anger and hurt on Erica's face was hard to stomach. She had to come clean with her now.

"It was almost love, Erica. But we never quite got there." The weight in her chest lifted. She'd finally done what she'd been trying to do for weeks. She glanced at her watch and then out the window again. She hoped Shay had to wait at the restaurant.

Erica moved into her line of sight, forcing her to look at her. "It could be."

She shook her head. "No. It will never be the same kind of love I have with Shay." She'd never have that again with anyone else. Definitely not with Erica.

"Have?" Erica moved closer into her space. "So, you've forgotten everything she's done to you?"

Chloe closed her eyes and took a breath as the reminder brought the pain back. She hadn't found a way to block it completely. *Forgotten, no. Forgiven, yes.*

"You're not even giving me a chance." The hurt in Erica's voice had morphed into anger.

"You're right. I don't know why you've stayed around this long." She had to let Erica go. Chloe knew that feeling all too well. She was never going to get over Shay, at least not in the near future. Miraculously, she'd been given one last chance to make it work, and she wasn't going to screw it up by letting Erica come between them. "I can't see you anymore, Erica." She shook her head. "I need to stay with Shay until she's fully recovered. She needs me." Making it work with Shay was the best thing for her. It hadn't been easy to admit, but she needed her too.

"That's where I think you're wrong. You don't *have* to stay. You *want* to stay."

"Maybe so." It was true, but telling Erica that would only make things worse.

Erica's lips thinned as her eyes narrowed momentarily, and Chloe thought she was going to blast her, put on a spectacle for everyone left in the gallery to see. Her smile returned as quickly as it had disappeared, and Chloe was confused.

"You think you can just let go that easily? Just ignore me like we never had anything?"

"Listen, Erica. I'm sorry if you're hurt, but we both knew this wasn't permanent. You're already dating someone new."

"Barb and I are just friends."

"We both know that's not the case." She raked her fingers through her hair. "You love many women, and I don't fault you for that. But I can only love one."

Erica picked up her purse from the table and slung it over her arm. "You'll regret this when she's done with you," she said as she spun and reached for the door. She left without looking back.

"I'm sure I will." The door closed, and she went to it and turned the deadbolt. "One way or another, I'm sure I will." She rested her head against the door pane. It would be a miracle if Shay never found out about her relationship with Erica. When she did, her last chance might be gone.

The rap on the glass startled her. She backed up to see Shay standing outside with their food. She unlocked the door, let her in, and held up a finger. "Let me get my bag and we can go."

"Was that Erica I just saw leave?"

"Yes. She's in town with her girlfriend for the weekend. Barb has family here."

"Barb wasn't with her?"

"No. I didn't see her."

"Maybe we should get together with them tomorrow for brunch."

"No." She kissed her on the lips. "I'm not sharing our time this weekend with anyone." Not in a million years. What a miserable time that would be.

She'd have to tell Shay about the extent of her connection with Erica someday, but not this week or even this month. The thought lurked in the back of her mind that Erica might tell her before she had the courage to, but that was a chance she was willing to take right now. She wasn't willing to risk returning to the way things were before the accident. If she came clean and Shay remembered, she might revert to being the Shay she'd drifted away from in the first place, and their relationship could change again.

CHAPTER TWENTY-SEVEN

The following week, the call Shay had received from Erica hadn't been unexpected. She'd seen her rush out of the gallery in St. Augustine Saturday night. She'd seemed upset, and Chloe had been as well. When she'd peered through the window and seen her with her head pressed against the door, she wasn't sure exactly what had happened. When they'd arrived back at their weekend place, Chloe had seemed fine, more relaxed than she'd been all day, and they'd made love again. Desire rushed through her just thinking about the warmth of Chloe's hands skimming across her thighs, her mouth between her legs. The night had been pure bliss.

She hadn't wanted to spoil it, so she hadn't pressed her about Erica. She'd hoped Erica was out of the equation for good, but that didn't seem to be the case. Erica wanted to meet Shay for lunch. She'd said Chloe had told her that she was doing the books for the gallery now and had used the excuse of getting receipts for Chloe's works she'd previously purchased. Shay knew that was bullshit, but she'd printed them off and folded them all neatly into an envelope for her.

The restaurant wasn't far from where Shay worked, so she'd arrived early and asked for a booth toward the back of the restaurant. The lunch was definitely not about receipts because a stamp and any US Post Office would've sufficed if that had been Erica's only concern. Even so, she had them out on the table in front of her as she waited for Erica to arrive.

"Thank you so much for meeting me," Erica said with a smile as she slid into the booth across from her. She was nothing if not cordial.

"Sure. All the receipts you asked for are right here." Shay pushed the envelope across the table. "Is there anything else I can do for you?"

It was a loaded question, but if Erica had something to say, she wanted it out in the open now when Chloe wasn't around.

"Why don't you stay and have lunch?" Erica asked as she picked up the menu in front of her from the table and focused on it. "I hear the chicken salad is delicious, as is the vegetable soup."

Neither one of those sounded appetizing. Shay opened her menu, perused the items, and opted for a quick bowl of conch chowder. She wanted Erica to get to her point, so she could get the hell out of there.

After they ordered, Erica continued with small talk until the food arrived. Shay had no interest in passing time discussing Chloe's art, the weather, or anything else with Erica.

"I know you're interested in my wife, Erica. Why don't you just tell me what you want?" Shay asked, taking the direct approach, since Erica was having trouble addressing the subject.

"It may not be my place." Erica hesitated like she might actually have a conscience, but Shay knew better.

"I'm sure it's not, but you're going to tell me anyway, so just get to it."

Erica looked up from the chicken-salad sandwich in her hands. "I just don't think it's fair to her or you for Chloe to keep things from you now that you've recovered from the accident."

"Just what exactly is Chloe keeping from me?" She spooned a bite of chowder into her mouth. It was pretty good. She'd have to remember this place in the future. She glanced up at Erica, who had now abandoned her sandwich and was staring at her. Maybe not.

"During the time period you don't remember, you and Chloe had separated. She and I have been seeing each other."

Shay dropped her spoon into her chowder, trying to make her reaction look good. "I don't believe you. We're ridiculously happy. Chloe doesn't have any reason to look anywhere else for attention."

"She didn't. You were fucking a colleague at work, and she caught you doing it in your office." Erica's callousness triggered something. The memory crashed into Shay's mind, and the devastated look she had seen then in Chloe's eyes almost crippled her. "You broke her heart, and I put it back together again." Erica stared at her, obviously waiting for some sort of reaction, but the memory had horrified her, and she couldn't talk. "You already know this, don't you?" The anger in her voice rose. "You remembered and haven't told her."

"No." She wiped the tears from her cheeks. "I didn't remember until just now."

"You deceptive little liar. You're keeping her under false pretenses."

"And you think you know what's best for her? That's absolutely ridiculous. You don't know her at all."

"Well, we'll just see what she thinks about you knowing all this time." She dropped a couple of twenties onto the table and got up.

Shay bolted from her seat and grabbed Erica's arm. "Please, Erica. I swear, I didn't remember." Her world was crashing down around her—again.

Erica wrenched it away. "I don't care." She spun around and left the restaurant. Erica had decided Chloe needed to know, and Shay couldn't stop her. She had no idea how to head off this disaster. Life as she knew it with Chloe would be destroyed in a matter of minutes. Not only had she had the affair, but now she'd kept her discovery of it from Chloe.

❖

Shay hadn't gone back to work. She couldn't. The thought of sitting in the office where she'd betrayed Chloe was too much. She found herself at the hospital waiting in Rachel's office as she finished with her last patient for the day. When Rachel had seen her distraught expression, she had stopped working with the young boy she was coaching up and down the practice steps in the corner of the room and told her to go into the office, that she'd be there in a few minutes.

As soon as Rachel finished with the boy and had successfully handed him off to his mother, she rushed back into the office. "What happened?"

Shay pressed her fingers to her forehead and then whipped her gaze to Rachel. "I remember it."

"The affair?"

She shook her head. "Not everything, but the whole fucking messy scene when Chloe caught me with Lila." The bits of memory were starting to come together, and she hated herself more as each piece of the puzzle became clearer.

"Were you at work? Was Lila there?" Rachel seemed to be trying to understand.

"I wasn't at the office, thank God. I had lunch with Erica. She made up some bullshit story about needing receipts. I shouldn't have gone."

"Erica told you...Oh my God. I wonder if she's told Chloe."

"Yeah. She thought I didn't know and took it upon herself to clue me in. As she was telling me, the whole thing came crashing back in vivid color."

"Okay. Okay." Rachel dropped into the chair next to her. "Just calm down. Have you talked to anyone about it besides me?"

"God, no. I can't tell anyone else that. I don't even want to think about it." She rubbed her face. "I don't know if I can go back to what we were after actually feeling what I did." She bolted from the chair and paced the room. "Before, it was like a story I'd written about myself. It wasn't actually real. Now I *know* I cheated on Chloe, felt how my stomach dropped when I saw the devastation in her face. She trusted me with everything, and I fucked it up. How stupid could I have been?"

"Was it really that bad?" The pity on Rachel's face hit her square in the chest.

She sank into the chair. "It was horrible, Rach. I feel like I'm about to throw up. What am I going to do?"

"You're going to do exactly as you have been. Chloe still loves you." She crouched on the floor in front of her. "You can't let that go. Not now after all you've both been through together."

"She'll hate me after she finds out I knew about what I've done."

"Maybe. Maybe not. Don't you think you should let her decide that?"

She nodded. Rachel was right. Nothing she could do now would change how Chloe felt if she found out. She'd just have to wait and be prepared for the other shoe to drop.

❖

Shay stopped by the apartment before going home to the beach house. She had no recollection of any feelings for Lila, only that they'd had sex. If Lila had any feelings for her, she hadn't made them known.

The only way to find out if Lila was going to become a threat to her relationship with Chloe was to read more of her journals. Most people would've read every one of them by now, but Shay hadn't been able to bring herself to face all the sordid details of the last year of her life just yet. At least she'd been smart enough to keep the ones dated after she'd started whatever it was she had with Lila at the apartment, where Chloe wouldn't find them. She went into the closet, found the journal preceding the time when Chloe had found her and Lila together, and thumbed through the pages. She stopped on a page that made her wonder.

Is it love?

Lila sent me another steamy text today, and I fell back into it again. The banter is just so easy, and it feels so good to be wanted. She makes me feel beautiful and sexy. I hate myself for needing that, and it makes me wonder about my future with Chloe. Am I in love with Lila— no. Does she make me feel wanted—yes. Chloe used to make me feel wanted, and that was all I ever needed. What did I do to change that? Can I change it back? She's been so preoccupied with the gallery lately that we aren't communicating much at all—and we're rarely spending any time together. We had sex a week ago, maybe two. I can't remember exactly when. It was good, as always, but not spectacular like it used to be. The emotional intimacy we shared isn't there anymore. God, I miss her and how we used to be together. I wonder if she does too.

Chapter Twenty-Eight

Rachel was working with a patient when Chloe entered the physical-therapy room. She should have phoned first, but she hadn't wanted Rachel to tell Shay she was coming. The visit wasn't so much to deliver a warning but to notify Rachel that she and Shay were together now, and she'd decided not to hold what Shay couldn't remember against her. Even though Chloe hadn't become involved with Erica until after she'd discovered Shay with Lila, she'd come to realize that she hadn't been entirely innocent.

When Rachel glanced her way, she drew her brows together and held up a finger. Chloe nodded and continued into her office, where she'd waited on occasion during Shay's therapy sessions before. As soon as she closed the door, her cell phone rang. She took it out of her purse and looked at the screen, intending not to answer if it was Shay. It was the art-supply store. She'd called earlier in the day and asked for pricing on some special-order items.

"Hi, Jan. I wasn't expecting you to get back to me so soon."

"I had some free time, so I went ahead and got all the prices you were needing. Do you have a pen and paper handy?"

"Hang on." Chloe scanned Rachel's desk and didn't find any, so she rounded the desk and pulled open the top drawer. She froze and stopped listening, unable to comprehend what was staring back at her from the drawer. It wasn't unfamiliar. She'd read quite a few of them over the past few months. Even though the woman was still chirping into her ear, Chloe hadn't understood a word of what she'd said, and the room had become eerily silent. "I'll have to call you back." Not waiting for a response, she touched the red button and dropped her phone to the desk. She took the journal from the drawer and sank into the chair as she opened the cover, read the date inside, and thumbed quickly to the page she knew it contained.

The office door flew open and clanged against the doorstop. She looked up, blinked, and refocused on Rachel. "Why do you have this? Where did you get it?" So many questions flew through her mind.

Rachel's face dropped like she was a fly caught in a spider's web.

Still not quite understanding how the journal came to be in Rachel's possession, she tilted her head. "Did Shay give this to you?" The realization hit her. "She knows what happened." It wasn't a question.

"Yes." Rachel rolled her lips in. "She knows. She read the journal, but she still doesn't remember it happening."

She narrowed her eyes as she got up from the chair, then shoved it back into place under the desk. "How long?"

"Honestly. I swear, she doesn't remember the event at all." Rachel was pleading with her now.

"How. Long?" She tried to hold an even tone.

"A month, maybe more." Rachel rounded the desk. "Listen, Chloe. I was with her when she read it. She was absolutely crushed."

"*She* was crushed?" Her voice wavered as a tsunami of emotions stirred in the depths of her soul. She sank against the wall. "How the fuck do you think I felt?" When the whole mess had happened, she'd become physically ill. Each time she'd thought of it since had been no different. And now the gut-wrenching feeling hit her all over again. She became dizzy and sucked in a deep breath. She'd thought she was over it, but clearly, she wasn't. The gashes had just begun to heal, her inner demons had moved on, and all the ugliness had disappeared. Now it had all come crashing back in one single moment. Rachel came closer and reached for her, but she pushed her away.

"Didn't you think she would be curious? You didn't want to touch her. It only makes sense that she'd go looking for her life in what she'd written."

"This is what you wanted all along."

"Honestly, I would've stepped up immediately if you hadn't stayed." She shook her head and leaned back against the desk. "But she doesn't want anyone but you. I would never ruin her happiness."

She held up the journal. "You just did." It wasn't Rachel's fault, but she didn't have anyone else to blame but herself right now. That self-destruction would come later.

❖

By the time Chloe had made it back to her car, she had five missed calls from Shay and more than double the number of texts. The phone calls from Shay had begun within five minutes of her leaving Rachel's office, and the texts had been commingled between them. It was clear that Rachel was no longer working against her. She glanced at the first few texts, all impassioned apologies along with pleas to talk to her, and then called Jackson.

Chloe hadn't responded to Shay yet. She couldn't. Her frame of mind was so unstable at this moment that every bit of anger she'd kept packed away inside was ready to spew out in a horrible backlash. She had too many things to say, to understand, to discover before she could respond. Anything she said right now would mushroom into a huge pile of regret. She needed the voice of reason. She needed Jackson.

When she'd called him, he'd immediately dropped what he was doing and agreed to meet her at her apartment. Now she glanced around the living room as she sat on the couch waiting for him. The furniture they'd left was still there, her paintings were on the wall, same as before, and not one picture of the two of them together was out of place. Shay hadn't changed a thing since Chloe had moved all her things out. She remembered her earnest pleas before the move, her apologies, her promises to make everything right again. She'd done all that over the past few months after the accident, but under false pretenses.

The knock on the door brought her out of her thoughts. She pushed off the couch, crossed the room, and opened the door.

"What the hell happened?"

Not wanting to go into the whole ordeal on the phone, she'd kept the conversation short. She held up the journal. "I found this in Rachel's office."

"Rachel?"

"Shay's physical therapist. You know, the flirty one?"

"Ooh, that's not good."

"I couldn't care less if she read it, Jackson. She got it from Shay."

"Oh, no." The words whooshed out of his mouth in a whisper as what she was saying dawned on him. "She knows what happened."

The journal's pages flapped in the air as she tossed it across the room, and it crashed to the floor like a warped Frisbee. "I'm just so mad at myself, Jackson. I did this once before, and now I'm right back where I started."

"It doesn't have to have the same resolution, you know."

"She lied to me. Again."

"Technically, she didn't lie. She just didn't disclose something." He crossed the room and picked up the journal.

"Something pretty fucking important not to disclose, don't you think?" She paced the living room. "It's bookmarked. Go ahead. Read it." She wanted him to know how it had happened, how she'd found out, how devastated she'd been.

"Hmm." He turned the page, continued reading. "Looks to me like she regretted what she'd done."

"That's the only thing that helped me let it go in the first place." She swiped a tear from her cheek. Being this weak made her hate herself so much more. "Now she's lied to me again."

He read a few more pages and then dropped the journal to the coffee table. "If the situation were reversed, wouldn't *you* have lied to get her back?"

"Damn it, Jackson. Stop trying to make this better." She flopped onto the couch. "I need to be pissed right now."

"Okay." He sat next to her. "Everything she did was wrong, from the very beginning. I get that." He put his hand on her knee and squeezed. "And even after everything that's happened, you still want her back, don't you?"

She nodded. She did. She wanted her so much she couldn't stand herself. "It's ridiculous, but I do. I just can't trust her after this."

"Can't you?" Jackson tilted his head. "Technically, she didn't remember. She just found out by reading her journal. Considering her state of mind, I'm sure that was a huge shock to her, probably the reason she's done everything in her power to make you fall in love with her again."

"Well, she succeeded." She raked her teeth across her bottom lip.

"And you were blissfully happy again, weren't you?"

She closed her eyes and let out a heavy sigh. "I was. Damn it, Jackson. Enough is enough." She vaulted off the couch and threw up her hands. "How do I forget this?"

"The heart wants what it wants, and there's no turning back," he said as he stared up at her. "Why don't you stay with us for a few days while you sort this out?" He stood up next to her. "We could use some help finishing the nursery. You know how horrible I am at decorating."

She laughed at the blatant attempt to gain a compliment. Jackson could walk into a room and make it more pleasing in ten minutes by just rearranging the furniture. "I need you to run interference for me, okay?"

"On it." He took his phone from his pocket and typed in a text to Shay. *Chloe is staying with us for a few days.*

The reply from Shay came immediately: *Understood. Please tell her how sorry I am for everything.*

He typed back, *Will do.*

He showed her the screen before he slid his phone back into his pocket and pulled her into a hug. "Now let's work on getting you back to that blissfully happy spot you were in yesterday."

She wasn't sure if that was even possible, but what Jackson said had made sense. How could she punish Shay for doing something she clearly would've done herself?

CHAPTER TWENTY-NINE

S hay sat in Rachel's office while she finished up her last patient for the day. She shouldn't have left the journal here, but she never thought Chloe would have any reason to be here and discover it.

Rachel came into the office and snapped her out of her thoughts. She reached into the mini-fridge and took out a couple bottles of water, but Shay waved her off, and she put one back before she sat in the chair behind the desk. She took a big gulp of water before she leaned forward on her elbows.

"I really am sorry," Rachel said. She'd told her how Chloe had found the journal when they'd spoken on the phone earlier. Shay didn't fault her for that. "She still not responding?"

Shay shook her head. "She told me the product of the equation would never change, and it has." That was something she and Chloe had always laughed about after they'd gotten together because Shay was so analytical. She had to work out everything logically.

"That's not her fault."

"I know whose fault it is, but it doesn't change the outcome. Maybe I should just give up."

"Oh my God, Shay. You have so many possibilities not to be alone here—take one."

"I don't want to be alone. I don't want to be who I was without her again. I like the person I am now. She's made these permanent changes in me, and I can't go back to who I was before—alone and closed off." She shot up and paced the room. "If I'd known it was going to be our last time together, I would've paid more attention. I should've paid more attention all along."

"What is wrong with you? Where's that determined woman who

sat in front of me just a few weeks ago telling me how in love she was with her wife?"

"I don't know what to do. Everything I ever wanted was right in front of me, and now I might not have it anymore."

"So, you're just gonna walk away?" Rachel had a valid question. "I recall you saying that she's the one who makes your heart feel one hundred times its size. The one who motivates you to be successful. Has that changed?"

Shay broke eye contact and looked out the window. "No. That hasn't changed. But when is it too much?" She honestly didn't know what would be best for both of them at this point.

"It's your choice, but I don't recommend leaving it like this." Rachel swiped the bottle of water from the desk and took a sip as she relaxed into her chair. "You'll always love her, and you'll be useless to anyone else because of that. I wouldn't touch you right now, even if you upped your wooing game a thousandfold and threw yourself at me."

"Jesus, Rach. Don't hold back on account of my feelings."

Rachel raised an eyebrow. "I won't because you're being stupid. You're assuming she's done with you."

"What should I do?"

"Wait her out. Give her some time and space. Let her make up her mind about what *she* wants. Then crawl back if you have to." Rachel stood and took her purse from the drawer. "Now let's get out of here. We can pick up some dinner and go to my place. There's another scary-movie marathon on TV tonight."

Shay had thought she'd lost Chloe a few months ago before the accident happened, and now she was sure she had. She'd wanted so badly to tell Chloe the truth about what she'd read but hadn't wanted to push her further away. When she'd gotten the second chance, she'd wanted it with all her heart. She'd needed it. She couldn't ignore a miracle like that. Now it all seemed out of reach again.

It would be difficult to take Rachel's advice. Shay wasn't good at waiting. She liked to take action, which wasn't always the best tactic. But she would wait, let Chloe have the time and space she needed. If they came out of this okay, if she remembered everything that had happened between them, including the bad things, Shay swore she would spend every day making it up to Chloe. If she would let her.

❖

Shay walked through the door of their beach house and set her keys on the counter. She'd sat with Rachel while she ate but left soon after. Staying at her place would only make the situation worse. She scanned the room, looking at the decorations Chloe had so painstakingly picked out and placed perfectly. Her life was so pathetically bare before Chloe came into it. There had been days when she'd told herself that someone, somewhere was having a worse day than she was—but not today. She felt like she was stuck in a fucking permanent Monday. She lived her perfect life with Chloe at night when she slept, and then she'd wake up to this nightmare of a life without her.

She couldn't deny that it was all her fault. She'd screwed everything up not once, but twice by not talking to Chloe. She'd been raised in a family good at concealing their true feelings until someone crossed the line. Living in that kind of environment, she'd never known what anyone was thinking or what might set them off. She'd thought she'd finally broken free of that pattern when she'd met Chloe. Apparently not completely.

When Chloe had come into her life she seemed like wildflowers in the field—a little patch of pretty surrounded by weeds. Now she'd mowed them under and didn't know if they'd ever grow again. Shay went into the bedroom, took out her latest journal, and began to write.

Chloe is a woman with a soul so beautiful anyone would be blessed to capture her. I truly believe I was blessed. The thought that I could be so loved, cherished, desired by her was a miracle. We have a love so strong my body aches when she's in anguish. How could I be so cruel? I'm crushed at this moment, not knowing what to do, how to fix this amazing phenomenon I have destroyed. Twice.

CHAPTER THIRTY

Chloe had taken all that was remaining of Shay's journals with her when she'd left the apartment. The stack seemed to be larger than it had been before, but after a couple of days, she finally found the courage to read them. She sat on the couch staring at the neatly stacked pile in front of her on the coffee table. She took the journal from the top, opened it, and read the final entry.

I fucked up in the most colossal way. All my assumptions were wrong about Chloe and Erica. What she has with Erica is innocent, purely business. I was the only one looking for comfort in the wrong place. I have no idea how to fix this, but I have to try again. I have to talk to her one more time, get down on my knees and beg her to forgive me if that's what she needs. All I can do is hope she will...forgive me.

The words Shay had written hit her square in the chest. Shay knew she'd made a mistake. Now she understood why Shay had shown up at the beach house the day of the accident. She replayed it all in her head—the apology, the pleas for forgiveness, and the hurt look in her eyes when Erica had entered the room, proving her right, even though she hadn't been before. She searched the binding for an earlier date and yanked it out of the pile.

The beach house will be such a surprise—my biggest surprise for Chloe yet. It's going to be a struggle but will be so worth it to see the joy in her eyes. I've told myself not to worry, that the extra money will come once I'm in the new job. I pray I get the promotion just in time for closing. I'll be working a massive number of extra hours, but Chloe will be at the gallery in the evenings anyway and shouldn't notice. I'm so excited she'll have the house for summer. She'll capture the beautiful sunrises and sunsets on canvas in ways I can only imagine, as well as the many nuances in the ocean, the breaking waves, the dolphins, the sea shells. I can't wait for her to see it. I can't wait to see her painting them, the way she glows when she's in that zone of creative bliss. My purest enjoyment in life is pleasing Chloe. I don't think that will ever change.

The heart drawn at the end of the sentence only made Chloe's tears fall heavier. That's when Shay had stopped going out of her comfort zone, stopped doing all the fun stuff Chloe wanted to do, that they used to do. They both had—working the long hours, never checking in. It all made sense now. Shay had thought Chloe had found someone else, and the frequent text messages she'd received from Erica had been just vague enough to fuel her suspicions. *What a fucking idiot.* A few words would have easily cleared up the whole mess.

The gallery was slow this afternoon. It was a beautiful day, and most people were outside enjoying the weather. Chloe had had plenty of time to think about her next move. Too much time. When the door chime rang, Chloe looked up from the desk in the back room and was annoyed to see Erica entering the gallery. When they'd talked over the weekend in St. Augustine, she'd thought she'd made it perfectly clear that any romance between them was over. Surely she wasn't coming to buy more of her art. Since she didn't wave or say hello as she entered, she apparently wasn't there to offer a truce. Chloe got up from the desk and went to the front of the gallery to meet her.

"Hi." Chloe forced a smile. "I didn't expect to see you today."

Erica crossed her arms in front of her. "You can be truthful. You didn't expect to see me again, at all." Her stare was penetrating.

Eye contact held, Chloe straightened her shoulders. "You're right. Honestly, I didn't really expect to see you again, ever."

"What I have to tell you will probably solidify that. I went to see your wife and told her all about our relationship and how it came about."

Erica took a deep breath but wasn't done yet. "I told her everything, and she claims she doesn't remember, but I could see that she does. She wasn't near enough surprised to make me think she didn't know."

The knot in Chloe's stomach tightened as her life became more complicated. After many sleepless nights, she didn't have the energy for this encounter today. "I'm busy, Erica. Can I do something for you that doesn't involve my personal life?"

"You're not surprised at all by this news either, are you?"

"Just get out, Erica." She went to the door, pulled it opened, and swung her arm in a motion for her to leave. "No matter what happens between Shay and me, this news definitely takes you out of the picture for good." The emotional roller coaster she'd been on was about to end.

Erica smiled. "Your loss." She walked out the door.

Chloe locked the door behind her and flipped the sign to Closed before she went back to the desk and flopped into the chair. The colorful squares of notepaper peeking out from under the stack of papers on the desk taunted her. Pushing the pile aside, she read her own jagged writing.

You love her—Shay is the one—your one and only
Never forget that—EVER

Drunk Chloe had struck many times over the past few months, and she was right. Even after all that had happened between them, she still loved her with her whole heart.

It was the middle of the day, but Chloe closed the gallery and drove to the beach house. After heading straight through the house to the back door, she stepped out onto the deck, walked to the railing, and took in the view. She didn't hold the tears back as she gazed at the beauty of the sand and the ocean. It was a gorgeous sight, but they'd lost so much because of it. Was it really worth it?

She stepped back inside, went to the bedroom, and took Shay's newest journal from the drawer of her bedside table. She didn't read the latest entry, only fished out a pen from the drawer and flipped to the next blank page. She had so much to say, she wasn't sure she could articulate all her feelings on paper like Shay was able to, but she would try.

Once she'd written everything she wanted to say, she tossed the pen into the drawer, closed the journal, and clutched it to her chest. The decision hadn't been an easy one. She had so many things to consider, so many memories to lock away. Life would go on, but it would never be the same. She gathered a few of her paintings and loaded them into the back of her Tahoe before she headed back to Tampa.

CHAPTER THIRTY-ONE

Shay had done most of her work on autopilot, just as she had been since Chloe had discovered she knew about what she'd done. The guilt and pain had all come back now, and she didn't blame Chloe for not forgiving her. She'd given it all she had and hoped for the best of their relationship to come from the worst with minimal damage.

The knock on her office door broke into her thoughts. "Come in," she said, and her stomach clenched when Lila walked through the door.

"You've been working nonstop since this morning. Can I get you anything?" Lila smiled and took the seat in front of the desk. "Or help with what you're working on?"

She bit back the emotion bubbling in her chest. "No. I'm fine." Lila had already done enough, and she refused to let her creep back into her life.

"Seriously, I don't mind."

She picked up a file on her desk. "There is one thing you can assist with." She leaned forward and dropped the file in front of Lila.

Lila opened the file and drew her brows together. "This will put me back in the Atlanta office for good."

She nodded. "That's where I need you to stay." She didn't intend to go into her memories and the reasons. Lila should already know them.

"So, there's nothing at all in Tampa for me?" She swallowed. "For us?"

"No." She wasn't expecting the disappointed look in Lila's eyes, but she pressed on. "And if you don't agree to the permanent change, there will be nothing at this company for you either, and we will need to sever that relationship."

Lila rolled her lips in and slapped the file closed. "Got it." She stood up. "I'll be out of here tomorrow."

As soon as Lila left her office, Shay signed off her laptop and packed it into her bag. She was exhausted and had just been spinning her wheels for the past hour. She'd done what she had to do to save her own career and possibly Lila's. Even though Lila's work was stellar, if word got out that they'd had an affair before she'd given her the promotion, she'd be done. Maybe she deserved to be, or maybe they both did.

Shay flopped onto the bed after coming home to the beach house early today. She'd been working nonstop since Chloe found out she knew about the reason they'd split, and she was mentally and physically exhausted. Part of her hoped she'd see Chloe's car in the driveway when she got home, but that hope might never be fulfilled again.

She reached into her nightstand drawer and took out her journal to write a new entry. The blank pages had been taunting her lately because she'd had nothing in her heart to express but sadness. She thumbed back to the last entry and stared at the beautiful script. It wasn't her writing at all, and the message it contained gave her more hope than she'd ever imagined.

How do you go from something spectacular back to ordinary?

You wouldn't just let me walk away from you again, would you? Just let go of the love of my life? God, I hope not. I need you to want me, to fight for us because you're crazy nuts about me. Letting you into my heart the second time was absolutely terrifying, but fear and uncertainty were running hand in hand with hope. Questions and doubts were clouding my mind, blocking my path. What if this wasn't about time and attention? What if you don't like the real me? What if there's some little something about me you can't take? An imperfection that turns you away. How can I ever be that beautiful to you that you could ignore all my imperfections once more? My faded heart is glowing again as I never thought it would, and now it's in your hands.

So many thoughts rushed through Shay's mind. When had Chloe come home? How long had the entry been there? Where was she now? The gallery, she must be at the gallery. Shay couldn't get to the car fast enough. She had to see Chloe now.

❖

Shay fought for breath as she raced down the walkway and into the gallery. Chloe glanced at her but didn't smile. She was helping a customer, so Shay waited patiently while she finished. As soon as the customer was out the door, Shay rushed to her. "Did you mean what you wrote?"

Chloe nodded as tears formed in her eyes. "I'm sorry it took me so long to see it."

"No. Don't be. It wasn't your fault. You loved me with your whole heart, and I gave you only a piece of mine." Tears sprang from Shay's eyes as well, and she moved closer. "I didn't believe anyone could love that way. Until now."

"Do you love me that way? With all my quirks and imperfections?" Chloe asked.

"Like the way you pick the raisins out of the raisin bran? The way you can only sleep on the right side of the bed? The way you order pizza with onions on it and then pick them off before you eat your slice because you like the flavor, but not the texture?" She wiped the tears from her eyes and laughed. "And you always eat the crust first."

Chloe nodded and let out a snort. "You get me in every way. I shouldn't, but I still love you."

"You do?" Suddenly the rock in Shay's stomach dissolved, and she had hope.

Chloe's voice caught, and she nodded as more tears welled in her eyes. "I finally get it. My heart hurts without you. But we have a lot to work on, you and I. Communication, time, trust."

Shay struggled for words as the wave of emotions rushed through her. Chloe wanted to try again. It was exactly the opposite of what she'd expected to happen a few days ago. "A lot of shit has blocked our paths, me being the biggest part of it, but I love you, Chloe."

Chloe anchored her hands on her hips and paced the room. "Don't say that if you don't mean it. I can't stand losing you again."

"I mean every word. I really fucked up, but I never stopped loving you." Shay took Chloe into her arms. "I'm different now—we're different now. There was a time when I didn't think our life could get any better, but now it's exceeded every expectation I've ever had for us. I don't want to live without you ever again. I'm not perfect. I'm probably gonna screw up again." Chloe's eyes widened. "Not like that, but when I make little mistakes, I want you to be the one who forgives me." Shay moved closer and brushed a strand of hair from Chloe's face. "All I know for certain is, if you let me, I will love you for the rest of my life."

Chloe raised her eyebrows. "Third time's the charm."

Shay smiled. "Third time's the charm," she repeated, and kissed her with everything she had.

CHAPTER THIRTY-TWO

Chloe finished helping the newest artist in the gallery hang her last painting, said her goodbyes, and raced to her car. She had a date tonight, and if she didn't hurry, she might miss the main attraction. She and Shay had mutually decided to bring in a few more artists as partners in the gallery to ease up on the maintenance workload and the hours Chloe spent there. Shay was still chief actuary at the insurance company, but she'd promoted Jackson and Amber and shifted some of the workload to them, as well as to Lila in the Atlanta office.

It seemed that Lila hadn't really wanted anything more from Shay than sex. At least she'd never brought it up after the day she'd given her the ultimatum. So Shay was happy to let her think she hadn't remembered any of it. She still wondered if it had been a move to get ahead in the agency. The work she'd done was competent, so there was no undoing Lila's promotion now without putting herself in the middle of a huge scandal. Since Shay really didn't remember much about it still, seeing her on occasion wasn't as awkward as it could've been. She'd eased Chloe's concerns by communicating with Lila via email and Skype only and making sure she remained in the Atlanta office permanently.

She hadn't received a single mirror-message, note, or text from drunk Chloe since she'd decided to make life work with Shay. Hopefully she'd taken the right path, and it seemed that she had because she was the happiest she'd ever been.

The pizza was half gone, as was the bottle of merlot Chloe had picked up on the way home. She sipped her wine as she gazed across the blanket, watching Shay take in the gorgeous sunset. Her face beamed with hues of red and orange. Chloe loved to paint the sunset, but she would never grow tired of trying to capture the beauty of Shay's face as the sun reflected upon it.

They'd planned a weekend away in St. Augustine again, with no event scheduled other than just to be with each other. Jackson and Whitney would be over in the morning to spend the weekend at the beach while they were gone. It was the only getaway they could manage, since the baby's due date was growing closer. Whitney was ridiculously uncomfortable and refused to travel for more than an hour anywhere at this point.

She and Shay had planned to leave early in the morning, but right now, Chloe was seriously considering spending most of the night exploring Shay's body. She pushed the pizza box out of the way, scooted closer to Shay, and took her face in her hands. She would never again question whether she wanted Shay to kiss her. In fact, she would always want so much more.

About the Author

Dena Blake grew up in a small town just north of San Francisco where she learned to play softball, ride motorcycles, and grow vegetables. She eventually moved with her family to the Southwest, where she began creating vivid characters in her mind and bringing them to life on paper.

Dena currently lives in the Southwest with her partner and is constantly amazed at what she learns from her two children. She's a would-be chef, tech nerd, and occasional auto mechanic who has a weakness for dark chocolate and a good cup of coffee.

Books Available From Bold Strokes Books

Beautiful Dreamer by Melissa Brayden. With love on the line, can Devyn Winters find it in her heart to stay in the small town of Dreamer's Bay, the one place she swore she'd never remain? (978-1-63555-305-5)

Create a Life to Love by Erin Zak. When sixteen-year-old Beth shows up at her birth mother's door, three lives will change forever. (978-1-63555-425-0)

Deadeye by Meredith Doench. Stranded while hunting the serial predator Deadeye, Special Agent Luce Hansen fights for survival while her lover, forensic pathologist Harper Bennett, hunts for clues to Hansen's disappearance along the killer's trail. (978-1-63555-253-9)

Endangered by Michelle Larkin. Shapeshifters Officer Aspen Wolfe and Dr. Tora Madigan fight their growing attraction as they work together to destroy a secret government agency that exterminates their kind. (978-1-63555-377-2)

Incognito by VK Powell. The only thing Evan Spears is focused on is capturing a fleeing murder suspect until wild card Frankie Strong is added to her team and causes chaos on and off the job. (978-1-63555-389-5)

Insult to Injury by Gun Brooke. After losing everything, Gail Owen withdraws to her old farmhouse and finds a destitute young woman, Romi Shepherd, living in a secret room. (978-1-63555-323-9)

Just One Moment by Dena Blake. If you were given the chance to have the love of your life back, could you ignore everything that went wrong and start over again? (978-1-63555-387-1)

Scene of the Crime by MJ Williamz. Cullen Mathew finds herself caught between the woman she thinks she loves but can no longer trust and a beautiful detective she can't stop thinking about who will stop at nothing to find the truth. (978-1-63555-405-2)

Fear of Falling by Georgia Beers. Singer Sophie James is ready to shake up her career, but her new manager, the gorgeous Dana Landon, has other ideas. (978-1-63555-443-4)

Daughter of No One by Sam Ledel. When their worlds are threatened, a princess and a village outcast must overcome their differences and embrace a budding attraction if they want to survive. (978-1-63555-427-4)

Playing with Fire by Lesley Davis. When Takira Lathan and Dante Groves meet at Takira's restaurant, love may find its way onto the menu. (978-1-63555-433-5)

Practice Makes Perfect by Carsen Taite. Meet law school friends Campbell, Abby, and Grace, law partners at Austin's premier boutique legal firm for young, hip entrepreneurs. Legal Affairs: one law firm, three best friends, three chances to fall in love. (978-1-63555-357-4)

The Last Seduction by Ronica Black. When you allow true love to elude you once and you desperately regret it, are you brave enough to grab it when it comes around again? (978-1-63555-211-9)

Wavering Convictions by Erin Dutton. After a traumatic event, Maggie has vowed to regain her strength and independence. So how can Ally be both the woman who makes her feel safe and a constant reminder of the person who took her security away? (978-1-63555-403-8)

A Bird of Sorrow by Shea Godfrey. As Darrius and her lover, Princess Jessa, gather their strength for the coming war, a mysterious spell will reveal the truth of an ancient love. (978-1-63555-009-2)

All the Worlds Between Us by Morgan Lee Miller. High school senior Quinn Hughes discovers that a broken friendship is actually a door propped open for an unexpected romance. (978-1-63555-457-1)

Falling by Kris Bryant. Falling in love isn't part of the plan, but will Shaylie Beck put her heart first and stick around, or tell the damaging truth? (978-1-63555-373-4)

An Intimate Deception by CJ Birch. Flynn County Sheriff Elle Ashley has spent her adult life atoning for her wild youth, but when she finds her ex, Jessie, murdered two weeks before the small town's biggest social event, she comes face-to-face with her past and all her well-kept secrets. (978-1-63555-417-5)